I0670395

THE INCEPTION WAR

A Dak Donahue Novel

Steve Dwight Nichols

Copyright © 2022 by Steve Dwight Nichols
ISBN: 978-1-7365728-3-2

Books

1. Murder and the Preacher's Wife
2. The Sinner's Reckoning
3. The Good Samaritans
4. The Last Revelations: The Beginning of the End
5. The Inception War
6. Tanger Gold
7. To Kill a Blueblood
8. An Angel Never Prays

Prologue

Aquarius held Zenith tight against his body. She tried to struggle free. He whispered; "I am truly sorry. I love you so much. Do not allow them to see you care or have feelings for this man. Stand strong." Zenith could feel her father holding her tight and listened to him say, "This is not me. They will kill both of us if they have to. Please Zenith, this will be over soon."

She whispered. "Father. I cannot watch as he is butchered. You do not understand. I love this man."

Chapter 1

The air was bitterly cold and felt like the dull blade of a pocketknife cutting into the exposed skin on Dak's cheeks as it blew from the northeast with the constant early morning wind. Dak wrapped his animal skin robe tighter around his shoulders to protect his neck. His seal skin shirt and pants were made to wear in the bitter cold weather of the north. The leather robe lined with bear fur provided the additional layer which kept him warm against the unrelenting bitter wind chill. He had become accustomed to the cold weather over the years living in the new world, located on the northeastern coastline just below the jet stream. The jet stream was the invisible barrier which separated the north frozen tundra deserts, and the evergreen forest of the northern continent. Dak had always lived in the north and only heard rumors of the warmer climates further south.

Dak's love for his village would not allow him to waiver or let his people down as he hid behind the rocks and waited. He loved his friends and would not be fearful as the pending battle approached. The six friends had grown up together in the wilderness located high above the cliffs on the now northeastern peninsula of the new world. They had spent their days hunting, fishing, working, training, and living but mostly having fun. They had been taught how to prepare for battle, but this was their first test. He knew the adults in his tribe questioned his ability and his friend's abilities to wage war at the age of sixteen. He also was aware a few of the men in the tribe had refused to fight and had taken their families and fled west into the Midlander territory.

Dak carefully peered between the small crack in the rocks located on the top of the six-foot high naturally formed jetty, which extended out close to one hundred yards and then turned and ran parallel to the shoreline about four hundred yards in between the open beach and the Atlantic Ocean. He glanced back to his left and made certain the path was clear to the landing area and the trail leading up to the top of the cliff. He could now see one rowboat had been dropped from one of the larger ships away from the main convoy. He counted ten men approaching, headed directly for his position. The main force of the Normand army would sail a larger warship into the jetty and once on the beach open their hatches to release the soldiers from below deck. He glanced at his friends in their hidden stations along the inside of the jetty. They were well camouflaged, ready for battle. He hated it when he was told he was positioned in the rear area to protect the route for the possible retreat for his friends and the tribe's other soldiers positioned at the bottom of the cliffs. He felt he deserved to be in the center of the battle, not hidden in the rear area. Someone less qualified could be watching the route of retreat. The embarrassment had been hard to hide. He had routinely fought better than all his friends and the other soldiers in the tournaments and practice rounds. Only the two instructors, Billy Ray and Little Jimmy, had been able to best him as he was being trained when he was a boy. They had not sparred in three years and now that he was sixteen years old, he wondered if he could not best the two men in the tournament ring. Billy Ray was a complete warrior, and Little Jimmy was too big, quick, and strong to handle in fighting hand-to-hand. Dak had strenuously argued with his superior, Billy Ray, against being positioned in the rear area to protect his comrades if they were forced to retreat. He felt this assignment could have been handled by one of the females or an elderly tribe member.

Billy Ray was fearless as a teacher of war and as a hunter. He not only was a great hunter but was a brilliant teacher of war. He had been part of one of the America's most elite fighting forces as he worked in the Green Berets of the United States Army and the Army Rangers in the old world. He had taught Dak and his friends how to fight, how to kill, and how to mentally prepare for battle. He stressed that planning for a battle versus preparing for war were two entirely different events. The battles might last a few minutes or a day, but a war could last for years. In both cases, you needed to understand your team and your opponent's characteristics, such as the weaknesses, strengths, tendencies, and fortitude to fight. The more information you understood about yourself and the opponent, not just the soldier in the field, but the people supporting the armies, the better position one would be in to make a life and death decision in battle and war. He taught them, once the battle started, even the best made plan could unravel, and soldiers had to adapt or be killed.

The elders in the tribe that had survived the collapse of the old world over sixteen years prior had united and built the city called Cliff Tops. Billy Ray had learned how to forge steel prior to the collapse of the old world, and he passed along his techniques. The six friends had forged their own weapons with Billy Ray's guidance. Billy Ray and Eric of Newport would take the six friends to parts of the tribal lands without crossing over into the dangerous areas of the nuclear waste. The group would crawl deep under the ground in caves to locate the old-world metal and carry it back to their city, Cliff Tops, to forge the metal into swords, arrow heads, axes, spears, nails and tools.

Dak had loved growing up with his friends and their families. Every day had been an adventure riddled with fun and excitement. They were taught how to live and be warriors in the new world and now Dak, his friends, and his tribe were sitting hidden behind the rock jetty wall and spread out on the beach and the above cliff top. The Normand army led by King Solman was attacking by sea with five large battleships full of mercenaries, slaves, and Normand soldiers. The battle was life or death for him and his tribe. Dak looked up to the cliff top and caught a glimpse of his mother watching from the top. He knew she was the reason he was placed in the back lines of the battle. She wanted her son to be protected. Now, he was in the rear of the battle lines with his five closest friends in the middle of the planned ambush.

Dak eased his head higher so the approaching men in the rowboat could not see him and peered between the small crevasse in the rocks at the top of the jetty. The rowboat was fast approaching and still headed directly for his position. He again glanced down the row of rocks at his friends, well-hidden and camouflaged to blend in with the rock structure located on the interior part of the jetty. He then peered along the trail and made certain the retreat route was still clear of Normand soldiers. No one had anticipated the Normand navy would send a small rowboat to his part of the jetty. He had one task, to keep the retreat route open.

The ocean side of the jetty was rough with jagged rocks protruding out of the surf in front of him and further along the jetty. This prevented a large ship from landing on the outside of the jetty. The Normand fleet was larger than they anticipated with three warships at sea while two warships fast approached the open jetty area which led to the smooth waters located within the beachfront below the two-hundred-foot-high cliffs.

He could see the first ship entering the channel of the jetty. He knew this was the beginning. His adrenalin was rushing with his heartbeat rising. He remembered the same feeling when he was eight years old before he had pulled the trigger on his crossbow and killed his first bear. He had been taught before battle; his nerves would try to persuade him to forget his training. He had to fight the impulse. His instructor, Billy Ray, had coached him on the placement of the arrow onto the crossbow. To instantly kill a large animal, the shot would have to be perfect, hitting it either in the brain or the heart. He did not miss the large bear with the arrow sinking through the heart. He did not want the bear to suffer.

He looked and saw Billy Ray watching and waiting from his hidden spot under the large cliff behind the boulder on the beach. Wayne was second in command of his tribe and had gone over the plan several times with the leadership group. They were vastly outnumbered, and the group had emphasized that in order to win, the Normand army had to be stopped at sea. They could not allow any of the Normand army to make it to shore. They wanted to hide their weakness, which was the lack of numbers of fighting men. His mother, Vicky, was the leader, and she had agreed on the plan. They had summoned the miners, hunters, and all the tribe's people to defend the city. Billy Ray had positioned them along the rock walls at the bottom and top of the cliff preparing for battle.

Hulk walked over to Dak and could tell he was ashamed to be stationed on the back lines. Hulk was his best friend and the son of Billy Ray and Delores. Hulk told him it would be okay. The fighting would be over quickly, and the Normand army would be left with no choice but to retreat to the sea. The stormy weather would not allow the Normand navy to drop anchor, and he said with a determined look on his face, "They will not make it to our beach. Today, we fight for our tribe."

As Dak waited, he remembered when the first Normand boat had arrived in the open sea over seven years ago. He was so excited. He and his friends were told to stay hidden, and he and his five friends had crawled behind the rocks at the top of the cliff and peered down on the rowboat which had approached the jetty rock wall. Dak remembered watching the large warship sailing at sea and marveled at the size. The only vessel that had ever sailed to his village located in the far northern part of the continent, was half the size of the warship. He remembered turning and looking at the open area and saw his mother watching him as she stood at the top of cliffs observing the approaching rowboat and the large warship further out at sea. She seemed to always be on the lookout for him and his friends. The tribal leaders were nervous. The rowboat had stopped just outside the jetty, and the man stood in the boat and announced they represented the Normand empire and in the name of King Solman, this was his property, and they were coming ashore to organize efforts to collect rent and taxes. Dak could not recall the rest of the message but had remembered the word trespassing. He also remembered the shot from Billy Ray's arrow striking the big man's center chest and had missed the smaller man reading the message. At first, he thought, how could Billy Ray have missed from his hidden spot behind the jetty wall? He had looked at Hulk's face and remembered the look of surprise that his father had missed. Dak then realized Billy Ray had not missed, "He did not miss. He hit the big warrior. Your father knows what he is doing." Hulk had nodded his head in understanding.

The people in the new world had not been able to manufacture gunpowder. His tribe had located charcoal, potassium nitrate but the sulfur needed to make gunpowder could not be located. The new world had also lost their ability to manufacture electricity, and the survivors of the world had plummeted back in time to a period similar to the tenth century. The choice of weapons was the sword, a spear, or a bow, and the world was at war over the limited resources available after the Armageddon events which ended the old world.

The large soldier had fallen into the ocean backward from the arrow impact, and he was never found. His metal armor weighed him down, and he sank in the fifty-foot ice cold ocean water. The ocean's cold temperatures prevented the Normand sailors from diving into the ocean to retrieve the body. The Normand personnel in the small boat knew what had happened. Their bid to take over the village located at the top of the cliffs had been rejected. They also understood they were going to have to take the land by force and kill the people of Cliff Tops. With that shot, his tribe had drawn the line in the sand, and they were prepared to fight. The small boat immediately retreated to sea. The larger ship was anchored a quarter mile offshore and could not have been able to discern what happened. When the small rowboat carrying the six men made it back to the large ship, the tribe relaxed and watched the Normand vessel pull the anchor and sail south. The tribe knew war was coming, and the Normand navy would return.

Dak's attention was brought back to the situation at hand as he now looked at the first ship, which was crossing into the calm waters between the jetty and the shoreline. He saw Billy Ray going under water from behind the boulder near the cliff and knew the battle had just begun. He once again lifted his head so as not to be seen by the approaching men and glanced through the small crevasse in between the rocks as the rowboat with the ten men were about twenty yards away and headed directly for his position. One man was standing in the very rear of the small boat watching while eight men were sitting down rowing. He could see the muscles in the men's necks flex as they pulled the oars through the water. They were dressed in heavy armor, thick coats and appeared to be men of war with swords positioned next to their seats. The tenth man, who was in the very front of the rowboat, had turned and was trying to determine when to jump for the shore. He was holding the tow rope attached to a cleat on the top front of the boat. Dak knew he could not allow the men to exit the boat. He wanted them in the boat where they would be limited with their ability to fight. He also knew he had to surprise them, and he determined the large warrior in the rear of the boat was going to be the first to die. He glanced, and the one-hundred-foot boat was now inside the jetty, and the second boat was just preparing to enter the narrow opening leading into the beach area. The Normand command wanted the two vessels to drop their landing gates, so the large number of foot soldiers housed below deck could exit and attack. Once on land, the Normand army could outnumber the tribe ten to one with just the army in the five large ships. Their armies down south were a thousand to one the size of his tribe. Dak knew his tribe was with fewer warriors, but he also knew they would fight to the bitter end.

At this very moment, Dak had no reservation about what he must do. He took his cape off, lifted his crossbow and jumped onto the top of the jetty. He noticed the surprised look on the face of the Normand soldier in the front of the rowboat. He also saw the large soldier standing in the rear of the rowboat reaching for his sword. He aimed and pulled the trigger, releasing the top arrow. The arrow flew true and hit the large man standing in the back of the boat in the center chest. The force of the arrow's impact pierced the metal chest plate and caused the man to fall backward into the sea. Dak did not hesitate. Everything happened so quickly, the second arrow had also flown true striking the front man in the forehead with the steel dipped arrow passing through his skull and sticking out the back of his head. He had been on the verge of jumping to shore with his weight leaning forward, which caused him to fall sideways into the sea. Dak immediately dropped his crossbow and pulled his two-foot-six-inch-long Sai swords. He took a running start and leapt from the jetty rocks into the rowboat. Dak was the only one in his tribe that had elected to make a Sai sword. Most of the men elected the heavier and longer swords, but in close with his swords, Dak could outwit and was quicker than his companions and win the mock sword fights. The Normand soldiers were still sitting with their backs toward him and did not have an opportunity to drop the oars and pull their own swords.

Dak came down hitting the first man to his right across the neck and then stabbed the next man in front of him squarely in the middle of the back with his left hand. With his right hand, he used the handle and smashed the small six-inch blade into the man's face who was sitting in the front of the left side of the boat. The boat was rocking back and forth from the waves and now with Dak landing in the boat and shifting his weight from side to side the boat was tilting more from one side to the other, which caused the men to fumble trying to stand and fight. Dak kept his momentum going forward and with his right hand swung the sword as hard as he could, catching the man under the chin decapitating the soldier. Dak released his grip on the sword in his left hand with the sword being stuck in the dead man's back. He switched hands with his sword and used his left hand to swing down, cutting the next man on the right across his head. Dak knew he could not hesitate. The men were ill prepared to fight in the small rowboat with large coats and armor. Their swords were four feet long and could not be easily swung in the restricted confines of the rowboat. Dak used the rocking of the boat to his advantage. The next man on his left had managed to stand and was trying to use the end of the oar as a weapon. When he lifted it to swing, he hit his comrade in front of him as he stood. The man had left his side open, and Dak sliced through the man's large coat into his side causing him to fall into the sea. Dak immediately took advantage of the fact the man had been hit by an oar and fell forward using his hands to brace himself as he fell. Dak came down with the sword cutting his right hand. The man was startled, losing four fingers with half his left hand being severed. He fell off balance into the sea while holding his injured hand. The last two men had managed to pull their swords and were standing on the last bench beside one another in the rear of the boat facing Dak. The man on the right lunged forward. Dak had been well trained. He knew this was an attempt to distract him. He stepped to the side and dodged the attempt. When the man on the left swung hard, Dak used the hook on the handle of his Sai sword to stop the sword blade, and then he twisted his Sai sword causing the man to lose his grip. He lunged forward while rocking the boat and plunged his sword into the man's gut. Dak reached for the man pulling him between himself and the man to his right. The man had done as predicted and swung his sword. Dak had held the dead man up and pushed him in front of the blade causing the blade to hit his comrade in the head. Dak reached under the now falling dead man and stabbed the last man in the lower stomach. The man looked into Dak's eyes as he pushed both men backward into the sea.

Dak heard the large catapult being released as the counterweight was being dropped. He knew the second ship must be in position. The tribe's plan was to trap the one ship between the jetty and the shore and use the second ship to block the entrance to the smooth waters inside the jetty area by dropping a one-hundred-pound rock from the cliff top onto the middle of the deck of the second ship. Then, the reinforcements could not sail or row into the inner waterway and provide support for the men aboard the first ship. Billy Ray's part of the plan was to plant a small explosive device under water on the bottom side of the first boat and force it to sink in the thirty feet deep cold water. The plan was to force the crew to the deck where they would be caught in the crossfire. The men and women from the cliff top could shoot arrows down onto the top of the deck and the soldiers hidden behind the jetty wall could shoot their arrows into the Normand army crew as they emerged from below deck. The level of the ocean would change with the tide moving out as the sun rose higher in the morning sky, and the large reef would prevent the three other large warships from moving close to the ocean side of the jetty during low tide. The approaching army would be limited to use only rowboats to approach the shoreline with the larger warships not being able to dock in the jetty or along the jetty wall.

Dak looked down the jetty on the seaward side and saw the rowboat approaching the jetty near Veronica's position. She was one of his best friends. She was the daughter of Little Jimmy and Mia. Dak then noticed the man who he had hit in the mouth was trying to stand. He ran toward him and sliced him down his back and then used the short blade on the handle located under the larger blade to slice into the rear of the man's head. He watched as the man fell limply into the ocean. He pulled his other Sai sword from the dead man's back and placed it in his sword sleeve. He placed the other sword in the other sleeve and jumped out of the rowboat onto the jetty rocks. He crossed the top of the jetty and grabbed his crossbow as he sprinted down the backside. He pulled an arrow and loaded the top of the bow and loaded an arrow in the bottom. He pulled the string tight and locked it in place as he raced along the rocks. He could see Robin Hood, Veronica, Trey, Tommy Boy, and Hulk firing arrow after arrow into the deck of the ship inside the jetty. There were dead Normand sailors lying all over the ship's deck. He could see that the ship was starting to sink from the explosive Billy Ray had ignited. He yelled for Veronica to watch out for the man about to jump out of a second rowboat behind her position.

The captain on the second large ship had observed the first large ship sail into the jetty area without conflict and now his ship was sinking after it had been split in half by the one-hundred-pound rock shot from the catapult on top of the two-hundred-foot cliff. The sound of the rock hitting the middle of the boat was deafening. The direct hit had caused the front and rear of the boat to rise out of the water as the center of the boat went further down in the water. Dak knew Little Jimmy and Wayne and the other men would be reloading another huge rock into place and resetting the counterweight in case a third shot was needed. All the prior practice, weighing of the rocks, and calibrating the catapult had paid off. Wayne and Little Jimmy had the rocks lined up next to the catapult according to their weight, and they knew the distance the different sized rocks would fly.

Dak could see the second ship sinking fast as he kept running down the rocks. The Normand soldiers who did not get killed by the two large rocks were either dying from arrows or drowning.

His friends were about to be attacked from behind by the men in the second rowboat who had been dropped off from the front of the first warship. There were several rowboats now being deployed to attempt landing at the jetty wall. They were staggered at different distances from shore. Dak jumped to the top of the rocks and balanced himself for the one-hundred-foot shot. He wanted to hit the front man before he was able to tie the tow rope to the rocks of the jetty. He knew as long as the men were in the rowboat, they were limited on what they could do. He also knew his friends could fire down into a rowboat from three sides from the jetty rocks, which made the invaders a sitting target. The men were moving inside the boat back and forth. Dak pulled the trigger as the man jumped. The arrow missed by an inch and slammed into the temple of the man sitting to the right front rowing position. The men in the boat had turned and were all preparing to jump to shore. They saw the man take an arrow in the side of his head. They looked at Dak as he pulled the trigger, and this time, the arrow hit the man on shore in the stomach. The man released the rope as he bent forward reaching for his midsection. The boat started to drift away from shore. The men in the boat started yelling at each other. Dak dropped his crossbow and ran down the rocks yelling for Veronica to turn and be prepared to fight the men from the seaward side of the jetty.

Veronica looked over and saw Dak running down the rock jetty toward her position pointing to the position behind her. She knew Dak was told under no circumstance could he leave his position. He was to guard the exit path, or they all could be trapped. She turned and stepped up on the rocks and peered over the ledge. She was shocked to see a rowboat full of men so close. She turned and yelled at Robin Hood. He was located next to her position on the interior of the jetty rocks. She raised her crossbow and saw the front man sitting to the right with an arrow through the side of his head. Before she could aim, the men in the boat started jumping out of the boat landing on the shore. The second man out had grabbed the tow rope and was trying to hold the boat steady. He saw the first man to jump with an arrow in the midsection and grabbed the rope.

Veronica shot into the group of men standing bunched together and trying to exit from the front of the boat. She had not had time to load her second arrow before turning around. She shot her arrow and immediately dropped behind the jetty rocks for cover. Her arrow had hit the fourth man in the group in the upper arm. The men in the boat fired at her position and had missed her by inches. She immediately reached for another arrow and started reloading her crossbow.

Robin Hood had been the first to reach her position and was using a bow. He could reload the bow a lot faster and was shooting as he ran down the rock jetty formation. He knew Tommy Boy, Hulk's younger brother, would be right behind him. The two had stopped firing into the men on the deck of the large warship and were firing into the group of men in the rowboat as fast as they could reload. The men had shields and were cowering behind the shields. None of the arrows were penetrating the shields. Dak ran from the opposite direction and when he was approximately ten feet from Veronica, he ran up and over the jetty wall and leaped toward the group of men cowering behind their shields facing the opposite direction. He caught the group by surprise and cut two men down with his two swords. He rotated down the ocean side of the rocks and cut another man in the midsection. The men turned to fight Dak. As the closest standing man swung his sword, Dak caught the sword in the handle of his left sword between the small blade and the two-foot-six-inch blade. Dak used his momentum to shove the sword in his right hand through the soldier's neck right at the Adams Apple.

Dak did not break stride as he moved down the bank. As another man swung his sword with great force, Dak caught it between the small blade and the two-foot-six-inch blade and again shoved the sword in his other hand into the midsection of the man. Veronica raised up over the rock ledge and fired her crossbow twice hitting two men. The last man laid down his shield and sword and held his hands up.

Dak looked toward the jetty opening. He saw Hulk and Trey firing arrows into men hiding behind shields as the third rowboat was fast approaching the jetty wall. Dak yelled for Tommy Boy to watch the one prisoner while he, Veronica, and Robin Hood would fight the Normand soldiers in the third rowboat.

Hulk yelled, "Our arrows are not making it past their shields!"

Dak noticed the men in the rowboat had placed their shields in perfect alignment so arrows could not hit them. Dak yelled, "Throw a large rock. When the shields give, we will shoot between the cracks of the shields." Hulk reached quickly, picking up a rock that weighed close to twenty pounds and grunted as he strained and shot putting the heavy rock into the fast-approaching rowboat. The large rock landed in the middle of the rowboat and the men holding the shields fell backward causing the shields to shift. Dak and his three friends were standing, appearing downward from the top of the jetty. They fired two arrows each into the shifting men hitting the five men in the middle. Dak's two arrows hit one man in the arm and a second in the exposed leg. Veronica fired her two arrows and hit a man in the face and the one man pinned under the rock in the hand. Trey had hit the man pinned under the rock in the neck and then hit the same man Veronica had hit in the back. Robin Hood had intentionally hesitated and fired his first arrow at the man at the side of the boat still cowering behind his shield. From his angle, his arrow flew true and hit the man in the shoulder.

Hulk was in the process of throwing another large rock, when the man in the rear of the rowboat stood and was preparing to throw his spear. Robin Hood had waited for another open shot and hit the man in the Adams Apple before he could release his spear. The man fell backward into the sea.

Hulk's large rock hit the four remaining shields in the middle causing all the men to drop the shields. The rock crushed the one man's left hand as it pinned his hand underneath it on the bottom of the boat. The remaining men had no cover and took several arrows at close range from the four shooters.

The group looked at sea and the other rowboats had retreated and were not approaching the jetty wall. Dak yelled, "I will return to my station."

Billy Ray stood on the shore under the cliff and motioned for the shooting to stop. The water line on the first warship was to the railing, and the boat was close to being under water. The small explosive made from condensed nitrogen had blown a fourteen-inch hole in the side of the boat below the water line. Wayne blew the horn to stop the shooting from the cliff.

Billy Ray swam to the boat and climbed on board and noticed the bodies of the Normand soldiers. He killed a couple of wounded men who were trying to stay above the water hanging onto the top of the railing. The rest were dead with arrows sticking into their corpses as they were floating under the surface. He noticed the lock and chain which had been placed on the lower cabin door leading to the deck. The door had been broken through from the inside of the cabin. He then dove off the sinking boat into the ice-cold water and swam to the jetty wall. He walked over to the group and yelled, "He is our prisoner. Bring him up to the top of the mountain. We will need to interrogate him."

Eric of Newport motioned from the bottom of the cliffs that the other rowboats were turning and rowing back to sea. Billy Ray said, "There is no one left alive in the two ships. The warriors were mostly slaves on these two ships and locked below deck."

Trey asked, "What about all the dead Normand soldiers?"

Billy Ray looked around and noticed most were in the ocean. "Leave them in the ocean. Feed the sharks."

Veronica motioned for the now tied prisoner to follow her. Tommy Boy fell in behind the prisoner as the three headed for the trail up the steep cliff. Billy Ray walked to the top of the jetty and viewed the battlefield. The three rowboats were pushed against the jetty wall. There were dead men who had washed up on shore or were hanging half out of the rowboats. He ordered Robin Hood and Hulk to secure the rowboats and feed the sharks with the dead men.

The horn sounded from the top of the cliff a second time which indicated the three warships were heading out to sea. Hulk ran over and hugged Trey. Trey was Veronica's younger brother. He yelled loudly at Robin Hood in delight. The three looked over at Billy Ray who glanced over at the sinking ship. He said, "We will start trying to salvage the metal from the sinking ships first thing in the morning. But first we need to check for survivors. The other men have already checked the other boat. The second 100-pound rock ripped it into pieces."

They wanted to secure the metal as salvage to forge it for weapons and more importantly, build an underwater barrier to prevent the large ships from entering the calm jetty water which provided a beach landing site. The oceanfront for hundreds of miles south and north were cliffs and further north the land turned to glaciers and was uninhabitable from the bitter climate and rough terrain.

Wayne reported to Vicky, "We have no casualties, all are dead in the two warships, and three row boats except for one prisoner. Some of the survivors from the second warship tried to swim back to the rowboats at sea. The men in the rowboats killed them in the water for being cowards and not fighting to the death.

***

Wayne made the prisoner look at his comrades who were lying on the beach dead. He told the warrior some had been killed by their own men as they tried to swim from the second ship to safety.

27

Billy Ray said, as he was out of breath from the hard climb of the cliff trail, "They would have shown us no mercy." Billy Ray looked into the eyes of the six teenagers standing in front of him, "This is the reason we pushed you so hard in your training. The Normand army would have killed every one of us and then raped all the women before killing them. There would be no mercy provided by King Solman, only death and misery. If they kill their own soldiers trying to survive the cold ocean, they will not hesitate to kill us. We will have to fight to the death to protect our tribe and you six did great. Thank you for being such good students."

Tommy Boy asked, "Do you think the plan worked? They lost close to three hundred men and two large ships in less than thirty minutes, and we had no casualties. The Normand commander has no way to tell our strengths or our weaknesses."

Billy Ray pointed to the captured man. "He is not a true soldier of the Normand Army. He is a captured slave who was forced to fight. The warriors on both ships were locked below deck. They were slaves force to die or be cruel in killing us." Billy Ray walked toward the captured man and abruptly turned the man around and pulled up his shirt showing the others the brand in the middle of his back. "I noticed this brand on several dead soldiers on the boat deck prior to it sinking. They were slaves with only two shirts and limited clothes. The Normand Army brands the slaves with a hot iron. These men were expendable." He pushed the soldier down on the ground. "They were just checking our fortitude to fight. When the Normand Army arrives, we will not survive."

Chapter 2

Vicky looked at her friends standing and sitting around the table in the banquet hall. The six of her closest friends had worked for the CIA either directly or indirectly in the old-world killing terrorists. They had escaped to this isolated area in North Canada during the demise of the modern world. They had taken on people who had survived and started the tribe located at the top of a cliff overlooking the ocean. They had helped build the homes for each other over sixteen years ago, as well as the banquet hall which was also used as the church. The portable sawmill, which had come in handy, was one of the things they had refined and preserved from the old world. Wayne had taken an interest in sawing lumber, and that had become his job. Everyone had taken a job and worked hard to survived.

Vicky asked, "Does the prisoner know when the Normand navy will return?"

Billy Ray replied, "He was a slave forced to fight. He indicated he wished we had killed him. His wife and kids will now be raped since he did not die with glory in battle. He has no useful information. He has no way to know when the main army will attack. He said he believes the main army is still bogged down in holding the two cities near the southern region. They held back their main force and only employed two of their ships which were full of slaves who were forced to attack us. The slaves were locked below deck, so they could not escape. The Normand captain had not opened the door to the lower cabin. They were waiting until they landed. The door was broken through by the slaves in the cabin as the boat was sinking. The other ships watched and were ready. They were observing and learning about our ability and willingness to fight. They also learned about the tide and the reef. They now know we will fight, and we will be prepared. They will try to figure out how to conquer us. Today was a recon mission for them. They know we have no navy to fight them at sea. The next attack, I am afraid, we will not be able to repel."

Wayne looked at Vicky, "They were just testing our defenses, trying to intimidate us. They know they cannot attack us from the south or west because of the nuclear holocaust. They cannot reach us from the north with an army because of the frigid temperatures, and there is no beach for them to land their ships along the shoreline. The terrain is too difficult. No army can cross the frozen tundra with all the ice cliffs and valleys."

Little Jimmy added, "If each of the ships was carrying one hundred warriors, then they held out close to three-hundred soldiers. Why?"

Billy Ray replied, "I believe they did not realize until today they could not land on the jetty wall with their big ships and advance their foot soldiers. Their commander made the correct decision to live to fight another day. They did not have nearly enough rowboats to transport an adequate number of soldiers to break our defense. They will adjust and figure out how to get through the surf and reach the jetty wall. They sacrificed the three rowboats and the thirty men in return for knowledge. They also were surprised with our catapult and us taking out two of their ships." He paused and looked at Dak. "Once they obtain control of the jetty wall, anyone cut off from the footpath or the lift will be killed. Dak, that is why you were placed to protect our retreat route."

"If they are willing to kill their own men who we turned back during the attack, they must not have a shortage of warriors. They will be able to bring as many warriors as the boats can carry. They must have a shortage of boats. I believe the prisoner is telling us the truth. The next attack, they will hit us with overwhelming numbers, and we will not be able to turn them back. We will need to make double the arrows we had for this battle, and we will need better arrows. They will try to flank us down the coastline and locate another landing zone and then attack us from land and sea." He looked at the teenagers in the room and continued, "During the interview the prisoner said they were farmers and then one day the Normand army came across their land and took it. They were all beaten, and the women raped. The ones that would be willing to kill their neighbor farmers, proved their worth and were led away to fight for the Normand army. They marched off and were told they were now soldiers. When the Normand army first came on their land, they acted as if they just wanted taxes. Then the General by the name of Cuez came with over two thousand hardened soldiers and the mass killing started. They took all the land, horses, cattle and freedom from the people." Billy Ray looked at his friends and family. He hesitated. "The commander is General Cuez. He will try to gain a foothold on the beach and somehow surround us. They need good weather to finalize an acceptable attack. I am certain they will have catapults on the next ships to hit our troops stationed along the jetty. The only chance we have is to not allow them the opportunity to make landfall. Once they make landfall, our defenses will start falling like dominos."

Delores looked around the room, "We will be trapped. We cannot escape north or west. If we go south, they will follow us to the New York Tribe, and they will not be prepared to fight. They cannot control their own people let alone place a skilled army in the path of the Normand army."

Vicky, knowing all this to be true, looked at her friends and tribe members. She hesitated, "We only have one choice. We will need to send a small group on a journey across the waste land to seek help from the Bluebloods and negotiate their help. At some point, the Bluebloods will have to stand and fight the Normand armies."

Delores shook her head no and then looked at the floor. Vicky saw her and asked, "You do not agree?"

"I hate to ask them for assistance. They will want our freedoms and our land in exchange. Some of the rumors we have heard over the last few years about how the Bluebloods and the city of Merlin have treated other people have to be true. They will not help us on our terms. Where there is smoke, there is fire. I am not certain we can trust the Bluebloods."

Vicky announced, "We cannot trust King Solman. There will be no compromise or treaty with him, and if the Normand army kills all of us, the next target will be the City of Merlin. Once they lay siege to Merlin and force the Bluebloods out in the open, they can kill them. They will have their city surrounded. The Bluebloods really have no choice but to throw in with us. Remember, I still have a friend in their city. They are the only hope we have. If the Normand army is as strong as Captain J.J. has indicated, they will capture our beach front and then they will figure out how to scale the cliffs. Besides, once they cut us off from the ocean, we will not have enough food to feed our tribe and supply the New York Tribe. We are at war, and we need to make certain everyone here in our City of Cliff Tops understands our situation. There are some in my realm who feel we should pay King Solman taxes and sign a treaty with him. We will allow the prisoner to tell his story to our citizens and then if there are some who are scared to fight or want out, they can leave. Captain J. J. can provide them passage south."

Eric looked at his friends, "Captain J.J. has provided us with updated information from the south for years while trading with us. At some point, we may have to be careful in dealing with him. The Normand commanders will figure out he is smuggling our coal to Asia and bringing us needed supplies in trade. They might use him against us."

The group looked at each other, understanding the next move.

Billy Ray stood, "I will go. I will take three other men with me."

Vicky countered, "Billy Ray, I need you here. I have discussed this with Wayne and with a great deal of consideration I made my decision. We will send Dak, Trey, Hulk, Robin Hood, Veronica and Tommy Boy on this journey." She looked at the parents. She knew how they loved their kids. She felt the same about Dak. "We will show them the map to cross the waste lands, and then they will need to head north and then proceed back around the great canyon and

35

the mountains. The trip might take them forty days if they ride fast and stay clear of the Midlander tribes."

Little Jimmy spoke up, "The Midlanders are nothing but outlaws and cut throats. Every time Billy Ray, Eric of Newport, and I ran into them near the great canyon, we had to kill them. They move around from place to place and are constantly at war with the other tribes within their area."

Vicky announced, "The journey won't be without tribulations, but we need the help of the Bluebloods to win this war. The Normand army is not going to stop until we all are dead. I hope the Bluebloods will escort them back home. Our six young people are more mature than we all were growing up. They have learned to survive." She looked into the faces of the parents, "They fought their first battle and each of them killed more than one Normand soldier. They respect life but will not hesitate to be lethal to survive and protect one another. The plan is they will go north of the Midlander's camps."

"The teenagers might be safer trying to reach Merlin than staying here, if the Normand navy returns while they are gone." Wayne did not finish his thought. He looked at Billy Ray, Little Jimmy, and Eric of Newport. "It could get dangerous here. You men are the managers. The workers look to you for your leadership. We need you here."

The group realized Vicky was agitated with making the decision of sending the teenagers. The understanding from the group had been silently perceived with the difficulty she had faced. They needed to stay and prepare the city to battle in case the Normand army returned. They all held hands and prayed.

Chapter 3

Vicky hugged Dak and told him she loved him. She said, "Remember, you are in charge, and you are responsible for the lives of the group. You will soon understand being in charge is not easy. You will have to make some unfair and unfavorable decisions. Your group will need to obey your command. Your trip will not be an easy one. I hate to send you on this journey at the age of sixteen, but we have no choice." She had to look up to peer into his eyes. He stood close to six-feet-three inches. He was starting to mature in his shoulders and had small stubble which he had to shave on his chin and jaw line. She knew he was capable of being a great warrior and leader. She said, "Promise me you will return. I love you dearly."

Dak was like most young men in their teens being coached by their mother. He stood still and hoped the talk would be over soon. As soon as she was finished. He said, "I love you. I will see you soon." He abruptly turned and jogged to his horse. Vicky watched him approach his horse with a frown on her face, wondering if he had listened to anything she had said. She thought about if he had been a teenager in the old world before the Transition Period, the girls would have been chasing him and asking him out. He was good looking, smart, thoughtful and had a commanding personality. She stood and watched the group ride away concerned with her decision. "Were they mature enough to cross the continent through the Midlander's territory?"

Chapter 4

Each person in the tribe's council had met with the six and provided them insight into the journey. Delores had been the first. She explained the map and how to use the stars to travel at night. "Polaris is the north star, the end star of the Little Dipper, and is always in the north location." She pointed to the night sky. She further emphasized the need to avoid the Midlander tribes at all costs. The mission needed to be in stealth as they traveled and avoided the nuclear waste areas and the Midlanders. "You have one objective. That is to reach the Blueblood command and convince them to assist us."

Mia had explained how to use the radiation detector monitors, and how to recharge the two in rivers. She explained they could not go into the fields of radiation. Their bodies would die a slow painful death. She asked each of them to remember the one Blueblood who had made it through the radiation field and died a very painful death from the radiation sickness. The animals that came through the fields of radiation had to be provided mercy and killed.

Little Jimmy further explained hand-to-hand fighting and how to attack the opponent's weakness. "Surprise and allowing the opponent to underestimate your abilities is one of the best strategies. Be smart and have courage in the face of danger."

Billy Ray confirmed all could shoot the bows and crossbows with great accuracy. He also made certain they all could hit a target fifteen feet away with a throwing knife.

Wayne explained to them the importance of strategy, which included an exit plan and to make certain each had the other's back. "You need to make the trip and return before the winter starts. You do not want to be much further north than you are right now during winter. You all know how brutal the winter will be."

Eric of Newport ensured they each could climb a tree with no limbs by using their hands to wrap around the tree and walk up the tree holding their hands around the tree trunk. They would use a rope on larger trees. He also made certain they knew how to rappel, climb ice walls with spikes, and rock cliffs.

This was all a refresher. All six had been doing these things for years. Vicky concluded the training when she explained that Dak was the leader, and he was in charge. The group indicated they understood. Vicky could tell they were eager and did not appear to be afraid. She looked at each teenager and told each of them she loved them, and the tribe would pray for them daily.

The meeting with the teenagers had provided the adults a sense of confidence in the decision. The teenagers were mature and ready for the trip. The teens had been going on overnight

41

hunting trips by themselves and fishing in the ocean overnight for the past few years.

Chapter 5

As the group rode away on the horses in a slow gallop, Delores walked up next to Vicky, "I hope they are ready for this mission. I hope they are not too young for the perils they will face."

Mia also walked over and looked at Vicky. She smiled a reassuring but worried smile. "I thought I would never convince Little Jimmy he had to stay here and protect our tribe. He said he understood. You really had no other choice."

Eric of Newport and Casey joined the group, "We have told Robin Hood to listen to Dak and do as he commands," said Casey.

"They all need to work together. We will pray daily for their safety until they return," Eric added.

Vicky announced, "They may be safer going on this trip, because if the Normand army returns while they are gone, they could be killed along with us." The parents looked at Vicky and acknowledged her statement.

Wayne knew the parents were worried about the long mission. When they were young, the group had gone out with some of the men for weeklong hunting and fishing trips. They had also made trips on their own as they got older. The tribe had watched each of them grow into teenagers. The teens were very much liked by the people of the tribe. They had helped each family by bringing them food from the ocean and spoils from hunting trips. They had also assisted with repairing homes and maintaining roofs and gardens. They worked continuously cutting and stacking firewood for the wood burning stoves. Forging metal found in the underground sponging trips and making iron skillets and iron pots for the tribe.

Once on the road away from the view of the tribe, Dak looked over at Hulk, "We will ride hard the first day and a half then rest at Old Thomas' farm. He will restock us with food and then we must ride cautiously through the nuclear waste areas and slip by the Midlander tribes."

Hulk looked over and nodded his head that he understood. He glanced back at his friends, "Let's go." He punched his horse in the sides as Dak had done the same.

***

Dak knew his friends were tired. They had ridden for eight hours straight at a fast gallop. The horses were all spent. He looked around, "We will camp at the next clear spot."

Robin Hood smiled, "The spot under the pine thicket is clear enough and would provide us plenty of firewood." Dak nodded his agreement. He knew Robin Hood was tired. Robin Hood had always been last in all the competitions except for shooting a bow, running, or climbing. Trey and Tommy Boy were each over six-foot-five and weighed over two-hundred-and-fifty pounds, and both appeared to have room for growth with their large bone structure. However, neither one of them were fleet of foot and never liked running long distances or climbing cliffs. Robert had a knack with shooting a bow and as he got bigger and stronger, he became very deadly with a bow and arrow. The adults started calling him Robin Hood, and the nickname stuck.

Dak knew his best friend Hulk would never stop riding as long as he kept riding. He also knew Veronica would never show any weakness. She was the only female in the group, and he loved her like a sister. She had to compete with the males in the group every day and would never back down or confess to any weaknesses. She would never give up or be last in any of their training.

Hulk was named after his grandfather from Texas. His grandfather had died either in the nuclear war or the worldwide plague. When the earth's crust had moved and rearranged the seven continents to only two, the population on planet earth had decreased by over five billion people. No one really knew how many people survived the plague, the nuclear holocaust, and the earthquakes which caused the earth to reshape into the two large continents. Now sixteen years later, the remaining groups were fighting for control of the limited resources.

The two largest groups were the Normand clan who lived in the southern region of the world located on the Atlantic continent. They had gone to war with the other tribes in the southern region killing them and taking the survivors as slaves. The Normand people were ruled by King Solman who set up work camps and ruled ruthlessly. King Solman was always looking to expand his territories, so he could acquire the limited natural resources. They controlled the oceans in seeking out the pockets of territories they conquered. The generals under King Solman were brutal and showed no mercy.

Almost as large of a group were the citizens of the city of Merlin. The people were governed by a small group nicknamed the Bluebloods. They were a genetically enhanced group of people formed prior to the Transition Period. The Transition Period was the time from the demise of the old world and the establishment of the new world over sixteen years ago. The Bluebloods derived their nickname because of the blond hair, dark brown skin, and their blood was genetically altered to fight off all viruses. The group was hidden in Europe and bred to be the group of people to advance humanity. The Bible had explained how this event had taken place in Genesis 6:4. This verse in the Bible documented how the Gods came down from space and impregnated the women on earth. This was thought to be the same method that helped humanity jump ahead of the rest of the animals on planet earth over four thousand years ago. A group called the Syndicate had tried to control the world. The Syndicate planned some of the transition by unleashing a deadly virus on the world, and only the Bluebloods or people who were provided the antidote would survive. The antidote had been destroyed in the nuclear war and now just the Blueblood's blood was immune from the deadly B12 virus.

The Blueblood colony had been moved to a safe location in the north Arctic and waited until after the worldwide Armageddon event. They were not only immune to viruses but were genetically programmed to have quicker reflexes, higher intelligence and stronger muscle tone. Some were bigger and stronger than the average person. Most were more intelligent and bred with empathy, loyalty, and other characteristics. They could be easily noticed with their dark brown skin and blond hair. Unlike the rest of humanity, their ears were pointed, and once they reached adulthood, the ears stopped growing unlike the normal person. Once the Transition Period ended, they moved south to the west coast of the Atlantic Continent located in the warm weather and lived in a beautiful city surrounded by large walls. The weather averaged between sixty-five and eighty-five degrees year-round. The City of Merlin housed over a million people with the outskirts reaching in three directions for several hundred miles. The city was on a large plateau overlooking the Pacific Ocean with vineyards and large fields of wheat and other farmlands to the east and south. Initially, the surviving people had migrated to the area to live and have the protection of the Blueblood warriors. The Bluebloods and a select few survivors lived inside the walls of the castle which was built in the interior part of the city. The people inside the castle worked as servants for the Bluebloods which guaranteed them food, shelter, protection from armed bandits, and access to the best doctors. Then, after the revolution, the Blueblood Senate enacted a stringent set of laws in the City of Merlin and the territories around them. The laws were enforced by the Blueblood army, the sanctioned guards, and local militias. Most of the population located outside the interior portion of Merlin City, those who had survived the holocaust of sixteen years prior, now faced starvation, illnesses, and the cruel judgements of the Blueblood Senate. The death toll was high among the young, elderly, and the weak.

The other continent was called the Pacific Continent and was ruled by the religious zealots. The land was mostly barren with harsh hot weather similar to the southern region of the Atlantic Continent.

Chapter 6

The group pitched in gathering firewood and preparing for the cold night. Dak ordered, "Trey, you and Tommy Boy see if you can locate a boar to eat. You should not have a difficult time finding one the way the ground has been ripped to pieces by them."

Trey announced, "We will see if we can locate supper. I look forward to some pork." The group agreed the beef jerky and stored food would in no way be as good as fresh meat. About one hour later, Trey and Tommy Boy reappeared carrying a dead wild boar which they had already gutted and skinned. The two men dropped the boar on the large rock and stuck the metal spear through it to hang it over the fire.

They were all enthusiastic for the opportunity to see the western part of the continent and visit the City of Merlin. They had never been outside the realm area owned by the City of Cliff Tops. They sat down and watched the meat roast over the hot fire. Tommy Boy looked over at Dak and asked, "What do we really know about the Bluebloods? The only one we ever met was the one you found at the border of the waste land three years ago."

Dak looked straight ahead, "It was close to four years ago. I remember his dark brown skin, pointed ears, and his sinewed muscled body. We were fortunate to have used his blood before he died to make us immune to the B12 virus. I wished more of the tribe could have benefited from his blood."

Veronica replied, "I remember your mother giving the speech to the people that the tribe needed everyone but not everyone was going to be able to receive the blood. Doc Johnson could not keep him alive long enough. They never had the antidote before the Blueblood showed up, and they were no worse off."

Hulk looked at Dak, "It is not easy being the leader and having to make those decisions. I know she struggled making this one sending us west."

Robin Hood said, "Hell no. It is not easy being in charge." He looked at Dak and smiled. "I know I am ready to eat. I am starving to death. Who gets the first strip of meat?"

Veronica laughed, "Robin Hood you eat more than any of us and yet you never gain weight. You are the runt of our group."

Trey announced, "I am going to eat four pounds of the tender pork, and then I am going to sleep like a baby."

The group kept talking and loved being in the woods away from the adults. They really enjoyed each other's company, and they knew how to have fun with Robin Hood pulling out his stash of weed and rolling papers.

Tommy Boy looked at Dak, "I know about the Blueblood's dark skin, pointed ears, and silver hair. I meant, what do you know about their ability to wage war? Do you really think they are better than us with a sword and a bow? I would put you and Robin Hood up against anyone with a bow. You two can hit flying birds all day long with an arrow."

Dak leaned back, "The stories are told that none of us have the power or the quickness they possess. We have been led to believe they are the greatest warriors on earth, and we would be no match for one of them in a one-on-one fight, but all of us working together should be able to take one down. The key would be us working together as a team. They are also rumored to be better than any of us fighting from horseback."

Tommy Boy stared straight into the fire understanding what Dak had just said. He then reached for Robin Hood's smoking weed and took a drag. Dak then added, "Some Bluebloods are better at fighting, and some are better at other activities. They are like us. Some of us are better at different things. What concerns me about fighting one of them is that I have heard they can block arrows coming at them with their swords and can fire a total of six arrows accurately from horseback at a full run before the first arrow hits the ground."

Veronica said, "That is what Eric and Wayne were talking about when we all went camping last year. Captain J.J. had told them the stories when he came to port. I just don't know if I believe they can block arrows with their swords. I get it. They are better than us with a sword but being able to block multiple arrows coming at them with the broad side of a sword blade, I just do not believe it. How would we ever hit them with a sword if they can block an arrow?"

Tommy Boy smoked some weed and handed the joint over to Hulk. "I believe it. I also believe we are all better at certain things." He smiled at the others. "I am the strongest in this group."

"Now I know you're high," mentioned Hulk.

Trey added, "Lord have mercy. Cut him off. He has had too much weed."

Dak added, "We are fortunate the tribe has kept and maintained these Geiger counters from the old world, and Mia was able to figure out how to recharge the batteries in running water."

Veronica added, "The man named Jacob would come over, and they worked on the battery rechargeable device on the kitchen table all night for weeks trying to figure the process out."

Trey announced, "Jacob was from some place called Princeton. He died about five years ago, and I am afraid a lot of his wisdom died with him. There just was not enough time to learn what he knew. The people of the earth were trying to survive in the new world. As far as we know, no one tried to preserve old-world technology. Matter of fact, mom indicated the Midlanders destroyed all the data from the old world. The old world had mass produced the Geiger counters because of the threat of nuclear war, and there are several of them around the world preserved. But not much else can be located."

Dak listened and watched the group as they started laughing. He knew as soon as Tommy Boy made the comment about being the strongest, Trey and Hulk were wanting to see who could do the most pushups and then the wrestling would start. He also knew the trip was going to be risky, and he just did not feel good about the Bluebloods. When meeting with his mother and Wayne, they instructed him to seek out a man by the name Ivan Chezon. Ivan Chezon could provide the needed advice in dealing with the Blueblood Senate. He was an old, trusted friend from the old Russian territory. She had known him during the time before the nuclear holocaust. She had indicated he could count on Ivan.

The group slept well after the long ride with Hulk, Tommy Boy, and Trey's wrestling providing additional entertainment. They had eaten a small amount of the boar for breakfast. They would ride hard again today, and then they would proceed at a slower pace once they entered the path between the nuclear waste areas. The path provided in the map had them traveling around mountains and then down across deep gorges and three rivers. They would have to always keep the battery-operated nuclear detection device turned on. The battery could be re-charged in a river with the cold flowing water. They had a second battery as back-up with a second detector. If one of them wandered into the middle of a nuclear bomb waste area, a slow death was certain. They had heard tales of several men dying over the years from the nuclear contamination. The radiation was invisible, and one could not always tell by the grass and trees if radiation was present. Dak remembered a group of elders sitting around the fire one night talking about the old world and the nuclear war. No one ever knew who fired the first nuclear missile. Even President Grant was not certain. He was one of the tribe's members and liked sewing the leather animal hides together making clothing and quilts in the back room of his small cabin. He had grown elderly and kept to himself most days, but he enjoyed coming to the gatherings and listening to people talk about the old days.

Chapter 7

Dak was leading as the group approached Old Thomas's farm. He had been one of the tribe members that wanted to live on his own. Wayne had told the group years ago when they were on a hunting trip that Old Thomas was the sole survivor from his family and his community. Wayne had hesitated before completing his thought. "He had a very difficult time accepting he was the only remaining survivor of his small Maine community. He had lost his wife, three kids, and all his friends during the Armageddon. We all feel sorry for him. He is a nice man."

His farm was located at the edge of the tribe's land and the border to the first nuclear waste area. He watched the western territory and sent a pigeon daily to the tribe. He was the lookout for the tribe for the west territory. He would check the boundary line daily for signs of Midlanders crossing into their territory.

He saw the six riders heading his way. His two dogs started barking as the horses and riders approached. The old man was a recluse, but he was nice. The group had met him from time to time over the years either in town, or when they were making a sweep of the territory with Billy Ray, Eric of Newport and Little Jimmy during the weeklong camping trips. Old Thomas welcomed the company, if the company did not overstay their visit.

Dak approached the front porch and announced they needed a place to stay for the night. At first light, they would be headed on the path through the danger zone. Old Thomas was always dressed in leather pants sewed up the sides with oversized seams and a leather coat with fur around the neck. He smiled at the group and asked, "Where is Billy Ray, Eric of Newport, Wayne and Little Jimmy?"

Dak spoke as he dismounted, "The tribe was attacked, and they are standing guard. Little Jimmy is needed to load the catapult and mom needs Billy Ray, Wayne and Eric in case of another attack. We were able to kill over three hundred attacking Normand soldiers, but we know they will return." Dak knew he did not want to overstay his welcome. He added, "We will leave at first sunrise. We brought you some salt from the ocean and some fresh meat from the boar we killed last night plus other items mom sent. She said you can list any items you would need, and someone from the tribe will deliver them to you." The older man relaxed. The group fed the horses and released them in Old Thomas's fenced corral in the small field. Old Thomas was surprised that the teenagers were going to cross the waste lands to seek out the Bluebloods. Dak could see the look on his face. Dak said, "You will need to release one of your pigeons in the morning once we have left with a note telling mom we have moved further west."

Old Thomas followed the group into the cabin and became animated reviewing the map and providing his insight into the territory. He spent the next hour looking at their map and explaining what he knew about the path. He was sincere with concern about their journey.

Old Thomas said, "When I find animals that made it through the waste land, I must kill them and bury them. You can see them from hundreds of yards off and tell they have the disease. They have large open sores that will not heal. The disease is not contagious, but there is only one outcome. The animals are not safe to eat, and I do not want my dogs getting sick." He further explained there is nothing alive inside the contaminated areas. "It looks like an area on the moon just barren with no life, but you cannot count on the looks. The winds can change, and the radiation can travel. Eventually the radiation will kill the trees and woods if the radiation does not dissipate in the air quickly enough. I have noticed over the past few years, some weeds are starting to grow in some of the outskirts of the areas, but the center spots will never recover naturally. It will take 1000 years for the radiation to disappear. If you enter one of the nuclear waste areas without protective gear, you will die a slow death." He looked at the group with a concerned expression.

***

The next morning, the group slowly rode west with Hulk leading the way. The group was quiet and understood the danger of circling around the nuclear waste zone. Trey said, "Old man Thomas seemed to be happy this morning. I guess he was glad we were all leaving."

Veronica added, "That is not why he was happy. Robin Hood gave him a smoke and got him high last night." The group all laughed.

Robin Hood blurted out, "That is not why he was happy and smiling. He smoked the weed to celebrate. He was smiling because he walked in on Veronica in the backroom while she was naked and sponging off." The group laughed more.

Veronica had not realized anyone had known that while she was washing and changing her clothes, Old Thomas had opened the door. She also did not tell anyone she discovered Old Thomas had a peephole in the door. She smiled to herself as she thought about how he watched her disrobe and wash herself as she intentionally positioned herself in front of the peephole before he finally opened the door. "He apologized several times. Opening the door was an accident."

Robin Hood smiled looking forward at the group. He wanted everyone to hear him, "I heard him tell you he felt he had truly been blessed, and you could come and visit him anytime as he pulled the door closed." The group of five males all laughed.

Hulk finally suggested, "You, Veronica, definitely got the looks in your family."

Trey, being Veronica's younger brother who weighed about one-hundred-fifty pounds heavier announced, "What are you talking about? I am the best looking one in the family."

Robin Hood, still smiling said, "On your best day versus Veronica on her worst day times two, she is still better looking. You look just like your father, Little Jimmy, and Old Thomas did not walk in on you by accident. He is a lonely old man and has not seen a good-looking naked female in years. Hell, it was no accident. He was just a little high after the scenery." They all laughed. Robin Hood added, "He will be glad to see Veronica when we return. As long as Veronica is with us, he will make room for us in his cabin, otherwise, we men might be sleeping in the barn." The group laughed.

Trey then announced, "I am two-hundred-and-fifty-nine pounds of twisted steel and sex appeal." The group laughed again and kept riding.

***

The group tried to stay close together, and Hulk used the nuclear detector every few minutes. They followed the old trail with Hulk leading the way. Hulk was the best tracker and best at traveling on horseback for an extended period. He was also the best hunter. They could see the green trees miles away as they crossed a hill. The path seemed to just stop with barren land directly in front of them. They dismounted from their horses and looked at the map and looked for signs. Finally, Dak announced, "We can camp here tonight. We will try to look for a path on foot. We hopefully will be ready to travel again in the morning. We might have to backtrack and head north."

Chapter 8

On the fourth day of the journey, they had been able to recharge the batteries in the detectors in a stream. They had traveled up the stream north and then west into a small forest. Dak said, "This forest might lead us nowhere. I believe we are going to have to go further north into the glaciers and then turn west. I hope not, because our horses won't be able to make the journey in the deep snow."

The group had stopped talking and were just moving forward. The trip had become harsh. All of them had body aches from riding and little sleep. Robin Hood had been the rear rider and had been placing markers along the path cutting into the tree bark with his knife. On the tenth day, they noticed footprints near the second river. The group all had heard the stories of the Midlander tribes. They were cannibals, and they were lawless cut throats. No one knew how many tribes there were in the waste lands, but Wayne had told them the numbers could be more than the Normand and Blueblood populations. They were commanded by whomever was the strongest warrior and then when he was killed, another warrior would take his place. The group realized they needed to travel at night to stay clear of the tribes. They agreed after crossing the river they would proceed further northwest. Hulk had recharged both his detectors in the river and felt comfortable turning them off. The forest seemed thick with life, and the water had no signs of radiation. They were able to cross the river upstream and then traveled up a valley leading to the mountain top. On the other side of the mountain, they could see barren land and knew the area was contaminated. Hulk checked the area, and the detector chirped. They pushed further north and then zigzagged through the rough mountains.

On the fifteenth day they saw additional footprints and horse prints. Dak noticed Hulk had jumped off his horse at the stream's edge and was examining the prints very closely. He mounted his horse and galloped back to where Dak and the others waited. Hulk reported, "I have never seen prints like this. They appear to be two individuals. The footprints are showing up in the mud along the river. It would appear they are intentional walking in the edge of the river to avoid being followed, and they have a soft leather bottom soles on their boots. Both have a larger arch than normal." He looked at Dak to verify if Dak was understanding the significance of what he had just said.

Dak announced, "They could be two Bluebloods on the run. We are deep in Midlander territory. Don't you remember the one lost Blueblood we found. He had a larger arch in his feet. The directions from Wayne indicate once we make it past the third river, we are two maybe three days ride from the west coast. There should be no additional nuclear contaminated areas. Merlin is located at the narrowest part of the new continent. We are getting close." He knew his friends would be happy to know the journey across the continent was about over.

Hulk looked at Dak, "There is more. They are being hunted. It looks like eleven riders came in from the south tracking them, maybe an hour behind. The horse droppings are still warm, and the tracks are fresher than the Bluebloods tracks."

Dak announced, "We will need to catch up. We need the Bluebloods to show us the way to Merlin. This might be the break we need. I need to talk with Ivan Chezon and then we need to head home. Our tribe will need us in the next battle if King Solman sends his army north. Can you find a way around them, so we can get in front? They have to be heading southwest at some point."

Hulk acknowledged with his head movement, "We can cross the river here and head west and see if we can cut them off. The Bluebloods will most likely head north in hopes of losing the posse. They then will head west in hopes of either outrunning the Midlanders or finding help from Merlin. I cannot help but believe after listening to Billy Ray and Wayne talk about the Blueblood clan, that the City of Merlin would not send out additional Blueblood soldiers and some of the regular army in an attempt to locate the two Bluebloods. The two will try to reach other Bluebloods before the Midlanders capture them. If we run into an army squad from Merlin, we need to make certain they understand our intentions, and that we are not Midlanders. If they believe we are Midlanders, they will kill us."

Dak looked at Hulk with concern, understanding they could be confused with Midlanders. Dak grimaced, "Just another pearl in our endeavor to cross the continent."

**

The group rode hard for two hours west with Hulk checking for tracks. They came to the edge of the woods on a hill facing east. Hulk held his hand up to signal for them to stop, "I would have thought they would have headed southwest by now. We have not crossed any tracks in two hours."

Dak ordered, "We will proceed northeast. We might have outrun them. We will need to keep quiet. The Midlanders must be close. The Bluebloods would need to head west toward the City of Merlin to seek safety and shelter. You lead the way at about fifty yards. We will ride ten yards apart with no sound." The group nodded their heads they understood.

The group rode hard northeast for another thirty minutes. Hulk was fifty yards in front when he suddenly stopped his horse and dismounted. Dak motioned for the group to halt as they each stopped next to him. "I am going to see what is ahead. Veronica, you come with me and secure our horses. The rest of you stay here," Dak announced.

Dak crawled up next to Hulk who was lying on his stomach at the top of the ridge line. He looked down into the small valley with a creek running parallel to the ridge through the bottom middle part of the valley. The hedge was grown up along the creek banks with tall grass and small trees providing cover with thick foliage. There was a pine forest a few hundred yards east and snow on a mountain directly north. Dak kept looking but did not notice anything unusual. He turned toward Hulk and asked, "What made you so jumpy? Ever since you saw the footprints at the river, you have been on alert. You have tracked people before and not been this anxious. What gives?"

"The tracks I discovered are the eleven hunters. They crossed the ridge here. Look twenty feet west of the rocks and then look east of the creek near the grove of trees. Look next to the creek directly in front of us. Then, tell me what you see."

Dak did so, and at first, he did not see anything. As he refocused, he saw a man camouflaged hiding in the grass. He scanned the area near the creek and then near the tree grove. "I count three men hiding and waiting."

65

"There are eleven men hiding, and they are spread out. They are going to trap something or someone. My bet is their horses are hidden either in the pine forest or behind the opposite ridge."

Veronica crawled up next to Dak. She whispered, "The horses are secure. What have you got?"

Dak whispered, "We count eleven Midlanders spread out below. It appears to be a trap." He showed her the men in hiding.

Veronica whispered, "They are going to try to capture the Bluebloods. Wayne said an imprisoned Blueblood is worth a herd of horses to the Midlanders."

Dak whispered, "That is my bet. They have the ambush set."

Hulk turned toward his two friends, "This is not our concern. We need to proceed west as fast as possible and deliver the message and return home. We do not need this trouble."

Dak whispered, "I am in charge. This is my decision. We need to help the Bluebloods. This might buy us some goodwill. We can't just sit back and watch them become slaves or butchered. We need to slip Robin Hood in range with his bow and take out the two men over there." He pointed next to the creek. "Veronica, I need you and Tommy Boy to ride around to the other side of the valley and slip down behind the hedge roll on the north end. Hulk, Trey and I will attack from horseback directly at their position from this ridge. You will need to make your arrows count."

Veronica whispered, "We need to get going. We will need to ride north in a hurry to cross the valley unseen and then get in position. They look like this is about to happen very soon." She ran back down the slope of the hill, jumped on her horse and rode further down the hill and told Tommy Boy he needed to follow her.

Hulk looked mad but did not say anything. Dak noticed Hulk's expression, "This is my decision. If it blows up in our face, I will live with it. Now get ready to attack."

Robin Hood crawled down the hill through the high grass and weeds. He slipped unnoticed behind some small trees and then crawled into position one-hundred feet away. Dak saw Veronica and Tommy Boy cross the opposite ridge in the distance. They also crawled down through the thick underbrush. Dak turned and saw Hulk and Trey sitting on their horses ready to ride into battle. Dak turned back around and looked at the far valley, and he could now see two blond-headed people heading their way. He kept watching as one was limping and was obviously injured. The other Blueblood kept trying to support the injured Blueblood. He readjusted his binoculars and noticed the one trying to help the other was a female. The two kept looking back as they hurried as fast as the injured one could go. Dak said, "Damn. They are going to be butchered." He got up and ran for his horse. He looked at Hulk and announced, "We have no choice but to go now." Hulk shook his head in understanding.

Dak jumped on his horse. "Shields up and follow me. We must come in from the south of the valley, and we need to hurry." The three rode south behind the ridge and then crossed the ridge and rode full speed down the slope.

The two Bluebloods saw the three riders and knew they could not outrun them. The older Blueblood looked into Zenith's blue eyes, "Child, you need to save yourself. You need to run. I will kill these three or at least hold them up and give you time to hide. I just can't make it any further. I am no good to you. I cannot breathe. I know my lung is full of blood." He coughed and blood flew to the ground as he wiped his mouth and looked at the blood on his rag.

Zenith looked into the pleading man's eyes and clinched her jaws, "You know what they will do to you. I am a Blueblood warrior. We do not run. I will fight to the death. I am not going to abandon you."

The older warrior looked into her eyes and pulled her close, "You must go and leave me. My left lung is punctured. I cannot make it. You must go."

She pulled her sword. "I will not leave you. We will fight to the death." She stepped forward and positioned herself between

Dak who was charging and her wounded friend. Out of her peripheral vision, she saw a Midlander stand and fall with an arrow in his back. Then, she noticed Dak lean to the side while holding the saddle horn and cut down a man hiding in front of them. The other two riders went toward the creek and took out two more hidden men. As she turned, she saw other men falling from being shot with arrows. She stepped forward twenty yards into the open area and was prepared to fight in the open ground. Her friend yelled as an arrow hit him in the center chest. Zenith ran toward him. He was out of breath, "I am sorry. My time has come." Zenith looked up and saw two men charging at her. One fired a bow, and she blocked the arrow with her sword and then charged the two men. She ducked low under his sword and cut the one man through the thigh and then recoiled quickly and hit the other in the side, killing him. Neither man could match the speed of her sword. She went back to the first man with his wounded leg as he was lying on the ground. She placed her sword tip at his throat and noticed his bow lying on the ground, "Did you fire the arrow that killed my friend?"

He was trying to apply pressure to his injured leg and smiled, "He just stood still and let it hit him. He did not try to deflect it like you did. I will be famous for killing a Blueblood in battle."

She knew her friend wanted to sacrifice himself, so she could run for cover. She felt guilty for his death. "How far behind is the main army?"

The wounded man looked at her, "Two hours." She knew he was lying and cut his throat. She turned and saw Dak pull himself to the side of the horse and use his shield to block an arrow. He then reached over from the saddle and cut down a man who had been hiding on the hillside and had shot the last arrow at Dak.

Zenith ran to her friend and knelt by his side. She checked his pulse and closed his eyes. Dak came down the hill in the open area slowly approaching with his sword in its sleeve, "We need to leave in a hurry. The main army will be marching over that hill in a few minutes. There were eleven of them tracking you, and all eleven have been eliminated. Hulk and Trey also approached slowly. "You two ride and get the others their horses." Zenith had walked to the side in the open area holding her sword while watching the three. Dak jumped off his horse and walked toward the Blueblood lying on the ground as he kept his eyes on Zenith.

Zenith did not take her eyes off Dak. She said as Dak approached the dead man, "You need to stay away from him, or I will kill you. You will not steal his blood."

"I do not want his blood. Can we help him?"

"No. He is dead."

Zenith watched him while holding her sword. Dak bent down and felt his wrist, "He has no heartbeat." Dak walked back to his horse. As he got on his horse, "I am sorry about your friend. We do not have time to bury him. We tried to catch up and intervene to save you both."

Zenith was still holding her sword in her right hand. "I must bury him."

"We need to leave now. Hear that sound. That is a thousand horses headed this way. I am sorry, but we are leaving. We need to head north and then northwest. You are welcome to come with us."

Zenith looked at Dak, "You need to get off your horse and give him to me. I am a Blueblood, and I command you to give me your horse. It is the law. You are to do as I say. Now get off your horse."

Dak grinned, "My horse is named General Lee. I really like my horse, and I believe he likes me. I believe I will keep my horse." He smiled at Zenith and in an urgent tone, "We just saved you, and I am not giving you my horse. If you want to jump on the back, we need to leave now. Otherwise, you are on your own."

Trey and Hulk rode to meet the others, and they watched to see if Dak was coming. Dak motioned for them to head up the valley for the cover of the pine thicket.

Zenith went over to the dead Blueblood and removed his leather strap and medallion from around his neck and shoved them into her pocket. She looked at her fallen comrade for the last time. She placed her sword into the sleeve on her right hip and ran over and jumped on the back of Dak's horse. "There are over a thousand Midlanders coming after me. That much of what you say I believe is true. I am a Blueblood. Maybe you should give me the reins."

"I believe I can manage just fine. You need to hang on." He spurred the horse, and they followed the five other horses.

After fifty minutes of hard riding, Hulk held a hand up. He jumped off his horse and tested the air for nuclear contamination. The gauge was green. The others caught up, and he announced, "We are still clear."

Dak rode up and the group looked at Dak and Zenith riding double. Tommy Boy looked at Zenith, "What is your name?"

"My name is Zenith, and I am a Blueblood warrior. You are all looking me in the face. It is not allowed to make eye contact with a Blueblood. You should know this. Who are you, and where are you from?"

No one answered, "You just come literally from nowhere." She thought about their actions, and they showed no fear in her presence.

Dak changed the subject and looked at Hulk, "Should we go straight due west or go north then go west?"

Hulk responded, "Midlanders will try to cut us off and catch us if we go west. I am not certain with you riding double, we can outrun them. The safe play is go further north then cut west and proceed south down the coast like the map suggests."

Zenith asked, "What map? Where are you going? You keep ignoring me. I am a Blueblood. You need to do as I say."

Dak responded, "We are heading to Merlin to meet the Blueblood Senate. I need to meet with a man by the name of Ivan Chezon. Let's take the safe route and go north." Zenith's wrinkles appeared on her forehead as she now was squinting. The group could tell she was mad as Dak motioned for Hulk to lead the way and spurred his horse and followed Hulk.

Chapter 9

Vicky picked up the note without reading it. She looked at the note she had received thirteen days ago from the pigeon dispatched by Old Thomas. She could not help but worry. She was mad that the Bluebloods had done nothing to stop King Solman and his conquering and terror of the southern part of the new world. She could not comprehend why the Bluebloods did not understand the threat. She knew it was just a matter of time before the Normand army had enough resources and men to wage war at the Blueblood City of Merlin. She also knew at some point her small tribe could not hold out under a massive long-term extended war. They needed to make the Blueblood Senate understand and act against the common threat. The other parents were worried. The group was too young to make the trip, but she knew she had to send someone she trusted, and she needed her closest friends for the pending battle.

If they were going to win and survive, she needed the help of Ivan Chezon. Ivan had been an employee of a Russian mafia leader who was friends with the Russian dictator. His boss lived in Russia in the old world. Vicky had walked into his mansion and killed Val Venwhik and five bodyguards who were hand-picked and trained in the Russian Special Forces. She spared Ivan's life. He, in return, had agreed to work for

Vicky and the CIA. The two had developed a friendship over the next few years. Ivan helped save the hidden colony of Blueblood people and then after the collapse of the world, he helped them relocate to a safe area on the western part of the continent. Now Vicky did not understand what had happened to the Blueblood people and Ivan. Ivan was too smart not to see King Solman as a threat. Sending her only son should send a message to Ivan. Her message needed to be taken seriously, and she required his help. They needed to work together. They needed each other. She laid the message down and walked out of her small apartment located on the top floor of the four plex and tried to be positive. She proceeded to the small store and greeted Delores. She knew Delores was also worried. She seemed to worry more about Tommy Boy, her youngest son, than her older son Hulk. Hulk was ten months older and took after his father, Billy Ray. He seemed to be able to take care of himself at an early age. Tommy Boy did not take after either parent. He was a good kid but was quiet, a follower, and seemed to be late to mature. He had a large boned frame and at some point, after he hit a growth spurt, he would be a huge, strong man. All the other kids seemed to be more athletic and more active.

Delores said, "I am trying to keep busy and stop worrying. I know the kids are not due back for a few days. I remember in the old world, how our parents would send us to summer camp for a week with several adult supervisors, and the parents would still worry. Lord have mercy, we sent our kids across the continent to fight people we know are killers, through nuclear waste lands without an adult present."

Vicky replied, "I saw Mia and Little Jimmy last night. We sat by the fire and talked. They are also concerned but are confident in the kids. I believe they will take care of each other. They are all more mature than twenty-year-olds in the old world. They had to grow up fast." She looked at Delores, "There is something that has been bothering Wayne and I. We just cannot figure out why the Normand army attacked us. We are located at the furthest most point north. We know the great mountain range divides the continent, but why not attack Merlin? They are on the west coast where the continent is now the shortest distance from one side of the continent to the other and is located closer to Southern City."

Delores looked perplexed, "We do not know why King Solman does what he does. I have decided, there is a great deal we do not understand about our new world. We need to live in the future in this new world, or we are all going to be killed. There is no going back in time."

Chapter 10

The group came up to a small open area next to a stream. The stream had icicles hanging in the rapids, and tree limbs hanging into the stream, weighted down with ice. The ground was lightly covered with a dusting of snow. Dak commanded, "We will camp here. Robin Hood, you can feed the horses and tie them to a lead rope. There is a little grass exposed under the snow at the edge of the tree line for the horses to eat. You might want to also hobble them. We cannot afford to lose a horse. Veronica, you and Trey can gather firewood. It will be cold tonight, and we will need plenty of firewood. Hulk, you take your spear and see if you can find fish in the stream. Tommy Boy, you can scout the area of about one-hundred-yards around us to see if there are any concerns. Robin Hood, after you attend to the horses, if you see any animals to eat, shoot them with your arrow. The fish might not be enough."

The group dismounted and went to their jobs. Dak and Zenith dismounted the horse with Dak giving the horse reins to Robin Hood. He looked at Zenith and noticed she was not dressed for the cold weather. Her robe was thin and not lined with fur, and he could see her exposed stomach muscles as her top did not extend over her midsection. Her boots were thin leather and also not lined with fur. He asked, "What is going on? What are you not telling us? An old Blueblood man and a young pretty Blueblood female do not happen to be in the middle of the Midlanders territory by themselves. Where are your people?"

"What are you talking about? I was on my training exercise through the wilderness. This is part of my apprenticeship to become a full Blueblood Warrior. There were twenty of us, and we were ambushed by the Midlanders. The two of us were separated from the rest. The older man was one of the trainers. He had been cut through his hamstring and had a punctured lung from an arrow. He was unable to fight or run. He lost his horse in the attack. We headed north on my horse in hopes of losing them. We figured they would anticipate us heading west or south. The plan worked at first. They have some very good trackers. My trainer could not move fast with his leg cut and his lung punctured. We had hoped to head north then go west until we reached the ocean and then go south back to Merlin. The same plan as you."

Dak observed her while she talked. She had dark brown skin, blue eyes, and long blond hair. He could see her pointed ears with her hair pulled back in a long ponytail. When she talked, she was very articulate and talked with confidence and intelligence. He noticed the dark rings under her eyes. He could tell she was tired and cold. He also could not help but notice she was very attractive. "How old are you?"

She looked into his eyes, "Why do you keep staring at me?"

"I am sorry. I just have never met anyone like you."

"I am fourteen. The same age as all other Blueblood apprentices trying to graduate into the brotherhood of being a Blueblood warrior. We mature faster than the normal teenager."

"You were separated intentionally from the larger group. The Midlanders wanted to wear you down and then capture a couple of Bluebloods and use the blood for the ongoing fight against the B12 virus. Your blood will make them immune. They would then trade you or sell you. Each one of you would be worth a hundred good horses."

She snapped, "I know what they wanted, and what they were doing. I was not going to leave him. He was on point, and the first one injured. We rode into the trap. He was injured by design. I was second in our march and ran to him. I killed several of their men, and we escaped and rode my horse until it died." She hesitated looking directly at Dak. "The trainer was not a true warrior. He was a nice gentle man who loved people and life and now he is dead."

Dak could tell Zenith had bonded with the trainer. He could see the pain of loss in her face. He thought Zenith might have been his apprentice. He could tell the dead man was more than just a trainer to her. "We are all sorry for your loss."

"He was a close friend to my father. He was watching out for us. He volunteered to go with our class on our final training exercise. I will greatly miss him."

She hesitated and then announced, "I do not believe you understand the Blueblood Senate. If you are allowed to talk to them, they will not help you. You will be arrested for looking a Blueblood in the eyes. You do not know how to act in the presence of a Blueblood."

Dak looked her in the eyes, "We will see about that. The leader of our tribe instructed me to talk to Ivan Chezon. Ivan will not allow me to be arrested. Do you know Ivan Chezon?"

"Ivan Chezon was arrested and hauled away to the dungeon a few years ago. When he escaped, he just disappeared. He might be dead. The Blueblood Senate has a large reward for him dead or alive."

"How could that be? I understood he helped the first-generation Bluebloods and the colony during the old world. Without him, the Blueblood colony would not have survived the Armageddon. Why did he get arrested?"

"Because he was a normal man." Dak looked at her with scorn. "The Blueblood colony was sick of the arguing and nothing getting accomplished. They decided they needed to be in charge and took over the senate. You now must be a Blueblood to be in the senate. The mass of people are either slaves or work for Blueblood families. The people lost their land and have no rights. All the property is owned by the Blueblood Senate and Blueblood families. The farmers and ranchers in the rural areas must have a Blueblood as an owning partner to sponsor them."

"You mean they had a coup and forcefully placed themselves in charge. Your people have been genetically enhanced, and your people should try helping the ones in need. That is our way." He clenches his jaws, "It is about doing what is right to help those in need. That is why we helped you."

Trey walked in with another load of firewood. Veronica had dropped several limbs which would need to be further cut up. Hulk was walking down further along the stream looking for trout. Tommy Boy had crossed the stream and the ridge and had walked south of the camp. Dak was starting to be irritated, "The Midlanders wanted to separate you from the group. They know they do not want to fight twenty Bluebloods at one time. They need your blood to fight the B12 virus. Your blood makes you immune to the B12 Virus. The B12 virus is very deadly."

In a conflicted voice, she said, "I said I know what they wanted."

Dak looked down and shook his head. "Have you ever considered helping the people and providing a little of your blood to save them?"

Zenith never answered the question. She looked at Dak with her jaws clinched. "You do not understand. Who are you to judge me?" She now was frustrated, "The guards of the castle will kill you when you approach them. The Blueblood soldiers will not allow you close to the senate let alone talk to them. You are delusional if you think you will be able to speak with them. If by some miraculous chance you appear in the presence of the senate, it will be for a trial or to be sentenced for being who you are. You and your friends will end up in the dungeon at best or beheaded at worst. They will not tolerate drifters."

Dak listened. He then noticed Hulk was starting to appear back up the stream carrying fish and Veronica had started a fire. Tommy Boy ran from the woods and reported, "I see no signs of people. I am surprised there are no people in this area. It is nice here."

The group gathered around the fire and started to talk, laugh, and eat. Robin Hood had shot two rabbits and cleaned them. He had placed them over the fire next to the fish.

Veronica looked at Zenith, "Do you like fish and rabbit?"

"I am good with either." Zenith was surprised they asked her what she liked. She was hungry. She had not eaten in two days.

She had assumed since she was a Blueblood, she would eat what she wanted and then give the remains to them. Zenith sat back and watched the group interact. She was surprised by their friendship.

Trey glanced at his friends with a smile. He stared at Dak, "I heard you say Zenith is worth one-hundred horses. How did you compute that figure? What am I worth?"

Robin Hood announced, "I would give one-hundred-and-one horses for her. I would not give anything for you." He then smiled.

The group laughed, and Zenith felt a little uneasy. She looked at the group who were all smiling. Hulk snapped, "You don't own one horse Robin Hood let alone one-hundred-and-one."

"Smokey is borrowed from your parents," Veronica announced.

Robin Hood said, "People base their value of me on my personality and looks and not on my material wealth."

Zenith looked at Dak and with her hand on her sword. "Are they kidding?"

"They are always joking."

Trey smiled, "If we are not careful, we might gain weight on this trip. We still have some of the deer from last night. All we do is ride, eat, and sleep. I am not getting enough exercise, and when we do exercise, I must hold back on doing pushups because I am afraid I will hurt your feelings if I do several more than the rest of you." He deadpans the expression.

Robin Hood smiled, "The Blueblood might have something to say about doing more pushups than the rest of us." He glanced at Zenith and smiled. Robin Hood then added, "Yes, after I eat, I will roll us some dessert. Give you something to look forward to. Nothing like a good smoke and a buzz before sleep." Dak and the others smiled.

Dak then became serious, "The five of you will need to head back south and then east across the mountain. You guys will need to stay north of the Midlander camps, and since Robin Hood has marked the path for the trip home, you should be home in less than a couple of weeks. You will need to travel at night to clear the Midlander camps."

Hulk was the first to say, "We are not leaving you. We are a team, and the team sticks together."

Trey interrupted, "What are you talking about? We are going to stay together."

Dak ordered, "Zenith has indicated we will be arrested and thrown in the dungeon once we reach Merlin. There is no way all of us need to be arrested. I will convey our position to the Blueblood Senate and then leave. Things have changed. Ivan Chezon is a fugitive hiding from the Blueblood Senate. The Senate might not help us, and I do not want you to be arrested."

Tommy Boy looked perplexed, "Why would we be arrested?"

"For being who we are," Dak announced.

The group kept eating and finally Veronica announced, "We are a group. We need to stay together. If you're arrested and go to the dungeon, we can be close by to break you out."

Dak looked at his friends, "You will need to head home. I will take Zenith to her people and then I will convey our declaration for a joint effort of war against King Solman. It is my decision and my decision alone. I have spoken."

The group sat in quietness and finally Hulk announced, "I will go with you and Zenith and the other four can head home. You will need back-up at some point."

Dak did not bother to immediately reply. He looked at Veronica, "Zenith can bed with you tonight. Her clothing is not made for this cold weather."

Zenith looked at Veronica and could sense she did not like the idea. Zenith said, "I will be alright."

Dak replied, "Our bedrolls are lined with fur and have a liner like a large pocket we can crawl into. The bottom is thicker material which helps keep our feet warm. Your clothing is not made for the cold climate. Your boots have no fur lining. You must remove them when you sleep. They are wet and will freeze tonight. When the fire burns down, and we have no heat, you will freeze. The temperatures will plummet to below zero.

The temperature may even get as low as thirty degrees below zero."

Zenith could not help but shiver. She knew these men and Veronica were not going to give up their bedroll. She looked at Dak and spoke up, "Okay, I will lie in your bedroll with you."

All eyes glanced at each other at the revelation, and no one said a word. The group finished eating. They each dug a hole and placed some of the hot ashes in the ground under the dirt and then got under their capes lying on the ground above the hot ashes. Hulk placed some large logs on the fire. Hulk then said, "I will take the first watch and then I will wake Trey." The group knew the night watch routine.

Dak watched the others get under their robes and into the warm layer pocket of the lined bedrolls. Robin Hood looked up as he was about to pull his bedroll over his head with a smile, "Everyone knows it is best to remove all the wet clothes before entering the bedroll. Veronica, you can remove your clothing, and you should get under my bedroll to stay warm."

"Not on your life. I would rather freeze to death one-hundred-times-over." The group laughed.

Dak noticed Zenith had not hesitated to remove her boots and placed her sword beside her. She pulled the bedroll open and slid inside. Dak took a deep breath and thought, "What am I doing?" He pulled from his saddle bag the honeysuckle lotion and rubbed it on his chest and neck. He removed his boots, knife and laid his belt with his swords attached next to him and pulled the bedroll back and crawled under the cover. He said, "When you breathe, blow out hot air under the cover. We will need all the heat we can generate. I am concerned about you contracting hypothermia which can be caused from cold weather but also over exertion, which you are at risk from both."

Zenith had never been so cold. When Dak rubbed up against her, the body heat was welcome. She placed her feet into the pouch, but they were still cold. When Dax placed his feet into the pouch, she immediately felt the warmth. He reached over and felt her leg. She was shivering. He said, "You are freezing to death. Your body is not acclimated to the cold climate."

He started rubbing her legs and then held her feet in his hands. He kept breathing heavily with the hot air blowing under the cape. He hugged her and told her she needed his body heat. "Keep breathing out the hot air. The heat will be trapped under this fur. I promise you will be okay." He held her tight and rubbed her body.

She finally murmured, "Thanks" as she fell asleep. Dak wondered how long she had been without sleep. He then started wondering about meeting the Bluebloods. He knew he had to order his five friends home. He had little doubt he and Zenith could now make it to the coastline and then proceed south to Merlin. The old map had noted the new continent and coastline was not contaminated, and they should be only one-to-two days' ride away from the coast.

Dak awoke with the noise of Trey talking to the others about something large that was approaching. He heard Hulk say, "Place a lot of firewood on the fire and get it started again."

Dak got out from under the cape and put on his boots and belt with his swords. He asked, "What is it?" Tommy Boy and Robin Hood held their bows and were looking for a target. Veronica held her crossbow and was checking the rear in case they were being tricked.

Hulk said, "Trey woke me and said there was something out of eyesight up the hill in the woods. He walked up the hill a small distance. We are waiting for him to return."

Dak was surprised, "Why did you not wake me before now?" He looked at Hulk with a frown and his eyes were staring intently at Hulk. "I should have gone up there with him."

"We did not want to disturb you and your concubine." He and Hulk were best friends. They had not been in a fight since the age of eleven. They basically would fight once a year until the time they were both eleven and then the next day be best friends. He started to hit Hulk with his fist, but he heard Trey walking out of the woods. There was a baby racoon following him. He turned and looked at the group, "I found this little guy. I fed him a mushroom, and now he is following me." He smiled really big, "I am sorry to wake all of you. I thought I heard something a lot larger, but the noise could have been his mother and the rest of his family."

As Trey made the statement a large shadow appeared behind him. Robin Hood raised his bow, "Trey, get down." Trey thought he was joking. Tommy Boy ran over and got into firing position. At that point, Trey ran behind the fire and looked over his shoulder at a two-thousand-pound bear charging.

Dak immediately grabbed a burning log and ran into the bear's path. "Don't shoot unless it goes toward the horses. He is out for a winter stroll. He is not hunting." The bear seeing the fire being waved back and forth halted the charge. The bear reared up on its hind legs and growled. Hulk grabbed another burning log and did the same. The bear sensed the danger of the fire with both men frantically poking and waving the burning sticks. The bear turned and ran back into the woods. The two watched and then placed the logs back on the fire.

Dak said, "Let us keep the fire going." He turned and crawled back inside his bedroll. He was surprised Zenith had slept through the entire episode. She moved over against him once he laid still. He could tell she was tired and cold. He knew she would be warm enough inside the bedroll. He welcomed her sleeping body pushing up against his trying to get warm as he wrapped his arms around her and held tight.

***

The group woke and ate breakfast. Dak could tell the others did not like his decision. Veronica mentioned the huge bear and Zenith asked about the bear. They all paused. Dak finally said, "You said you have not slept in days. We all are sorry for the loss of your trainer. You must have had a hard journey. We are glad we could help you."

"I had been a few days without sleep. Part of my training is to go without sleep. They want to see how we react when our body is pushed to the limit, and how we perform under stress. They also want to make certain we are committed to have the honor to be a Blueblood warrior. The failure rate is fifty-four percent. We were about finished with the week-long exercise when we were attacked."

"The Brown bear was over a ton and ten feet tall when it stood on its back legs," Trey mentioned as he was eating the last of the fish.

"Why did you not kill it?"

Veronica smiled, "It is not our way to kill something for no reason. If we cut a tree or kill an animal, it is for a need. We knew we could protect you and run the bear away with fire."

She snapped. "I am a Blueblood warrior. I do not need to be protected. I will protect you."

Robin Hood announced, "That is twice we have saved your life. If we stepped back, the bear would have walked over to you while sleeping and devoured you for his midnight snack." Zenith looked mad.

Dak looked at Zenith, "They are teasing you. Do you not listen to them talk to each other?" Zenith looked at the now smiling faces of the six and walked away.

Dak knew he would have to be forcible in telling Hulk he was not coming with him. He finally ordered, "Zenith and I are leaving. You five need to load up and move east and pick up your old trail once you cross the mountain. Hulk will be your leader on the trip home." He watched Hulk for a reaction.

Veronica asked, "How about you? We will be free of the Midlanders once we cross the fourth mountain and the second river. What if you run into them going west? They may not give up so easily. You know they need her blood. You cannot outrun them riding double."

Zenith announced, "I will protect Dak. I am a Blueblood warrior."

Hulk was angry, "Like you did last night when we were confronted by the giant bear?"

Robin Hood added, "If we ever want to attack a Blueblood, all we need to do is wait until they fall asleep. You would sleep right through the entire attack."

Veronica and Trey both looked at Zenith with angered expressions. Zenith looked at Dak in surprise, "Are they teasing now?"

Dak said, "The two-thousand-pound bear would have woken you, and you would have killed it. We ran him off with fire to protect him. It was not really an attack. The bear was looking for a place to hibernate. He knows winter is coming. He must have come out of his shelter prematurely. He was not looking for food. He was just on a walk. Sometimes they do that."

"Why did you not kill it? That would have been the safe thing to do. Then, you would not ever have to worry about it again."

Tommy Boy said, "We never kill an animal unless we need to eat. That is our way." Zenith looked at the group and was not certain they were telling the truth. She could not believe she slept through an attack. She knew the Brown bears were territorial, killers, and assume humans to be part of their food chain.

Tommy Boy pointed, "Over at the tree line, you can see the footprint in the snow. When it stood on its hind legs, it was close to ten feet tall." Zenith walked over and inspected the ground and noticed the bear footprint was about twice the size of her hand.

Tommy Boy announced, "If he had been hungry, he would have gone after our horses. Like Dak said, the bear was just walking around the neighborhood. My best bet is he smelled the fish cooking from earlier and wanted to meet us."

Hulk walked by Dak as he was tightening his saddle, "I hope you know what you are doing, brother. This isn't right. You will need me at some point. Do you trust her?"

Dak looked at his friend, "I have made my decision."

Robin Hood said from the other side of the camp. "Dak, why don't you take my horse? You two might need another horse. We can ride double going home."

Dak replied, "Smokey is your horse. You will need her. You guys will have to face more than one Midlander tribe. We will make it to the coast in two, maybe three days, and then we will be safe. Thanks for the offer. I will see you in a month. I am going to try to beat the cold winter and make it back home. I love you guys."

Trey looked at Zenith. "Where we come from, if a person saves another's life, that person is indebted to that person for the rest of their life or until they save their life. It is called a life credit. He has now saved your life twice, once in the valley and once with the bear. You owe him two life credits. You better protect him."

Dak turned his head with a smile. The other four also smiled while Trey had a deadpan expression. Trey was not known to be funny or a prankster. Zenith could tell the group did not like her leaving with Dak. She came over and jumped on his horse behind him. "I will protect him. I am a Blueblood warrior." She then looked at the faces and noticed the group was now smiling and trying not to laugh. "Are you guys ever serious?" The group started laughing with Robin Hood looking at Trey and asking, "What in the hell is a life credit? Can you explain that once more?"

They rode off without saying goodbye while the five watched. Hulk finally announced, "We have done our jobs and now we are ordered back home. Everyone load your gear and let's go."

Veronica asked, "You are not going to follow him? You know he would follow you. I do not trust the Blueblood. She will leave him for dead and take his horse if she must."

Robin Hood asked, "What about the life credit?"

Veronica replied, "The joke is over. This is real. We should not be allowing Dak to ride off by himself."

Hulk had known Veronica had always seemed to like Dak. He had wondered if she did not have a crush on him. Although Dak had never tried to flirt with Veronica, he wondered how Dak really felt about her. Robin Hood seemed to always flirt with Veronica, and she just turned him down. She was not interested in Robin Hood. Hulk said, "We five have been ordered home and that is what we five are going to do. No one is going to follow Dak." He made eye contact. He then added, "Now, we need to get moving. Load your gear and let's get on the trail. The sooner we get home the better."

Veronica asked, "The better for who?"

Trey replied, "The better for all of us. Dak will be alright. The Normand army is real, and they might be returning as we speak. I have been worried about my parents ever since we left."

Chapter 11

Dak rode the first two miles without saying a word. He finally said, "I like your name Zenith. What is your last name?"

"That is my name. I only have one name."

"What does Zenith mean?"

"It has a couple of different meanings. I choose the one that indicates when something is most powerful or successful. The other meaning is the point directly above a particular spot in the atmosphere. In the old religion Islam, it means the passing of a star over Mecca." She hesitated and then said, "Your friends really like you. They wanted to come to Merlin knowing they would be arrested and not treated fairly."

"That is what friends do. Tell me about your friends."

"I don't want to talk about that subject. You know the City of Merlin is not going to welcome you. Let me take your message to the senate and you catch up with your friends. The Blueblood-controlled government will not be nice to you. You do not understand. You will not be allowed to speak to them. There is no venue where you will be able to convey your request."

"You do not understand. It is about doing what is right. I was entrusted to deliver the message, and I am going to do so. My tribe is depending on me." He could feel Zenith shift her weight to the other side. "You need to hold on tight as we ascend this hill." He felt her reach around him and tighten her hold as the horse climbed up the hill in the snow. After a few more hours they came down the other side, and Dak said, "We have ridden for eight hours. We will camp here tonight."

"We still have a few hours of daylight."

Dak replied, "The horse is tired, and he can feed on some of the grass and rest. There might not be grass available tomorrow in the mountains. Besides, it will give you time to gather firewood and set up camp."

Zenith jumped off the horse and a wrinkle appeared on her forehead as she looked at Dak. "I am a Blueblood. You need to gather the firewood and set up camp."

"Without firewood, we won't eat. I am going to take care of the horse and then I am going to try to find a rabbit. You need to learn to work. It is an honor to work. It is how we serve each other. Jesus was the greatest man to ever live, and he washed the feet of his disciples knowing one of them would betray him. The meal was called the last supper. He was trying to teach his disciples how to love each other. You show love by helping others. Some people talk about how they love others, but they never show it. Actions speak louder than words. The more you help others, the more you grow with love in your heart." Dak walked the horse to the creek and the grassy area. He tied off the rope, pulled off the saddle and bridle. He laid his cape, bedroll, and saddle bags on the saddle on the ground and pulled his bow. He noticed Zenith had not started to pick up firewood as he walked down the creek looking for animals. When he came back to the camp area carrying a turkey, he noticed Zenith had a large stack of firewood and was cutting it down to size. He walked into camp and announced, "I will clean the turkey, and you can start the fire."

Zenith seemed to be proud of the firewood and the stack. He said, "I have flint in my bag if you need it." Zenith went to the bag and pulled out the small bottle of honeysuckle lotion. She held it up, "What is this?"

As Dak was about to start cleaning the turkey, he looked over and smiled, "Take the lid off and smell it."

Zenith smelled the flagrance, "Perfume. I love the smell."

"Sometimes on long trips, I do not have an opportunity to bathe. The lotion was my mother's idea." After dinner and the hot fire burned for a couple hours, Dak suggested, "We need to get some sleep. We have a hard day tomorrow and then we will travel into warmer weather as we head south down the coast."

Zenith had watched Dak bury some hot coals under the ground and then lay his large bedroll on the ground. She did not hesitate. She hated being cold. She pulled her boots off and laid her sword beside her. She totally disappeared into the bedroll. Dak waited a few seconds and went to his bag and rubbed the lotion on his chest and walked over and crawled into the cape. This time, Zenith was facing him. She shivered and Dak rubbed her. He held her feet in his warm hands. She asked, "Why did Robin Hood ask Veronica to sleep under his bedroll with him?"

"Robin Hood likes Veronica, but Veronica does not like him to the extent that she wants to be romantically involved with him. She does not want to be under a bedspread with him."

"I heard Hulk whisper to Robin Hood that she has a body like Venus. What does that mean."

"Veronica has been blessed with a beautiful smile and perfect chiseled body. Those guys think she is very pretty"

"Do you like Veronica?"

"No, I do not like Veronica. I love Veronica like a sister. She is truly a great friend. Robin Hood just likes to flirt with Veronica."

"What do you mean flirt?"

"I will have to teach you how to flirt. You will someday meet the Blueblood of your dreams, and you will need to flirt with him."

She turned over, "I am still freezing." She shivered and placed her butt against his lap, "Please hold me tight and keep blowing out hot air. I hate cold weather." Dak held her tight and rubbed down her thigh to her feet trying to generate heat. Zenith turned back over and kissed him on the mouth. She turned back over and shivered again as she pushed her bottom into his midsection, "Is that flirting?"

He smiled with surprise as he tried to control his sexual impulses. "Yes. That is how to flirt, but to be good at it, you will need to learn how to use your tongue when you kiss." He licked her ear and then blew hot air in her ear. She shivered, "Okay that is enough flirting for one night. I get the picture. Are you not freezing? I am so cold. How are?" She never finished her sentence as she could feel his body become fully charged pushing repeatedly against her bottom. She hesitated, "You are now crowding me. Do you mind rolling over on your back? Please."

Chapter 12

Hulk was tired. He intentionally rode faster after the sun had risen. His plan was to ride for two hours in the early morning and then rest and eat breakfast. He wanted to make up for lost time after being forced to ride at slow pace in the darkness of the night. The woods were thick with foliage and the route ascended over a thousand feet and then dropped down the other side of the mountain after crossing one ridge and back up another. He had seen the tracks of buffalo, sheep, and deer as he rode. He was on constant lookout for the Midlanders. He knew his friends had all been pushed to the limit. The horses were all spent with their heads hanging low as they walked. Traveling through the mountains at night made the journey more difficult. He thought to himself, "If we can make it to the open area at the ridge line, we will camp, rest, and eat." He knew Robin Hood would be the one who complained. He was always sarcastic and complaining. That was his personality. He worried more about his brother enduring the long trip than he worried about the other three. Tommy Boy was now bigger and stronger, but he was not suited for long journeys, as he weighed over two hundred and eighty pounds. He appeared to Hulk to still be growing. Veronica and Trey would never give up. Their personalities were competitive, and they both were in better shape and exercised more than Tommy Boy growing up. He also knew Robin Hood might complain, but he would keep moving forward one step after the other.

Hulk rode around the low hanging thick Mountain Laurel bushes as the mountain ridge leveled. He felt the sudden shock of fear as he glanced ahead along the ridge line. He saw the column of men on horseback riding toward him in tandem fifteen yards away. He had not heard them or the horses for the wind blowing through the tree limbs. He could not see all the men for the forest, but he noted at least a dozen leading the hunting group. Hulk yelled, "They see us." He turned and motioned for the others to retreat down the mountain. They each ran their horses with the fear of being caught. They did not dare look back as they rode. They were all tired from the long ride the prior night. They thought they were clear of the Midlander hunting group and rode right into the hunting party.

Trey was leading the way, and his horse was giving out. After twenty minutes of hard riding, Tommy Boy's horse fell with a broken leg. Robin Hood circled back around and picked up Tommy Boy. Tommy Boy had hit hard on the ground and rolled downhill close to twenty feet into a log. He saw his horse try to stand and start limping. He knew the front right leg was broken. He could see the Midlander riders fast approaching. He did not hesitate to jump on the back of Robin Hood's horse.

Hulk knew they had to fight. They could not outrun the Midlanders and with Tommy Boy and Robin Hood riding double, they could not keep up. He yelled, "We are going to have to make a stand. We cannot outrun them. The horses are too tired." He eyed their surroundings and yelled, "Get ready at the next opening in the woods. We fight to the death. You know what we must do. You have been trained for this."

The group jumped off their horses with Veronica tying the horses up. Tommy Boy jumped from the rear of Robin Hood's horse as they approached the open area. He tied the rope across the path twelve inches high. Robin Hood jumped off his horse with his bow in hand and shot the first two riders as they approached the opening. They all pulled their bows and let one arrow after another fly. The riders were surprised when they rode into the wall of arrows, and they fell from the horses one after another. A few had made it along the trail and the horses were tripped by the rope. Once a rider was thrown to the ground, Tommy Boy would run from behind the tree and slice them with his sword. Once a couple of riders had gone around the trip wire and came up from the south side, Hulk had cut the leg of the charging horse with his sword and then Veronica cut the man on the ground before he had a chance to fight. The Midlander leader observed the group had dismounted and started circling around their position. Tommy Boy looked at Hulk, "What are we going to do? I lost my bow when my horse fell. Robin Hood is about out of arrows. There are too many of them, and they are trying to surround us."

Hulk knew they were running out of arrows. He thought, "We can't run; we can't stay here in the open, and we can't hide." He looked at his four friends, "We only have one choice. Pull your swords. We will have to surprise them with a frontal assault at their position. If we kill their leader, they might back down. We need to cut the head off the snake, and the rest will flop around and run off. This is my plan."

The group looked at each other and pulled their swords and lifted their shields. Hulk whispered, "Here we go."

They ran through the woods spaced out about four feet apart toward the group of Midlanders who were off their horses standing behind thick downed trees. The Midlanders were close to one hundred feet in front of them out of sight. The tree limbs and undergrowth prevented a clear view. The Midlanders had sent most of their men north and south to surround the group. The Midlanders had watched as over twenty of their men had been killed by the arrows as they charged. The Midlanders had no one watching the front line while they were talking about when to attack from all four directions. Hulk's plan had been both fortuitous and risky. By the time the

Midlanders were aware of the frontal assault, there was not enough time to prepare for the battle. The five ran through the group swinging the swords and firing the last of their arrows and killing the enemy. The leader lunged to fight Trey. Trey had pushed one man down and killed him with a downward swing of the sword. He had not hesitated and took on two other men, one being the leader. He tried to fight one at a time and always kept the other one out of strike distance. He was able to finally kill the smaller man when he cut deep into his arm and then slammed his shield into the man's head. Trey did not have enough time to set his feet with the larger warrior trying to catch him off balance. The larger man wore a buffalo head as a hat and was unshaved, had long dirty hair and was shirtless. He looked like a big monster who no doubt was a killer. He swung his sword with great force and grunted with each swing pushing Trey backward.

Veronica had seen her younger brother in distress and ran behind the large warrior cutting him deep across the shoulder as she came up behind him. This caused the man to hesitate between swings, and Trey finished him with a powerful swing as he decapitated the large man.

Robin Hood turned to fire another arrow and was shot by an arrow from a crossbow from a man behind a tree. Hulk had seen Robin Hood go down and had charged the man with the crossbow. Hulk had thrown his knife as he was reloading the crossbow. The knife caught the man in the center chest sinking all the way to the hilt. Hulk kept running toward the injured Midlanders picking up the fallen crossbow and shooting the next man. He reloaded the borrowed crossbow and shot another man. Veronica had finally used her last arrow on the men approaching from the other direction. They heard the horn and the Midlanders broke off the attack. The woods got quiet. The battle had lasted less than thirty-six minutes, and they had killed forty-six men and the others had ridden off.

Trey was the first to reach Robin Hood. He had an arrow sticking in his shoulder. He was sitting on the ground hunched over in pain. Trey announced, "It went all the way through and is sticking out the front. Dammit, hang in there."

He could see the sharp point of the arrow pushing against his shirt on the front of his shoulder. Trey noticed the arrow entered from the back and went out his front upper chest area below his collarbone. Veronica ran to Robin Hood then Tommy Boy and then Hulk. Trey looked up, "The arrow went straight through and missed the bone. He is lucky. We will have to break it off and pull it through." Robin Hood sat on the ground. His face was red, and he was quivering from the pain. Veronica lifted his shirt to inspect the arrow in the front.

Hulk looked around to make certain the area was clear of the enemy. Without further hesitation, Hulk walked over and cut the shirt back and then cut the end of the arrow off with his knife, and he pulled the arrow through his back. Robin Hood yelped and rolled over in pain. He said, "Dammit, that really hurt. I thought we were going to talk about that first."

"Hell no. We were not going to talk about it. If we started talking about it, we would be talking about it this time tomorrow." The group laughed.

Veronica placed a cloth on both holes, and said, "They took our horses. We are on foot. We need to place a bandage on him, and we need to start walking."

Hulk looked at his friends, "We will need horses. We will need our supplies. Robin Hood will need a proper bandage, and we will need our radiation detectors. All that is in our saddlebags. Does anyone have any suggestions?"

Robin Hood was still in pain. He blurted, "Someone should have been holding our damn horses."

Veronica looked at Robin Hood while still holding the cloth on both holes, "We were fighting overwhelming numbers. I did not have a choice."

Hulk looked at Veronica, "It is not your fault. It is my fault. I knew we should have never ascended straight up that hill. We should have ridden up slowly at an angle and been cautious as we approached the apex of the ridge. I took us right into the hunting party." Hulk knew they were all too tired, and he had pushed them too hard.

"The plan worked once," announced Trey. "Let's attack them. We need to slip into their camp and take our horses. They won't be expecting us if we hurry and hit them. They know we are on foot and limited in being able to travel. If we wait, they will be rested and at some point, they will come for us with greater numbers. There is no way they are going to let us go. Do you not remember all the stories about the tribes living in the midlands from dad, Billy Ray, Wayne, and Eric of Newport?"

Hulk considered the plan. "First, we need to gather all the supplies from these dead bodies. We need to dress like them. Robin Hood, can you make it? We will try to locate a horse for you. Trey's right, we only have one move."

"Hell yes, I can make it. If you get a chance, get my bag of weed from my saddlebags. I could use a good smoke right now." Despite the tremendous pain, he stood up and was obviously in agony as he balanced himself, ready to walk.

Chapter 13

The two had traveled close to six hours. They passed through the mountains and the terrain had turned flat with less trees. Unlike the first day, the two had talked the entire trip. Dak had explained what he knew about the old world and his tribe. Zenith had not mentioned Merlin or her family but talked about the requirements to graduating to becoming a Blueblood warrior. She listened to Dak talk about how close he and his mother were and his friends. Dak was surprised when finally, Zenith explained how her parents were paired, and they had never been in romantic love. They were ordered to have a child by the governing council. She mentioned once she returned and her apprenticeship was complete, she would be promised to one of the other warriors for breeding. The two rode in silence for another few minutes.

Dak finally said, "The pairing by the Blueblood leaders would take a lot of the anxiety out of dating, and the flirting process would not be needed. You do not have to worry if your mate likes you are not. You would not need to try to win someone over. I guess that is why you do not know how to flirt. That would be a more efficient way for two people to copulate. What happens when a Blueblood is a parent of a child with a normal person? I also wonder who gives the

Blueblood leadership the right to choose a mate for someone?" He could feel her shift her balance to the other side of the saddle.

She looked at the back of his head and raised her upper lip to one side in frustration, "There are no half breeds. It is not allowed. My people have a very strict set of rules. There is no deviation from the rules, and I am very good at flirting. I am very proud to be a Blueblood. Thank you very much for your thoughts." He smiled to himself with the last comments.

"I am sorry if I struck a nerve with the statement about you not knowing how to flirt."

"You did not strike a nerve. You just have no clue what you are talking about."

"Certainly, cross-breeding has to happen."

"I have never known of it happening." Zenith had gotten quiet, and the two rode in silence.

Dak noticed the sky was turning cloudy, and it felt like a snowstorm was possible. They arrived at a small pond, and above the pond was a small circle area with a spring, which fed the pond. The pond had a thin layer of ice over it and snow all around the ground. He could see some deer tracks and other small animal prints in the snow. He noticed around the spring area there was no snow or ice. He stopped the horse and stared. The spring area was a small area with clear water with some fog rising blocking the view of the small mountain west of their location. He then stated, "There is no fog above the pond, just the spring."

Zenith noticed and reached for her sword. She asked, "Why did you stop? What scared you?"

"I think we found a hot spring. Notice how there is no ice or snow around the spring."

Zenith asked, "A hot spring?"

"Yes. That is when the hot gases deep in the earth push upward and the heat warms the water. We can camp here tonight. We need firewood and wood to build a small shelter. It feels like snow tonight."

Zenith jumped down from the horse, "Maybe we could build the fire under the rock ledge near the spring." Dak dismounted and removed the saddle and bridle and tied the horse up so it could eat the exposed grass near the spring. He walked over to the spring and felt the water. He smiled, "It is warm. I will take a bath later, but first I will try to find us some food." He looked at Zenith who was already gathering firewood. He came back about an hour later with two pheasants. He noticed the pile of firewood, and at first had not seen Zenith, sitting by the spring with her feet in the warm water. He said, "It is really going to storm later. We need to hurry and eat. Can you start the fire?"

After the two had eaten, Dak stood, "Before it snows, I am going to take a bath." He stood and took his clothes off and walked into the warm spring water. He said, "My goodness, this feels great. There is room for two."

Zenith could not help but notice his good looks and muscled body. She had never seen a normal man naked up close. Without waiting too long, she pulled her clothing off while sitting on the rock next to the spring. She walked to the edge of the spring and removed her hairbow and walked into the spring. She sat opposite Dak. She smiled and leaned back allowing her head to go under the clear water. Dak could not help but notice her perfect brown skin and long blond hair. She had the Blueblood look with the athletic looking body with her firm breasts and large nipples. He went under water and when he came up, he said, "I believe I am sitting over the actual spring. There is a surge of hot water boiling up next to me."

She smiled and moved over next to him and laughed. "That tickles." She looked him in the eyes. "I have been wondering, why have you not asked me for some of my blood? I know you know the importance of my blood. You mentioned it when we first met."

The question caught Dak by surprise. He explained they had only met one other Blueblood. "The Blueblood was a man of science. He did not appear to be a warrior. The man had come through the nuclear waste and was dying. He had been running from the Midlanders, and his horse had already died. Hulk,

Robin Hood, and I had found him at the tribal boundary when hunting a few years ago, and we carried him back to the tribe. Once he entered the dead zone full of nuclear radiation, the Midlanders stopped chasing him."

"Doc Johnson checked his blood daily for nuclear poison. An adult male required a half pint of blood to become immune to B12 virus. The small kids required an eighth of a pint. Doc Johnson would not take more than one pint per day. He explained his medical diagnosis, and the Blueblood agreed to allowing our tribe to use one pint of his blood a day and in exchange we feed him and cared for him. Since we found him, the three of us were the first. Every day our tribe prayed for a good result from Doc Johnson. The focus at first was the kids because of their body weight. More could be vaccinated, but the leadership also recognized the need for the workers and the parents. Basically, everyone needed the blood. Death by the B12 virus is a painful death. The tribe had nourished him back to health just to watch him slip into a coma and then die. There is no cure for radiation poison. I was one of the one-hundred and thirty-seven who received his gift. Once he went into a coma, he never came out, but he suffered no more."

The two looked and noticed the darkness had set in with a heavy snow. They both talked and laughed with their bodies totally submerged, only their mouth, nose, and eyes sticking above the warm water of the three-foot-deep spring. The cold air was well below freezing and the spring water was in the upper seventies. The two would casually rub up against one another while going under water. Dak reached out and held Zenith's right foot and massaged it. "We are taught to help each other." He kept rubbing the arch in her foot. Zenith smiled at him. He set her foot on his lap and then massaged her other foot.

She went under water and came up while he kept messaging her foot. The two looked at each other. He held her feet apart and pulled Zenith's feet toward him pulling her under water. He pulled her tight against his body facing her while she was straddling his lap. Dak noticed as she came above water her smile and natural beauty. She had tilted her head backward to allow her hair to fall on her back. He whispered, "You are so lucky to be here with me. I can teach you about flirting. Maybe you will need this knowledge at some point."

She could feel his hands holding her tight around her waist. She felt his male part pushing against her stomach as he pulled her against his body. He leaned in for the kiss and at the last second, she turned her head. He kissed her on the cheek. She pushed backward against his chest. She turned and looked him in the eyes, "I need to go to sleep." She did not break eye contact, "Please let me go." He released her and watched her walk out of the spring placing her boots on and then walking up the bank carrying her clothes. She walked next to the cape and slipped her boots off without looking back at Dak and got into the bedroll.

He finally got out of the spring. He felt embarrassed with his actions. He said to himself, "Way to go you stupid thick skull knuckle dragger." He knew they could not have a relationship. He thought, how stupid am I? Once inside the bedroll he laid on his back looking at the bedroll covering his face and thinking about nothing. He finally said, "I am sorry. I am truly sorry for my behavior. It is like you said, we are from two different worlds, and the two worlds do not mix. I should not have tried to flirt with you. But for the record, you certainly are pretty."

Zenith rolled over and looked at him with a smile and kissed him on the cheek and then rolled back over. She hesitated a moment and then said, "I do not believe I will ever get used to this cold weather. I am freezing. Can you hold me and help me warm up?"

Dak rolled over and held her. "My feet are really cold." He reached down and rubbed her legs and then held her feet. "That is so much better. Remember to blow out your hot breath under the bedroll." She fell asleep a little later. Dak kept blowing out the warm air and then he fell asleep holding her feet while lying with his body pressed against hers. The trip had been wearing on both, and both were exhausted.

The snow stopped as quickly as it had started. The main storm had gone north of their location. They had made it to a road heading south as the sun was rising. Dak knew the well-traveled dirt road had to lead to Merlin. Most of the land to the east was for the cattle and horse ranches with some large fields for crops in between the ranches. Dak had never seen flat land and fields such as this. The Pacific Ocean was to their west, and he tried to take in the scenery. They rode for a couple of hours on the dirt road, and then they saw a farmer and then another. The people watched as the two rode south along the road. They finally came to an establishment with the word "ELA" written in red on a wooden sign. Dak announced, "We can stop and eat. I have not had a cooked meal in weeks."

He had not noticed Zenith had pulled her hood tight around her head and face as they rode double with her behind him. She knew the people in the farming communities disliked the Bluebloods. One Blueblood would never travel this far from Merlin alone with a normal human. She knew she needed to hide the fact she was a Blueblood. The two dismounted with Dak tying the lead rope of the horse off at the watering trough. Dak smiled at a boy and pulled a small sack out of his inner jacket pocket. Dak wanted to impress Zenith with his generosity. He pulled a coin and flipped a boy the gold coin and asked him to feed his horse. The boy caught the gold coin in midair. He inspected the coin and his dirty face lit up with a smile. He reached for the lead rope and took the horse toward the stable. He turned, "Thanks mister. I will bring him back to the front and tie him in the same spot. I will take very good care of him."

The man standing in the shadow of the soffit leaning against the front log wall of the building a few feet from the door was lighting his smoke and acted like he did not notice the gold coin and the two young travelers. Zenith kept her eyes looking down but also attempted to notice the people in the area. There were three men dressed as farmers leaving the establishment and several horse riders on the road. The man in the shadow turned his head the opposite direction as Dak and Zenith approached and entered the front door. Both Dak and Zenith noticed the man standing a few feet past the front door. Dak sensed something amiss about the man not looking at him and also not being neighborly and saying hello. He was not dressed like the farmers and ranchers. His attire was black leather and an old brown coat unbuttoned and hanging open in the front. Dak noticed the sword end protruding from under the coat near his left leg.

They walked into the restaurant and took a seat near the window in the corner with Dak wanting to be facing the door. He set his saddlebag down on the floor next to him. Once they located an empty table and sat, the waitress came, and the two ordered bread and stew with ale to drink.

The open area roared with chatter as the customers were eating and talking. Most of the tables were full with the two waitresses trying to bring the food and collect gold coins in payment. Several of the customers were heading to Merlin to discuss the taxes and meet with their Blueblood business partners. The conversations were mostly in anguish with the farmers and ranchers being overtaxed and not liking the forced partnerships with the Blueblood run government. Dak tried to act like he could not hear the table next to them as the men were cursing the Blueblood Senate. Dak heard the middle-aged farmer sitting at the end of the table say it would be better to not plant the ground next year and work his sons to death and then pay all the earnings to the Blueblood scum. Zenith kept her hood pulled tight and ate her soup. She tried to keep her eyes looking down but kept glancing out the window as she ate. Dak could tell she heard the men cursing her government and her people.

As they were about finished with their meal, the front and rear doors simultaneously abruptly opened, and six bandit type men entered. The man who had been leaning against the wall was the last one to enter. They were not dressed like the farmers or ranchers they had passed on the road or inside the restaurant. These men were dressed in armor with protective chest plates and extra knives, hatchets, and swords. One was carrying a shield and another a bow hung over his shoulder. They were blocking the two exits with their hands positioned on their swords. They immediately looked around trying to intimidate the farmers and ranchers.

The entire restaurant got quiet, and the twenty customers watched the men. The one man in the front looked around at the people, "I want to know who gave this gold coin to the boy outside. Taxes are owed, and we are here to collect." He held the coin up for all to see. "It does not sparkle as gold now for the blood stain because we had to cut the hand off the boy for punishment. This gold coin is considered stolen, and property of the Merlin Senate. You know the penalty. We are not here to bother you ranchers or sodbusters. We want to talk to the young riders about their gold. They must pay their taxes."

Zenith saw the rage in Dak's eyes. She said under her breath, "This is not your fight. You do not understand these people."

He whispered with clenched jaws, "I understand the boy is missing a hand. It might not be your fight but it sure the hell is mine. You can stay here in the back of the restaurant with your hood pulled tight around your head and hide if you want." Zenith reached for his hand, and he pulled it away. Dak stood and walked toward the man with his head tilted downward. He noticed the man was not the biggest or the oldest, but he appeared to be the leader. The man stood with his weight on his front leg. He noticed Dak was approaching, and he smiled while shifting his hand to the long knife hanging on his right side. When Dak got three feet away, he smiled at the man and then dropped on his right foot and extended his left foot into the man's left kneecap. The knee immediately bent inverted, and Dak rotated back into the standing position as he brought the knife from his boot up and cut the man's hand off as he was falling. Dak caught the gold coin in the air in his left hand. He said, "This would be my gold coin. A hand for a hand is a fair deal for you. Now crawl back under the rock you came from."

He placed the knife in his belt loop and the coin in his pocket. He turned and looked at the other five men with his now pulled sword level in front of him. He had his left hand on the handle of his other sword ready to pull it. The men started to surround Dak and move inward cautiously making the circle smaller and smaller. The customers sitting at the nearby tables immediately moved out of the way providing plenty of room for the apparent sword fight. The men noticed Dak did not retreat, and he did not appear scared. They hesitated to try to figure out what to do next. They realized this young man had just taken out their leader in less than a second. They glanced at each other. The man on the floor started crawling toward the back door holding his wrist and dragging his leg. The man grunted, "Kill him. That bastard cut my hand off and broke my knee."

Zenith looked at the five men approaching Dak. She knew they would kill him if she did not intercede. She stood and removed her hood and cape. She pulled her sword. She heard some of the other customers gasp with surprise. She announced as she approached the men from the rear of the restaurant, "I am a Blueblood. If you don't back down and leave out the back door, you will be killed. You choose."

The men all turned and saw her. They were obviously surprised at the revelation that a Blueblood was so close to them. The men knew they did not want to fight a Blueblood. Their chances of survival would be slim. They reached and picked up the injured man from the floor and hurriedly carried him out the back door. Dak walked back to the table as all the other customers and two waitresses watched. Zenith could tell Dak was still upset about something. She did not want to talk inside the restaurant. Dak drank the rest of his ale and left two coins on the table. He said to the waitress, "Find the boy and give him his gold coin. This coin is his." She reached for the coin, and he did not release it. He made certain the waitress understood she was to give the boy the coin. He released the coin to her and noticed the other customers had heard him tell her to give the coin to the boy. The farmers and the ranchers sitting at the table next to them stared in disbelief that a

Blueblood was so close to them while eating and the man with her was willing to pay for the meal. The Blueblood warriors and tax collectors had always demanded to be fed for free.

Dak picked up his saddle bag, and they headed for the front door. Zenith jumped on the back of the horse behind Dak, and they headed south. Zenith said, "Dak, you can't fight everyone that does not have the same moral code as you. These people are different. They have a different set of morals. Our people have tried to govern them, and they feed off the weak and kill those who oppose them."

Dak asked, "Do you really think he cut the boy's hand off to get the gold coin? I have never heard of such cruel behavior. What gives them the right."

"Yes. The penalty for stealing is the loss of one's hand. They most likely were with a group of drifters and maybe part of a Midlander gang at once. They turned into hired mercenaries. Killing and stealing are all they know. They prey on the weak. The bandits normally leave the farmers and ranchers alone because the farmers and ranchers are partners with the Blueblood Senators, and they do not wish to draw attention to themselves from the Blueblood warriors."

"I wished I had killed him. He deserved to die."

"You are a hard-headed man. I just explained, you need to look the other way and walk away. This is not your fight or your people. You are going to get killed. Did you not hear me? These men are hired killers. That is what mercenaries do for a living is kill other people. They collect bounties on people issued by the Blueblood Senate. If the Blueblood Senate has an issue with anyone in this area, they will hire these mercenaries to kill the people causing the problems. Then, if the problem does not go away, the senate will send out the Blueblood warriors to remedy the situation. Either group will kill someone like you."

"It is about doing what is right. Zenith, I am sorry if you do not agree. The weak need to be helped. Besides, the group of men were there for my gold. I should have considered killing all of them. Then, they would sin no more. Sometimes it is hard for a man to change his heart. There was a man named Paul who used to hunt down Christians and kill them. Then, he had a life changing event on a road to Damascus and became one of the best Christians ever. Men can change."

"You need to take the road to Damascus. Maybe you can have a life changing event before I watch you get killed. I hope you can change before you meet the Senators in Merlin. No wonder your friend Robin Hood and the others smoke so much weed. Hell, if I keep hanging around you, you're going to drive me to smoking weed. Hell forbid someone breaks your moral code."

They rode in silence for a short distance, and Zenith finally exclaimed, "I will try and see if my father can assist you to meet the Blueblood Senators. He works for one of them. I am concerned when you talk with the Blueblood Senate about what you might say. You need to understand, they do not care about you or your opinions. You need to say." She stopped and took a deep breath and then exhaled, "You need to be humble. You need to be gracious and thank them for allowing you the opportunity to speak to them. Do not look the senators in the eyes. You need to keep your head tilted down with your eyes viewing the floor in front of you, and the first thing you need to do is kneel on your knees and bow to them. Then, ask if they would graciously honor you by listening to your request. Would they consider helping fight against King Solman? That is what you are going to do, isn't it?"

He smiled as they rode. "Something like that. So, why did you not tell me earlier that your father worked for a Senator?"

"I guess I thought you knew someone, and you had a plan. You do have a plan, right?"

"I do now that I know your father might help."

"Listen to me. If you show any disrespect, you will find yourself in lockup down in the dungeon. I wish you would turn and leave right now. I can convey your message."

"You know I can't do that. I have no reason to be disrespectful to your senators. What I am requesting is logical and beneficial to both our people, and I will not be getting on my knees in front of them. I will not present myself or my tribe as beggars."

She flipped her hair back in anger and adjusted her body to peer from the other side of the horse. "They consider you the same as the drifters with very little value to them. You are not their equal. They would just as soon you be taken to the dungeon and beaten until you submit to being a slave for them. They will force you to show them respect."

"Then, if that is their attitude, I will be disrespectful to your senators."

"Dammit. You are the most hard headed person I have ever met. I am trying to help you." She twisted her body to the other side on the back of the horse and was frustrated. They rode in silence with Zenith staring into the passing scenery of trees and fields while she bit down on her lower lip in frustration.

Chapter 14

The group spread out ten feet apart and walked toward the Midlander's Camp. They were quiet and on the lookout as Hulk set the pace and followed the horse tracks. They would move from one concealed spot to another and run quickly through the open areas. They had stolen some of the dead men's clothing in hopes of blending in, in case they were spotted. They had confiscated all the arrows they could carry. The dead men had very little of value and very little food or water. On the path near the top of the ridge, they came to an opening that transitioned from woods to a field area covered in high grass, small bushes, and a few smaller trees. Hulk had cleared the area and proceeded to a small grove of trees. Tommy Boy was third in line following Veronica. Tommy Boy recalled the area where he fell off the horse. He said with a sudden excited voice, "Look, that is my horse behind the small stand of trees." The group noticed the three-colored horse, seventeen hands high, had a broken leg. It would try to walk and just hobbled. The horse was beautiful with a white face, black body, and brown legs. They noticed the horse's pain as it hobbled on the broken leg. His excitement turned to grief.

Hulk walked back to the group, "We can retrieve your bridle and other gear. I am sorry about your horse. Do you want me to do it?"

Tommy Boy looked at the others then looked down. He knew the horse had to be put down. It would not be merciful to leave it live in pain. It would die a slow death. Tommy Boy said, "Big brother, wait here. It is my horse, and I will do it." He was about to cry as he walked toward the horse.

He rubbed the horse on the neck and face as he pulled his saddle bags off and then the saddle. He again rubbed the horse's face and side and then removed the bridle. "I am truly sorry, Big Ben." He pulled his knife and cut up into the throat. As the horse slowly fell to the ground, Tommy Boy held it and whispered, "I am so sorry. I love you." He picked up the bridle and other items and walked back to his friends.

Trey said, "I am sorry you lost Big Ben."

Tommy Boy walked past the group carrying his equipment and uttered, "That was the hardest thing I have ever done." He kept walking with a determined expression, and the others followed.

They waited until nightfall and crawled into place. Hulk whispered, "I cannot believe they have no guards."

Veronica whispered, "I believe they are still trying to decide who is going to be the leader. We killed the leader back in the opening in the woods. See the dead man over in the field. He lost his bid for the title. It is the strongest who will be the leader of this village. They must have had men traveling in from the south. There are more horses in the pen."

They watched as the camp seemed to be involved in drinking and yelling. There was a large bonfire, and the group of men were arguing in front of it. Veronica suggested, "If we wait, they will be too drunk to fight or hear us."

Hulk responded, "That may be true, but we have not slept in two days. We need to move now to take our horses back. We will release their horses from the corral. It will be light soon. We will ride southeast for a few hours. Then, we will need to sleep and rest. If anybody gets separated, remember to head southeast. Without horses, they won't chase us. They have dogs, so we need to stay downwind if we can. These clothes will help us smell like these people. Maybe the dogs will not pick up our scent."

The group crawled through the grass and crossed into the horse corral. As they got closer, they noticed the men were arguing and cursing one another. One man swung his sword and missed another man who jumped backward. The man shoved his knife in the man's gut and then scalped him while he was on the ground. He stood with his foot on the other man's belly where the knife had entered holding the scalp and proclaimed, "I am your leader. Bring me his wife." The man on the ground was moaning in pain as the other man bent down to castrate him.

They spotted their horses walking among the herd with their bridles, saddles, and saddle bags still on. Tommy Boy was nervous. He and his friends knew they each needed to be mounted, in the saddle and open the fence to the corral before anyone knew they were there. If they were discovered while on foot, they would be killed. He carried his saddle as he climbed over the top of the railed fence with his bridle. He carried the equipment slowly so as not to spook the horses. Trey held him a horse, and he quickly saddled the horse. The herd of horses seemed not to notice. Trey tied his rope to the fence post and had his horse pull the wood fence post out of the ground. Close to ten feet of the fence collapsed and the group started yelling, sending the entire herd of horses running into the field heading toward the woods. They all headed southeast with no one following.

After about two hours of riding through the wilderness, Hulk pulled his gauge out and checked the area for nuclear waste. The gauge depicted a small trace of radiation. He said, "We need to find our marked trail tomorrow and head home. I believe we need to head further north to clear the radiation and find the trail." He explained they were in a low dose zone. They agreed to head north and camp.

Once the gauge cleared an area, they tied the horses and went to bed under their bedrolls. The group started waking up after the sun was well up. They had not slept past daybreak in years. They were all hungry but wanting to move east. The group agreed to travel a few hours and then eat an early lunch. They hoped to spot a deer or something on the way. The group changed Robin Hood's bandage and placed additional ointment on the wound. They knew he was in pain. He would not talk, and his face reflected constant anguish. He was able to climb on his horse inside the corral back at the Midlanders camp, but the others knew he was hurting. They were concerned about riding into another Midlander's tribe and having to run with Robin Hood not being able to use his arm. Hulk looked at Veronica and both silently nodded their understanding of his condition. Hulk figured they would rest more and ride slowly for the next couple of days. They would check his bandage and tear clothing from their shirts to place on his wound. They made certain the bleeding was stopped.

Hulk found at midday the first marker on the trail leading back to their homes. This represented peace of mind knowing they were heading in the correct direction and would now be clear of the nuclear waste areas. This seemed to brighten the mood of the group as they rode close to eight hours and picked a camping spot. Hulk had shot a deer as they came into the meadow.

The group was extremely hungry. They sat around the fire talking in the dense thick foliage of small trees and weeds. Trey looked over at Tommy Boy, "I am certainly glad you tied that trip wire before that little battle we had with the Midlanders. Once they broke through all the arrows, the trip wire took several of them down."

Veronica said, "I was surprised Tommy Boy ran and jumped on the back of the horse killing the Midlander and then killing his two companions. What got into you?"

Tommy Boy smiled, "I knew the tripwire would work. Eric of Newport told me about doing that to stop someone on a horse years ago. He explained that you need to be smart in battle."

Hulk nodded, "I remember when we all were camping in the summer two years ago. He mentioned it would work on either someone running or a horse running. That was a good call, Tommy Boy."

Tommy Boy announced, "I ran across the open area and then jumped off the log while the rider was turned looking at Trey. I knew I had to do something."

Trey said, "I could not have lasted against all those men by myself. Veronica helped me with the leader after you took out those three men. The leader was a huge strong man. He was a little bigger than a bear and twice as mean. I am not certain I could have taken him down without Veronica stabbing him in the back as she ran behind him. Hell, Veronica where were you going? You just ran behind him and sliced him as you passed him. You acted like you were pissed at him for being in your way." The group laughed.

Trey looked at his sister, "Right before that, he overpowered me with four straight swings which I kept blocking and falling backward with each block. I could not get my balance to attack him between swings."

"That was right when Robin Hood got shot. I saw him take the arrow and that big ugly man was in my way. I was afraid we lost you, Robin Hood." She smiled at Robin Hood.

"Thanks for caring. I will let you have the first smoke after dinner. I cannot believe the Midlanders did not get my stash from my saddle bag."

Veronica smiled, "The Midlander clan was more concerned with who was going to be their leader. They were totally consumed with their upcoming election and the guy without his scalp and his testicles and the dead man in the field both lost the bid to be in command."

"I am glad they did not get your stash. After spending the last few weeks with you guys, I need a smoke."

Hulk laughed, "I wonder what Dak is doing?"

The group got quiet and somber watching the deer cook. Finally, Robin Hood said, "I wish we could have stayed together, but Dak may have been right."

Veronica was adamant, "He was not right. We should have all stayed together."

Robin Hood grimaced in pain as he shifted his position, "He will be okay. All he must do is tell the Blueblood leadership what is going on with King Solman killing and conquering cities in the south. He either will be able to convince the Bluebloods to send an army or not. It is the only logical thing for the Bluebloods to do."

Hulk was tired from traveling with no rest. He was also tired of Veronica second guessing him. He looked at Veronica and said in a harsh tone, "A good soldier takes orders. Anybody can disobey. We had a direct order from the one in charge. Veronica, when you are placed in charge, we will all go to the dungeon together instead of five of us heading home."

Veronica looked at Hulk and jumped up and walked off into the tree thicket.

Robin Hood said, "Damn Hulk, chill out. I am the one in constant pain, and I am not as pissy as you."

"I am not certain I trust the Bluebloods to do the right thing. They must know what King Solman has been doing the past ten years. He has totally wiped-out city after city and conquered territories all in the southern part of the continent.

The news would have had to spread north along the coast to Merlin. There would most likely have been a ship sailing from the southern region with the news or people fleeing north along the western coastline seeking help with the brutal stories. I am also worried Dak will not leave without getting in trouble. You guys know how he speaks his opinion, and Veronica is right. We should not have split up. The decision I had to make has been eating at me, but I made it and now I am tired of being second guessed."

Trey mentioned, "Let us eat. The food is ready. Veronica will return in a few minutes." The group was very hungry after missing breakfast and lunch, and deer meat was a welcome meal. They all agreed to go to sleep early and try to ride hard the next day. Hulk wanted to get as much distance between them and the Midlanders as possible. He also hoped for a hard rain to cover their tracks, so they could not be followed. His goal was to make it to Old Thomas's home before the rain. He hated riding in the rain. The seal skin clothing repelled the damp weather but still the cold rain would penetrate the tops of their boots and their hoods. The wet weather was hard on the horses. He did not mind getting wet, but he hated staying wet and having to travel in cold wet clothes. He also knew he would tell Veronica he was sorry.

Chapter 15

Zenith pulled her cape around her head tight and tried to cover her brown legs. She did not want anyone to notice her. As they got closer and closer to the suburbs of Merlin, they observed more and more people. Dak noticed most of the people looked poor and the children were living in poverty, in unhealthy conditions with kids covered in flies. The houses were shacks made with whatever materials could be attached to form a dwelling. Most structures had dirt floors with no interior plumbing. Dak noticed as they got closer to the city, there were more beggars, and more misery. The people looked like they were just trying to survive a meager existence with most having brown teeth, if they even had teeth. He also perceived no one would look him in the eyes as they walked along the dirt road. From time to time, there would be vendors selling food and other items along the road. The merchants would yell at them to buy whatever they were selling.

Zenith knew Dak was observing the poor people as they rode. He kept looking on both sides of the street at the slums. He stopped the horse once and stared at a little boy bare footed with no shirt, covered in flies with open sores. Zenith for the first time, felt ashamed that the Bluebloods had done nothing to help these people. She had never considered their way of life.

The only time she had been outside the castle walls was during training to be a Blueblood warrior or when her father took her sailing as a child. They were taught the poor people were not human. Their lives had no value. She remembered her first training mission when she was eight years of age, and they rode their horses out the gate and into the country. She was surprised to see the dirt floor shacks and poor people as they passed them. The guards would run over the poor people on their horses and beat them if they showed any disrespect and looked at her group of students in training. As they approached the main gate to the inner walls of the castle, Zenith whispered, "You better allow me to talk. The guards are not Bluebloods, and they have their strict orders. They will not allow you to pass without me telling them to stand down."

As they approached the gate, the large guards were not nice or polite. The local people were void of the general area and knew to stay clear of the guards. The one on the right yelled in a commanding voice to stop as the horse kept walking. Then, the group of six guards approached from the gate with swords drawn. Zenith knew she had to stop the guards, or they would kill Dak. She hopped off the horse pulling her hood back and ordered, "We need to pass. He is my guest. You will take his horse and tend to it."

The six guards hesitated when they saw a Blueblood giving them a direct order. Her voice was harsh, "I told you to take his horse." She then softened her voice, "Come on Dak, dismount. We will walk." Dak stared at the six guards and then glanced around at the people watching from a distance located at the small retail stalls which lined the area against the castle walls and the street located opposite the gate.

Once they cleared the gate, they walked for close to a half mile with Dak looking at the inner castle. The people were better fed, and better housing was apparent. Dak saw some Blueblood kids playing chase in a small park. The kids were being watched by normal adult humans. Dak noticed no one said hello as they passed, and no one tried to be friendly.

Zenith walked fast and pulled Dak by the hand into a large building and up two levels of concrete stairs. She kept hurrying, pulling Dak faster and faster with her face tilted down, under the hood of her cape with her eyes viewing in all directions. He thought she acted like she was embarrassed to be seen with him. He then remembered she was promised to a male Blueblood and being seen with him might have been difficult for her to explain. She knocked on the door to an apartment and then opened the door pulling Dak inside. She very quickly closed the door behind him. Dak saw a lady who was a little older than Zenith walking in from the balcony. Zenith said, "Mom, this is Dak. He is a friend." There was a second delay with her mother's expression showing a worried and surprised appearance.

Dak smiled, "It is very nice to meet you."

The lady cut Dak off in mid-sentence, "No, this is not permitted. He must leave before the neighbors see him and your father arrives home. You are on the verge of being paired with a Blueblood Warrior. What were you thinking?"

"Mother, he and his friends saved my life. The Midlanders had us surrounded, and I was either going to die by suicide or be killed in battle."

The lady looked at Dak, "Thank you for saving my stepdaughter, but this is not permitted. You need to leave."

Dak looked at the lady and then at Zenith, "What is not permitted?"

"Number one, she is an unescorted Blueblood female teen and being seen with you is not permitted. Number two, she is not allowed to be associated with a drifter. Number three, you are not allowed in our home unless you are working for us in some capacity. Looking at us with eye contact and smiling at us is not permitted. Who do you think you are?"

"Mother, he is my guest, and he has no other place to go. He has business with the Blueblood Senate, which I was hoping father could help facilitate the meeting with the senate. Dak is from the far east, and he will make his request hopefully with the senate tomorrow and then leave. He is on a diplomatic mission."

She looked at Dak with pity in her eyes. "I am afraid of what the senate might do. Your father will not like this. The Blueblood Senator your father works for will not tolerate his employees who work for him as consultant's or the consultant's family members being involved with a drifter. Your father is expected home in a few minutes." She turned and looked at Dak, "We do not trust drifters. I would suggest you leave before Zenith's father arrives and finds you in his home."

"Are you not happy to see your stepdaughter and the fact that she is still alive? You have not even acknowledged her, and you have not seen her in three weeks. Who are you?"

The stepmother looked at Zenith and then back at Dak. She started to say something, and the door opened and in walked a male Blueblood. He had the look of a warrior with an athletic well-developed body and quiet steps when he walked. Dak had not heard anyone approach the exterior door.

He looked at the three people and then looked back at Dak as he placed his hand on his sword handle and unsnapped the strap holding the sword in the sleeve. Zenith with a hopeful look on her face announced, "Father, this is Dak. He has come a long way to make a request from our senate and then he will head east, back to his home. I was hoping you could make the arrangements at the first available opportunity. He is very busy, and he is in a hurry to head home. He would like to beat the cold winter weather, and he has a great distance to travel."

The father clenched his jaws and looked at his daughter and then back at Dak. "Where are you from, and what request are you going to be making? Tell me now."

"Sir, I come from the furthest point east on this continent. It is the end of a small peninsula which is past several nuclear contaminated areas and then further east of a large forest and open country. Then, past an additional nuclear waste area perched overlooking the Atlantic Ocean. The land is located where the glaciers and the frozen tundra meet the first tree line. We are just south of the jet stream. I was sent by my tribe to talk to a man named Ivan Chezon. We believe we have common ground with the Blueblood empire against a known enemy, the Normand armies. Do you know this man I seek?"

His expression did not change. "You crossed the waste lands?

"Yes sir."

"I will be back in a few minutes. Do not go anywhere." He turned and walked out, closing the door behind him.

Zenith looked hopeful and turned to her mother, "We are hungry and tired."

Her mother said, "We have food. The servants have all left for the day." She hesitated and then said, "I will get it and then we will talk after you eat."

Her father abruptly opened the door about thirty minutes after he had left. He refused to make eye contact as he walked into his apartment and four dungeon guards followed him. Dak noticed Zenith's father step to the side, which allowed the largest of the guard detail to pass him in the foyer. The guard pulled his sword and looked at Dak, "You will drop your weapons on the floor and come with us." The three had just about completed their meal with Dak offering to wash the dishes. He had been very courteous to Zenith's mother and had graciously thanked her for the meal. Her mother had been quiet and watched the two eat. She had not responded to Dak's request to wash the dishes.

Zenith looked at her father, "Father, what have you done? He trusted me, and I trusted you to help." Her father did not say a word. He stood against the wall and allowed two additional guards to walk into the apartment.

The first guard looked at Dak with a stern expression, "Listen here you scum. If I must repeat myself, we will carry you out of this apartment in pieces. The senate has ordered us to take you for questioning. Now do as I say, or we will beat you into submission." He stepped forward and pointed his sword at Dak.

Zenith at once stepped between Dak and the first guard. She faced the guards with the sword now aimed at her. "Dak, do as they request. It will be alright. Please drop your weapons."

Dak noticed the fourth guard had now positioned himself to the side and was slowly moving in position. Dak thought Zenith was going to be hurt. The guard's sword was leveled at her. He stood and unfastened his belt, allowing his swords to drop to the floor. He pulled the knife from his boot and dropped it. He looked at Zenith's mother, "Thanks again for the meal. It was very gracious of you. I have not eaten fresh fruit in four weeks." He bowed slightly to her, looked at Zenith, and walked out the door.

The fourth guard picked up the belt with the swords and the other gear. As he closed the door, the guard standing in the hall hit Dak in the left kidney knocking him to the concrete floor. Dak had not expected the punch and yelped as he was falling. The big guard leaned down into Dak's face with a clenched jaw, "You scum. I can't wait to get you in the dungeon. We are going to teach you how to respect the Blueblood people and the next time I give you an order, you will respond."

Zenith hearing the noise rushed by her father pushing him backward and opened the door. She kicked the large guard as he stood in the stomach. "This is no way to treat a diplomat from a distant kingdom. You will not touch him again. Do I

142

make myself clear? He is here to meet with the Blueblood Senate. They will not want him harmed." The guards looked at her and motioned for Dak to get up. The one guard rubbed his stomach area and walked in front down the stairs.

As soon as the door closed behind her, Zenith looked with a look of disbelief on her face, and asked, "Why did you summon the dungeon guards? He has done nothing to be arrested. He saved my life and helped me return home. He would like to make a simple request of our senate."

Aquarius raised his voice and looked at his daughter. "You know nothing of what you have done. He mentioned he wanted to meet with Ivan Chezon. Anyone associated with Ivan is an enemy of the senate. You have jeopardized your opportunity to become a Blueblood Warrior by being associated with him. The guards at the gate have reported you were riding double on his horse. This is not our way. A Blueblood demands the horse and forces the drifter to walk. Your actions show weakness, and a Blueblood warrior does not show weakness." Her father looked at his wife and then said, "She just won't listen." He looked back at Zenith, "You have jeopardized the future we have worked so hard to provide you."

Without even considering her father's position, she responded in a very calm voice, "If he is weaker then he should ride the horse, and the Blueblood should walk. It does not show weakness. It shows humility. I do not like who we have become. We hide in this palace and allow the weak to be chopped to pieces. I used to look at you two with respect. There is no respect for your actions."

The stepmother stepped in between the two and turned to Zenith, "How dare you raise your voice. How dare you bring that filthy, long haired Midlander into our city and into my home. You know they cannot be trusted. You do not remember the old days when they tried to be in charge. You also know there is a standing warrant dead or alive for the man he wants to meet, Ivan Chezon. Anyone associated with Ivan is our enemy. What were you thinking bringing him here? Your father had no choice but to have him arrested."

Zenith now realized this was an argument she could not win. She needed her parents to assist directly or indirectly to have Dak released from the Blueblood dungeon. She knew someone had given the order to have him taken to the dungeon and possibly mistreated. Zenith looked at her parents, "You are right. I guess I am tired. I am sorry." She turned and walked toward her room.

Chapter 16

As Hulk kept looking forward, hoping for a view of Old Thomas's home, he knew for the last twelve miles they were getting closer. He tried to recall the surroundings, so he would know how close they were. His body was sore, and he was tired of riding. He heard Trey mention to Veronica his lower back was sore, and Robin Hood had mentioned he was in constant pain all over. When he came over the ridge and saw the sun reflect off the glass window of Old Thomas's home, he felt relief. He yelled out to his four friends, "I see his home." The five riders all were relieved, tired, and hungry.

Tommy Boy said so low that only Robin Hood and Trey could hear him, "Not another foot further. This is physically the hardest day of my life." They all felt the constant body aches and were all happy to have finally pushed east and made it to Old Thomas's farm.

Old Thomas had seen them coming from a mile away as they crossed the ridge. The trip had been brutal with the fast pace. A couple of times they fell asleep while riding the horses. Once they located the markers and cleared the area of the Midlanders, they had made the trip in six days with limited sleep and food. Hulk asked Old Thomas for some food and a place to rest.

Old Thomas grunted when he spoke, "I have been smelling you for two days and hearing you for the past day. I assumed you would be hungry when you arrived. I have prepared a groundhog in boiling water and then finished it by frying it. Tie your horses up and come on in my home."

The group ate without talking. Old Thomas had been rushing around trying to provide water and food. He finally stood still and remembered, "Where is the sixth member?"

Hulk looked up, "Dak will be coming behind us in a few weeks. We escorted him into Blueblood territory, and then he ordered us home." Hulk went back to finishing his last few bites. He then said, "We need to rest."

Old Thomas glanced at the group, "I don't know when I have ever seen a group of people this tired. You each look like you could fall over at any time."

Veronica said, "We wanted to rush home. Robin Hood took an arrow in his upper back a few days ago, and he needs a new bandage. We need to check it for infection, and we are worried about the next battle with the Normand army."

Old Thomas said in a surprised voice looking at Robin Hood, "An arrow? I will provide you with a new bandage." He looked closely at the group wondering what they had been faced with fighting the Midlanders. He looked at Tommy Boy as he went for the bandage and asked, "When you left, you were on a beautiful horse. I noticed the one you rode in on is half the horse. What happened to your horse?"

"He broke his leg when we were running from several dozen Midlanders. I had to put him down." He went back to eating.

"That is a shame. I will go put each of your horses in the corral and feed them. You all need to find a place to sleep, and we will talk more tomorrow."

Old Thomas provided a new bandage to Veronica and walked out the door talking to himself about how he had never seen a group of people look so ratty and tired. He fed the horses and placed the saddles, saddle bags, and other items in the barn. When he was done, he wrote a note and placed it around the pigeon's neck. He released the bird and watched it fly off heading toward Cliff Tops with the note addressed to Vicky Donahue.

Chapter 17

Dak was sitting in a block cell on a concrete floor. The temperature in the room was in the eighties during the day and never below the mid-seventies in the night. He could smell the mildew from years of moisture seeping through the mortar into the blocks below grade. There was a small open window at the top of the exterior cell wall which had iron bars installed into the masonry. The window was open with no glass to prevent the flying insects from entering the cell. He was not certain how long he had been asleep. The guards had provided him little food and had left him alone. He was happy to see Zenith when she appeared in front of his cell. Dak knew she was not at fault, and she was trying to sound cheerful. Zenith smiled, "I thought I would check on you. How are you holding up?"

He loved to see her beautiful smile. She looked very attractive in her city attire with her long hair hanging down. He smiled at her, "You were right about one thing, and here I am in the dungeon. Any word on me getting out of here?"

She stopped smiling, "No. I have not heard any news."

Dak could tell something was bothering Zenith. She would look away when she wanted to say something, or something was bothering her. He asked, "What is bothering you? What is it you are not telling me?"

"I went in front of the Blueblood Army Custodians in charge of our army first thing today and requested they release you. I also submitted my written chronicle on my training and two-half-weeks journey inside the Midlander territory. I was told no cadet had incurred such an adventure. I tried to convey that this was no way to treat a foreign diplomat. They changed the subject and told me the ruling on me passing my trials from being an apprentice to a Blueblood Warrior has been placed on hold because of you."

Dak looked up into her eyes. "I am sorry if anything I have done has caused you not to achieve what you deserve. You are a great warrior, and I would be proud to fight next to you in any battle." She looked into his eyes, and after an awkward silence, he continued, "I never thought I would be treated like a criminal and be locked in a dungeon. I thought I would be able to make a simple request of your government to benefit both your people and my people. I miss my home, my mom, my friends, and my way of life. Your city is so big, and there are too many people. I am certain I could not live like this. Plus, ever since I arrived in the south, I have been sweating nonstop, and these damn flying pests are everywhere. This cell is full of them."

Zenith smiled, "The further you go south, the hotter the weather. Along the beach, the people do seem to have a constant breeze which helps one deal with heat and humidity.

There is a lot more swimming in the larger lakes, and the ocean is warmer. We can travel for days down the coastline before we reach a nuclear waste pit. We call a nuclear contaminated area a waste pit." She had not mentioned the flying insects. Everyone hated them.

"Where I am from, we have a huge forest of evergreen trees, but the forest transitions a few miles away from the ocean to hardwood forest and then fields. The old timers say because the winters get so cold, the extreme cold conditions help the plant life. Most of the insects and the fungus which can damage plant life die in the cold temperatures. The key is for the plant life to go dormant before the winter. In the spring all the plants grow better without the fungi and insects, and since the plant life is doing so well the wild animals are doing much better. Did you know that in the second year of a female deer's reproductive year, she is more likely to have twins and maybe triplets?"

Zenith could tell Dak was lonely and by him mentioning his home in a nostalgic manner, she was worried he might be giving up. She thought he must have realized his chances were not good. Dak talked for about an hour of his homeland and Zenith had pulled up a stool on her side of the bars and listened. She asked a question from time to time. She finally indicated she would check on him tomorrow and hopefully have news of his request. She cheerfully said goodbye and apologized for him being placed in the dungeon.

As Zenith walked out the door to the cells and by the guard, she turned and looked at the guard. "He needs more food and water. You need to double what you are providing him. You also need to get rid of all those insects." She looked into the harsh face of the guard with her hand on her knife strapped to her belt and said, "I will check on him tomorrow and his living conditions had better be improved, or I am going to place you in the cell with him." She turned to walk out the second security door. She heard the guard tell the other guard, "I would like to have that high born blonde Blueblood bitch."

Zenith immediately turned and walked back in front of the guard. She still had her left hand on her knife and placed her right hand on her sword handle. "What did you say? Please repeat it for me, so I can make certain you are gelded before noon tomorrow."

He looked down at the ground. She turned to the other guard and demanded, "What did he say? If you do not speak the truth, you will also be gelded."

The second guard seemed nervous and stuttered, "I did not hear what he said. I thought he mentioned you were a very pretty Blueblood. Please show us mercy."

The first guard said, "I am sorry. I should not have spoken. I will get the prisoner extra water and food immediately. I will also place some liquid sugar outside his window to draw the bugs out. I guarantee you; you will see an improvement in his cell tomorrow. Please forgive me."

She turned and walked out of the dungeon. She was upset. She could not believe Dak was being held against his will with no charges being filed against him. She laid in bed and thought of him, and she had trouble sleeping. She missed him pushing his warm body up against her underneath his large bedroll holding her feet keeping her warm and pushing his hard manhood up against her bottom.

She walked out into the sun and felt the warmth the following morning. She knew her father was a busy man, but this could not wait. His title was Senate Consultant, and he had worked as a liaison for Senator Blackmon for the past few years. Her father was a first-generation Blueblood, which meant he had no parents. He was made in a test tube before the demise of the old-world in a lab with close to one thousand other Bluebloods. Out of the original one thousand, there were close to six-hundred-and-fifty still alive. The other three-hundred-and-fifty had been killed in battles and a few had been killed by going too deep into the nuclear waste pits. Some others had been murdered in the city without anyone knowing who killed them. His blood was pure, and his genetic imprint was perfect. Unlike her stepmother, who was a second-generation Blueblood.

With the collapse of the world, the science behind the screening of the chromosomes had been lost, and her chromosomes could not be checked, but Zenith was the genetically enhanced offspring of her parents. She was immune to the deadly B12 virus and obtained all the other qualities of the first-generation Blueblood. All breeding was strictly controlled and reproducing with a normal person would result in a government forced abortion. The Blueblood Senate had ruled no uncontrolled breeding was allowed. The senate wanted to keep the perfect genetic imprint.

She walked up the steps to the large senate building and past the human guards. All the dungeon guards and most of the gate guards were normal men who had to take orders from the Blueblood wardens. Most of the guards were cruel men. They had all been taught to kill the poor and starving people as they tried to gain access to the inner castle. The guards were instructed to show no mercy, or no mercy would be provided to them.

The people located in the outer city rim and further outer territories had no laws or protection. The strong survived, and the poor were beaten down and victimized. The Blueblood Senate allowed the bandits and gangs to rule the territories as long as the Blueblood's interest was not disturbed with the farmers and ranchers.

Zenith walked into the main office. She said hi to the male secretary and never slowed down as she walked into her father's office. He was reviewing papers on his desk. He looked up and saw Zenith and quickly closed his folder. He looked into his daughter's beautiful face with her big blue eyes, "Good morning sweetheart. I left early for work and missed you at breakfast. What brings you downtown?" He smiled and looked hopeful.

Her frown was obvious, "You know why I am here. Dak has been in the dungeon far too long. I was hoping you could help with his request to meet our senate. I get the feeling you are not working on this, and if you don't tell me some good news, I will make the request for Dak. I am prepared to go in front of the senate and demand he be released." He noticed her clinched jaws and wrinkle in her forehead.

Her father jumped up from his chair. He was horrified by the thought of Zenith appearing in front of the Blueblood Senate making a request for a drifter. The men in the senate were professional politicians. They could act so sincere, but he knew their true nature. They were sharks looking for blood. He walked around his desk and hugged his daughter. He loved her, and he also needed to protect her. He said, "It is not that simple. You do not understand what you request, and you will not appear in the senate."

She had a tear come down her face, "Yes, Father it is that simple, and what I request is very simple. You need to do the right thing. Placing an innocent man in the dungeon is not what we should be doing. I cannot talk to mom about the situation. She is so full of hatred toward the people of our realm, I cannot communicate with her. She hates all the people except the Bluebloods. This is not right, and our actions should be deemed illegal." She looked into her father's eyes with a pleading look. "I hope you can see what we as Bluebloods have done is wrong."

"We are trying to start a family together. She is a good mate. Do not speak ill of your stepmother." He glanced at his door and was concerned if the secretary could hear them. He then looked at her and now realized her strong feelings for this man. He realized the relationship could not be allowed to grow. He knew he needed to stop it. He whispered, "Do you not care about becoming a Blueblood Warrior? The Blueblood board has placed your commission on hold because of your actions. They will not like you becoming attached emotionally to a normal man. This is not acceptable. You cannot have an offspring with him. It is not allowed."

Zenith was frustrated with her father changing the conversation and asking her about her career. "I believe they are your and my stepmother's dreams. You want your daughter to be a Blueblood Warrior at all costs. Have you ever asked what I want?"

"Listen here little girl, this is what is best for you. The board will decide your mate after you become a Blueblood Warrior, and let me tell you something, your mate will be more significant if you finalize your apprenticeship. Your life will be so much easier, and your kids will have a great deal more liberties. I had to go in front of the Blueblood Board and plead for them to postpone their decision to grant you passage from a cadet to a Class One Warrior. Out of the twenty cadets in your class thirteen passed and your status is in limbo. They have the reports of you entering our territory up north and our city riding double with a drifter. They were prepared to grant you a failing score without reading your debrief report with regards to your unbelievable journey having to deal with the Midlanders by yourself. After the meeting, one of the wardens who read your report came up to me and said you were at the top of the class tied with Apollo and the top female in the history of the class. No cadet has registered as many killings as you. The other cadets noted in their reports that instead of running away you fought several Midlanders and pulled the trainer over to his horse after he had been wounded, and you two escaped. You registered a perfect score and showed no fear in the face of the attack. The warden said you would have been paired with Zeus's son Apollo. He would be great for you." He looked her in the eyes. "Please do not throw this opportunity away."

She thought of Apollo. The Blueblood adults all thought Apollo was great. He was smart and good looking and seemed to always attract positive attention from the leaders of the Blueblood community, but Zenith knew his true nature. He was a bully, selfish, and self-absorbed. She could not stand the thought of being held by him or being in a relationship with Apollo and forced to conceive his children. Zenith had been getting angrier and angrier with each word from her father. She pulled away from his hug, "I do not want Apollo, and I was not alone. I was being assisted by the man you had imprisoned." She clenched her jaws, "I do not want this." She walked out his door slamming it behind her. As she turned the corner of the office, she walked into Senator Blackmon. The two stepped backward after the bump and stared at each other.

Zenith had never liked the senator. He had always come across as a con. He would seem so sincere when he talked, but he just did not seem to care about anything but his own agenda. She knew he did not feel empathy toward others. She had heard his oldest son was a bully to the younger cadets who had entered the elementary Blueblood warrior academy. She had always thought, "Son like father."

Senator Blackmon smiled and looked at Zenith, "Speak of the devil. You and your journey are the talk in our senate. Everyone is talking about how you survived all those weeks fighting the Midlanders."

Zenith's father Aquarius appeared in his doorway. Zenith glanced at her father and then looked into the Senator's eyes. "Yes, it was an unbelievable adventure. Unfortunately, one of the trainers was killed. But if it had not been for the man in our dungeon, Senator, I would also have been killed. He does not deserve to be placed in the dungeon. He is a diplomat and has a commission to speak on behalf of his tribe to the Blueblood Senate. Senator, this is no way to treat a foreign diplomat."

With every word the Senator raised his hands as to say let me finish. Senator Blackmon glanced at Aquarius, "I have been working on getting him released and the Senate has agreed to meet with him in an open forum in two hours."

Zenith was surprised with that revelation and looked at the Senator, "So, he can state his position and then he will be allowed to leave the city? He wants to go back home."

Senator Blackmon said, "I worked hard to be allowed to let him make his request to the Blueblood Senate. He will be taken to the senate floor. There were some that opposed this meeting. They mentioned he could be a spy. They also mentioned the fact that he wanted to meet Ivan Chezon is reason enough for him to be taken to the guillotine." The Senator turned to Aquarius, "You have been asked to attend with Zenith."

Aquarius did not like the sudden feeling in his gut. His sixth sense was telling him to be careful. This could be a trap. He said, "Yes Senator, we will both be present. It is both an honor and a blessing." Aquarius turned and walked back into his office.

Zenith had a shock of surprise with Senator Blackmon mentioning the guillotine. She had spent her time writing her report of the journey, talking with the other cadets while they celebrated their graduation to being a Blueblood Warrior and her taking praise from the commanders in the military for surviving the three-week ordeal in the Midlander territory, all while Dak was in the dungeon. For the first time, she realized the trouble Dak was facing. She tried to hide her disappointment and walked through the exit door.

Chapter 18

Vicky reached for the unsealed paper. She knew Wayne had already read it as he handed it to her. "What is the news?"

Wayne looked directly at her, "Read the message from Old Thomas. Five of them have returned. There is no mention of the sixth one."

Vicky gasped, "Who did not return?" She thought about the loss of Dak. She remembered how her husband died from gunshots in the old world and the feeling of regret and emotional loss. She still had not dated anyone and had decided against dating for the past sixteen years. She read the message and laid the note on the table.

Wayne said, "A few of us will ride to Old Thomas's outpost. It will take us one-and-half days at a fast pace. Please do not jump to any conclusions. Old Thomas does not understand how to communicate with people. He has lived by himself far too long. He is awkward at best."

"Take Old Thomas some supplies and tell him thanks. We need him as a lookout for the west territory."

Wayne turned and walked out of Vicky's room. Billy Ray, Eric of Newport, and Wayne saddled their horses and headed out at a run. The village stood and watched. Little Jimmy stayed behind. The group knew Vicky always wanted one of them in the city in case someone became unruly, or an attack occurred. She knew some of the men, especially those who had joined their tribe from the New York group, questioned her being in charge. Mia, Delores and Casey stood together and watched. Little Jimmy walked up, "We sent a pigeon to fly to Old Thomas's outpost. He should reply who did not make it within the next few hours."

Vicky reached up and rubbed the cross around her neck. Whenever she was concerned about something or someone, she seemed to rub her cross which had been a gift from her now deceased husband. She had been doing this subconsciously for years and had never noticed she did it. The ladies all looked at each other with worry. They all hugged and prayed.

***

The three men had ridden hard for about twelve straight hours. The horses were tired. Wayne turned, "It is close to midnight. We will camp here and make it to Old Thomas's by noon."

"Yes. I will pull the food from my saddlebag," said Billy Ray.

Eric said, "I will gather firewood." Wayne could tell both men were worried about their kids and the possible loss. He knew Billy Ray loved his two sons, Hulk and Tommy Boy. He knew they had tried to have additional kids and were unable. He also knew Eric loved Robin Hood. Eric and Casey had a younger daughter, who had just turned eight, but still the loss of his son was a concern that no parent wanted to consider.

Wayne announced, "The tribe will know by now who did not make it. The pigeon would have returned by now." Both men walked into camp with Eric carrying additional firewood and Billy Ray carrying the food. Both men nodded they understood. Wayne then remarked, "All the kids are loved by the tribe. No matter what, we could be faced with a huge loss." Billy Ray looked at Wayne understanding the situation and knowing Eric felt the same as he did. They loved all the kids, but you just prayed your child was not the one missing.

Chapter 19

Dak heard the guard open the door. He did not feel good about the situation and had become bitter being left in a cell. The guard walked to the cell door and demanded, "Get up, scum. You are to report to the Blueblood Senate. Then, they will order me to beat you. That is their way. The beating will not be personal. It is part of the job."

Dak knew they limited his food to make him weak, so he would not have endurance to fight. He had not bathed in days. He looked at the guard as he stood. The other three guards were waiting at the outer door. Two of them led the way, and two followed Dak. Dak noticed all four men were very muscular and appeared to be indifferent to administering pain or killing a prisoner. They were dressed in black leather with leather handled swords. He noticed the one guard had picked up his swords and belt but not his bedroll and his saddle bag. He now suspected they were not planning to release him otherwise the guard would have picked up all of his items.

Dak was pushed through the large double doors. He was surprised with the large auditorium. He noticed the windows around the dome in the ceiling, and the sunlight at first blinded his vision. It was nice to see the sunlight after being in the dungeon for days. He saw the Senators all sitting in a row on a stage behind a large marble platform looking down from behind the wooden podium onto the senate floor. He counted nine Blueblood Senators all wearing black robes. He looked over to the side of the senate podium and noticed several Blueblood warriors standing along the wall, and Blueblood people sitting in the audience. There were additional guards blocking another exit on the far side of the auditorium. He then saw Zenith and Aquarius standing behind the balcony. He turned a circle looking at the large doors directly opposite the Senators which he assumed led to the exterior. There were two additional guards standing in front of the doors. He turned and faced the stage. He then glanced at Zenith, who had a worried look on her face. She smiled when Dak looked at her.

The Blueblood Senator in the center announced in a loud commanding voice: "Let us get this moving along." One of the guards pointed for Dak to walk further into the middle of the senate floor. The guard carried Dak's belt with the two swords and his knife and announced, "He arrived carrying these weapons." He held them up for everyone to see and then carried them back to a table located at the door to the hallway leading to the dungeon.

Dak did as he was requested. Once in the middle, he turned and stared defiantly into the eyes of each senator. The senator in the center looked at Dak and pointed his finger, "Let the record show, we are doing this against our better judgment. We are holding this meeting at the request of a couple of our senators, but we will not accept any controversial request. If this is so important, why not send someone more important than you? Now what is it you want?"

Dak looked into the face of Senator Dale, sitting in the middle with four senators to his right and four to his left, making certain eye contact was well established. Dak knew he must have been the chairperson of the committee. "First allow me to extend my thanks for your hospitality. I have committed no crime, yet you ordered me to your dungeon. The dungeon you have kept me in for days without adequate water and very little food is commendable. Your four hostesses are extremely well educated on how to torment your guests." He looked at each senator. "Thank you again for your hospitality. Maybe you can visit my tribe one day, and we can provide you with the same amenities." The Senators all looked angry with two leaning forward wanting to say something. The Senator in the middle waved his hand for them to be quiet.

Zenith instantly felt worried. She knew too well what the Blueblood Senate would do to a defiant drifter. She looked down at the floor and rubbed her forehead, hiding her concern.

"I come in peace. I have come a long distance to request your help fighting alongside us in a war against the Normand armies."

Senator Dale interrupted Dak and asked, "What war? We are not at war with anyone. Why would we start a war with King Solman?" Several Senators started shaking their heads in agreement.

"Certainly, the Blueblood Senate has heard of the Normand war efforts against the southern region. They have killed all armies in their path and have taken over a million people prisoner. They do not offer compromise, just death and destruction."

Senator Dale raised his voice, "This is all lies. There is no war. What proof do you exhibit?"

Dak was taken back that at least one of the Senators was not at least acknowledging the known war. He asked in a surprised voice, "Proof? All you must do is send your soldiers south, and they will find the war. The cities now are all flying the Normand banners."

The senator sitting two over to the right asked, "Have you been to Southern City?

"No. I have not been to Southern City."

The Senator cut him off. "So, you come into our senate and make fun of us and then demand we go to battle against the Normand people because they have allegedly attacked cities far south of here and you have no proof. Certainly, you have a witness or a written decree from the southern cities describing these wars."

Dak was still surprised. How could the Bluebloods not know? There had to be refugees running north around the nuclear pits or merchant ships sailing from the south. Someone had to have told the people in the city of Merlin. "Senator, I have no witnesses. I assumed you were aware of the people pleading for help. The Normand Navy has attacked our city, and we turned them back to the sea. They will attack us again and with overwhelming numbers at some point. Once they breach our walls and kill my people, they will come west and attack Merlin. They will attack you on three land fronts and the fourth front will be by sea."

Senator Dale, in the middle, raised his voice, "This is all lies." He struck his gable on the desktop and declared, "This meeting is terminated. We have heard enough. Take him back to the dungeon. We will pass judgment on his treasonous lies next week. You, young man, will learn a lesson. You do not come into the Blueblood Senate with lies. We do not tolerate your insurrectionist acts."

Dak demanded, "I am not lying, and I am not suggesting violence against the city of Merlin. I was commissioned to speak to a man named Ivan Chezon. Do you know Ivan Chezon?"

Senator Dale was older than the other senators. Every one of the Senators paused when he spoke and looked to him for clarity. He looked at Dak with pure hatred. He said, "How dare you question me or anyone on this senate. You have no rights. And yes, we all know the name of Ivan Chezon. If he is ever located, he will have his head removed for treason against the City of Merlin. Anyone found to be helping him will be taken to the Guillotine. We do not tolerate treason."

He looked at the guards and commanded, "I expect next week when we see this prisoner again, he had better have been taught better manners, or we will teach you." The guard that had hit Dak in the kidney smiled at Dak.

Dak said, "I want to have a trial. I deserve to be treated with justice and have a fair trial, or does the Blueblood Senate not believe in justice?"

Senator Dale pointed his finger, "You just had a fair trial. We will sentence you next week."

Dak interrupted the Senator and commanded, "What about trial by combat? I understand you still have the trial by combat system set as one of your guarded rules." The Bluebloods in the audience laughed with surprise and watched with interest. Zenith said, "No Dak." She then looked at the nine Senators, "He does not understand. Please no."

Dak turned and looked at Zenith. The four Senators in the middle seemed to agree with trial by combat. Dak had noticed one of the larger Blueblood warriors had taken a step forward. The Senators had also noticed. Senator Dale looked at the large soldier and asked in a gracious tone, "Apollo, do you have something you would like to add to this meeting?"

Apollo smiled and then in a very stern voice declared, "Yes Senators. It would be my honor to fight in the trial by combat to represent the Blueblood Senate and people of Merlin. It will be my duty to teach this scum manners and also those in the audience that support this dirty, filthy drifter."

The Senator second to the right immediately said, "This would be fitting and fair. Apollo has just completed his training and apprenticeship. He has taken his vows and is a sanctioned Blueblood Warrior."

Aquarius said, "A contest with Apollo would not be fair. He finished first in the junior competitions and came in second in the tournament only to Samuel." Everyone knew Samuel was the leader of the Blueblood armies. He had also won all the tournaments since their inception ten years ago. He was considered the greatest warrior on the planet. Samuel was also a pure Blueblood and had been one of the original thousand created in the old world. "Allow the stranger to fight one of the guards instead." He knew all eyes were on him and his daughter, and he knew he needed to protect her. "When this trial is leaked to the citizens of Merlin, and it is said the contest was not fair, then the people outside the walls could cause an unnecessary uprising."

Senator Dale looked at Aquarius and smiled. "You are right, it would not be appropriate for Apollo to fight this contest." He raised his voice as he spoke. "But since Samuel is on an assignment south of Merlin trying to clean up some scum activity, we are forced to allow Apollo to fight in his place. I have ruled."

Dak did not hesitate. He knew his opponent had to be overconfident, and he needed every advantage, "I choose a sword fight. I also understand if I win, I will be allowed to ride my horse out of Merlin and head home. Is that what you have agreed?"

The Senator was now aggravated. He looked at Dak, "Listen here you scum. You do not tell me what I have agreed on."

Dak interrupted him, "You have monoculturalism and expect others to conform to you. I have no inclination to conform to your way of life. I have agreed to fight this quintessential warrior to obtain my freedom. You have placed an unfair stereotype label on me, and because of your actions, I do not trust you, Senators. I want to hear you say the agreement so all can bear witness. I do not want to stay in your disgusting filthy city. This is a disgrace where there are so many poor and just you and a few other wealthy people. This is a sin for those in charge to have so much and the common people have nothing."

Senator Dale looked at Dak and in a monotone pleasant voice, "If you win, you will be allowed to ride out of Merlin on your horse back to your home and when you lose, the janitors will be instructed to haul what is left of you out the basement door and feed your dead worthless body to the dogs. Now, let us put this trivial matter to rest."

Dak waited while Apollo took off his cape. Apollo seemed to draw out the preparation and enjoyed the attention while he took his time folding his cape into a nice-looking fold with the emblem on the rear of the cape now showing on top of the cape sitting on the bench for everyone to see. As he had removed his cape and folded it so nicely and neatly, he had glanced at Zenith with a smile on his face. He then pulled his sword and smiled at the sword as he glanced at Dak. One of the guards had carried his swords and belt out from the side. Senator Dale said, "You can only use one sword. We want the contest to be fair and, in the name of fairness, if you want to borrow a long sword from one of the guards, I will permit it." He smiled.

The guard tried to hand one of the swords to Dak. Dak reached for the other sword. He did not trust the guards. He felt they might have intentionally broken his handle on the sword and covered it up. "Senator, thank you for your offer and your sense of fair play, but I am fine with one of my two-foot-six-inch swords. I will need just the one sword for this trial." He looked at Apollo as he was walking toward the middle of the senate floor holding his four-foot sword which glittered when the sunlight reflected off the shining blade. The sun reflecting off the sword could be seen on the floor and walls as Apollo kept swinging the sword back and forth as he walked. Dak then turned directly to Senator Dale waiting for the procedure to start.

Senator Dale exclaimed, "Let the record show the scum did not want to use another sword, and we the Blueblood Senate have made every attempt to make this a fair trial which the scum has requested, so the common people won't see a need to cause a riot." He looked at Aquarius and smiled.

He then looked at Apollo, "Do not request permission of mercy. We expect you to execute the scum."

Apollo was three inches taller and fifty pounds heavier than Dak. His sword was shiny perfect crafted metal, and the standard size for the Blueblood male warrior. Dak had molded his sword with two six-inch curved small blades coming out of each end of the handle where the handle and the longer blade met. The two smaller blades extended parallel to the larger blade and were just as sharp. Apollo stood with a smile of confidence facing Dak in his shining armor waiting for the competition to start. He pulled his mask down from his helmet. "You should have requested a longer sword you scum. Your Sai sword is laughable. Only a female would fight with such a sword."

Apollo then whispered under his mask, "I am going to teach Zenith the importance of taking orders from me. You scum."

"I will be your huckleberry." Dak could feel himself getting angry when Apollo mentioned Zenith's name. He thought to himself, "I need to stay focused."

Senator Dale could not hear the exchange between the two men standing in front of him, but he wanted to give them an opportunity to hate each other. He suspected Apollo would be describing how he was going to kill Dak.

Apollo shifted his weight, "You dirty scum. It would be better for you, if you would keep your mouth shut."

Dak had listened over the years sitting around the bonfire and the older men talking about the old days and the television shows. He also had recalled his mother saying the line over the years, I will be your huckleberry. He quietly whispered, "I got news for you, This isn't Dodge City and you ain't Matt Dillion."

Aquarius held Zenith tight against his body. She tried to struggle free. He whispered; "I am truly sorry. I love you so much. Do not allow them to see you care or have feelings for this man. Stand strong." Zenith could feel her father holding her tight and listened to him say, "This is not me. They will kill both of us if they have to. Please Zenith, this will be over soon."

She whispered. "Father. I cannot watch as he is butchered. You do not understand. I love this man."

Aquarius felt the pain in his daughter's voice, and he felt for her loss of a loved one. He knew he loved her. He felt her sadness and emotional pain. He remembered the sickening feeling when his first wife had died while she was pregnant with their second child. He also thought how this would affect Zenith's future. He pulled her tight against his chest and held her. He glanced around to see who was watching. He knew they needed to cover up her feelings for this man. He also knew for her to be a Blueblood Warrior; she would need to watch the match. A warrior would not turn away. The other Blueblood families would be watching her and having emotional feelings for a normal man by a young female Blueblood was not acceptable.

Senator Dale smiled and announced, "Let us have justice. Let the trial began", and he hit his desk with his gavel. He, like the other Senators, was certain of the pending outcome. They all watched with an edge of excitement. Zenith started to yell something. Aquarius pulled her into his chest. "You need to watch. Now is the time for you to be strong."

She buried her face into her father's chest and wanted to cry. She thought, "Why did I not convince him not to come to Merlin? He was so damn stubborn. This is all my fault." She had to fight her impulse to jump into the arena and fight for him. She also knew she was no match one on one with Apollo. He was too big and strong.

Dak noticed Apollo was right-handed. He figured he would aggressively attack and try to show how quickly he could kill him. He knew Apollo would want to impress the Blueblood Senate, the Blueblood families, and most of all Zenith. He approached fast, yelled as he swung his sword right to left. Dak jumped backward and noted the speed of the swing, and his feet positioned prior to the swing. Apollo smiled and said loud so everyone could hear, "You're scared. Don't worry. I will not allow you to suffer. The dogs are hungry for an early dinner." He smiled behind his mask.

Dak did not answer and switched his sword to his left hand as he bent forward standing more on the balls of his feet. He waited for the second swing. Then as Dak anticipated, Apollo's second swing of his sword was left to right as he stepped with his right leg toward Dak. Instead of jumping backward, Dak stepped forward into the sword and caught the sword between his larger blade and the small blade, stopping the swing. The two swords made a large clashing sound, and Dak twisted his sword just enough to lock swords with Apollo. Dak kept moving forward and bent low and completed a frontal kick by placing his left foot on the concrete floor and drove his right foot through the kneecap of the right leg of Apollo. When Apollo had swung, he had placed his weight on his front right leg. As Apollo registered the pain in his knee, he grimaced with the shock of the fact his knee had lost the ability to support him. He felt an instant sharp pain and a nauseating feeling registered in his gut. He made the mistake of reaching for his knee with his left hand leaving himself open for the attack.

Dak still holding Apollo's sword locked between his two blades twisted the grip of his sword further, forcing Apollo to lose his grip entirely on his sword handle as Dak quickly rose after the kick. Dak switched his sword to his right hand and grabbed the right fingers of Apollo holding the arm out to the side as the large sword fell toward the concrete floor. He swung his sword downward with his right hand and while holding Apollo's right hand outward with his left hand cutting off the right hand at the wrist. Apollo fell backward to the floor landing on his back with his helmet falling off and rolling across the concrete floor. The sound of his sword landing on the polished concrete floor could be heard throughout the auditorium. The witnesses had a sudden look of surprise with a collective gasp coming from the audience as Dak stepped over

Apollo and pointed his sword at Apollo's throat. The two men stared at each other for a second. Apollo's father yelled, "Don't. Please." He was in the middle of the audience sitting in the benches and jumped over the rail onto the senate floor. He started to run toward his son, and Dak watched him. Zeus realized if he charged, his son would lose his head, and Dak would kill him.

Dak glared at the man and the Blueblood Senators and held the sword piercing against Apollo's neck. The man looked with a pleading expression and raised his hands in a pleading gesture and said, "I beg you. No. He is my son."

Aquarius said in a low voice, "It is over." Zenith slowly turned and anticipated Dak being cut into pieces. She had never been more surprised when she turned and saw Dak standing looking down at Apollo with his sword against Apollo's throat. She immediately felt relief. She smiled in disbelief. She saw the blood on the floor and noticed Apollo's hand. She yelled, "Please Dak no. You have won."

Everyone in the senate was very surprised. There was not a sound. Dak looked at each Senator and then stared at Senator Dale in the middle. "Like I said, I do not want to be in your filthy city. I can finish him, but you are going to need every warrior when the Normand armies roll across the eastern plains and come crashing down on Merlin." Dak looked at the scared eyes of Apollo lying on his back with blood pumping out of his right stump. Do you surrender in the name of the Blueblood Senate and the City of Merlin?"

Apollo said quietly, "Please don't kill me. Yes. I surrender."

Dak clenched his teeth, "I do not believe everyone heard you, and you need to finish your testimony, or I will cut your Blueblood head off and let the dogs eat you for dinner."

He cried out with urgency in his voice, "I surrender in the name of the Blueblood Senate and the City of Merlin." Dak pulled back his sword from Apollo's throat and held it to his side. He looked at the Senators.

The Chairman in the middle commanded, "Blueblood Warriors, arrest this scum and give him to the guards to be taken to the dungeon."

Dak did not move. He was not surprised with the actions of Senator Dale. He looked around as the twenty Blueblood warriors surrounded him with their swords pulled ready to fight. Dak finally turned and looked at Zenith and Aquarius. He dropped his sword, and the captain of the Blueblood soldiers came forward gathering his sword. A medic ran over to Apollo and placed a bandage on his stump, and another picked up his hand. A gurney was brought to the center of the senate floor and picked him up and rushed him to the sickbay.

The Blueblood warriors walked Dak to the hallway where the four guards were waiting. The big guard whispered, "Now I will teach you respect."

Dak with his jaws clinched quickly turned and grabbed the big man by his shoulders and rammed his forehead into the large guard's forehead. The large guard was not prepared for the headbutt. His eyes rolled back into his skull as he went falling backward on his back. Dak said in a loud voice so not only the other three guards could hear him, but the Blueblood Warriors and the Senators could hear him, "How can you have any respect for that Blueblood Senate?" He hesitated and then announced, "If you touch me, you better kill me because it only took me eleven seconds to take down the runner up to the Blueblood City Champion. I will come back into your dungeon and cut you into pieces in less time. Besides, I am just an envoy. Wait until the real warriors from the far east hear how you treated me. You all will be cut down."

The captain of the Blueblood soldiers looked at the three standing guards and then glanced at the other Blueblood soldiers standing behind him. He quickly contemplated what he had witnessed and what Dak had just announced. He ordered the guards, "Do not touch him until you hear from us. Now take him below."

Chapter 20

The pigeon flew true and delivered the news. Vicky looked at the note and was reluctant to open it. She knew no matter what, the news was not going to be good. One of the teenagers had not made it. She looked toward the door as Mia, Delores, and Casey rushed into her room.

Mia said, "We understand a pigeon came back from Old Thomas's outpost."

Vicky held the note up. She unrolled it. She said, "The five are okay. Thank God. Dak did not return with them. Hulk said they were ordered by Dak to leave him and head home, and Dak went to Merlin alone escorted by the Blueblood."

Delores was relieved her two boys had made the journey. She was also hopeful Dak would be alright. She said, "If Dak is with a Blueblood Warrior, then he will be alright."

Mia said, "There must have been a reason they split up. Don't worry, Vicky. Dak will be okay. I believe this is better news than we all expected."

Vicky said, "You are right. We all thought one of our kids was killed. Now we know five have returned, and Dak is on his own. I am going to ring his neck when I see him next. There is strength in numbers."

Casey, being relieved that her son, Robin Hood, had made it back said, "We all will help you ring his neck."

They all walked over to Vicky and hugged her. Delores said, "Now is the time for you to be strong. He will be alright. I know he will."

Chapter 21

The three men rode into Old Thomas's ranch in mid-morning. Old Thomas was on his front porch skinning a large deer. He saw the riders coming. Old Thomas asked when the riders rode up, "How would you men like some fresh deer?" The riders got off their horses. They heard a voice from the roof. It was Tommy Boy. "Hi Dad."

Thomas said, "Tommy Boy is repairing my roof. Trey and Hulk are cutting logs and dragging them in that stack. Veronica has been cleaning the inside of the home. She has made it dust free. Hulk shot this deer at daybreak. They are good kids. I have never had so much help."

Robin Hood walked out the front door of the home and looked at Eric of Newport, "Hi Dad." Tommy Boy walked around the side of the home after coming down from the ladder. Tommy Boy smiled, "We all have been working hard helping Old Thomas except for Robin Hood. He took an arrow in the back just so he did not have to work."

Veronica walked out the door and smiled at the three men. She said, "I am fairly certain Robin Hood would have rather not taken the arrow, and we wish he had not been shot. He has done nothing but complain the entire way home."

The men looked at Robin Hood standing. He looked alright and the three teenagers seemed to be happy. The men seemed to relax now knowing everything might be okay. Wayne walked over to Robin Hood and said, "Let us look at it. Take your shirt off."

"I do not recall complaining one single time." He pulled off his shirts.

Wayne and Eric of Newport looked, and Wayne said, "That will heal and looks like one of my many scars. You now have what I call a conversation scar. There is a story behind my scars, and I assume there is a story behind your scar."

Eric smiled, "That damn arrow went all the way through. The bottom silk undershirt must have helped. The fabric did not tear."

Eric then announced, "Well, it does not look to be infected. The blood fusion from the Blueblood is still in your system and must have helped with fighting off the possible infection and accelerated the healing."

"We changed the bandages daily and kept it clean. Believe me when I tell you, it was a group effort," mentioned Veronica.

Wayne then realized Dak's name had not been mentioned. "Where is Dak?"

Veronica told the three men the events of the trip while they sat around the kitchen table. Old Thomas had finished cleaning the deer, and Trey and Hulk had ridden back into the outpost dragging logs behind their horses. The three men listened while Tommy Boy and Robin Hood would add their accounts to the events. They all felt better about the journey now that they saw the five teenagers and heard Dak was with a Blueblood.

The three men helped cut firewood and repair the roof and barn siding. At night, they all gathered around the bonfire and talked further about the journey into the Midlanders territory. Billy Ray said, "The reason we have not been back into the waste land was we did not want to leave tracks so the Midlanders could follow us. Old Thomas sends us a message every day to let us know if the Midlanders have broken through. They do not know how to get around the contaminated nuclear waste areas. Eric of Newport, Little Jimmy and I have had several run-ins with the Midlanders. We made it all the way across to Merlin one time. We wanted to meet with Ivan Chezon and check on him. Merlin at that time was a growing city. There were a great deal more people who survived the old world in that area. The people seemed to be happy. The city was prospering with farmers, large cattle herds, sheep herds, and industries were starting to grow. The Bluebloods protected the people and were not involved in the government. A lot can happen in ten years."

Chapter 22

Aquarius whispered, "We need to leave. This is not good. Follow me." He noticed they were the first ones to reach the hallway. He looked and made certain it was clear. He turned his daughter around in the hall and said, "Listen to me. You do not understand. I need you to leave the city of Merlin."

Zenith pulled away, "You do not understand. I know corruption when I see it." She felt relief with the outcome of the trial and then she got mad at her father. So, mad she could barely control herself. Her jaws were now clinched, and her face was red, "You were prepared to watch an innocent man die on the floor of our senate just so your daughter could be forced to mate with Apollo. I do not know you. What man would knowingly force his daughter to be with a man she did not covet. Now those guards are going to beat an innocent man in our dungeon. You know what they do to people in chains. This is all wrong. Now let me go."

Aquarius looked around to make certain no one could hear them. He tried to pull Zenith in close. He whispered, "I am afraid they will try to kill us. I won't be able to protect you."

"Who are they? You and mom are part of them. You are all one big group of ruthless corrupt mean people. Now leave me alone."

Aquarius was rushed. He glanced around a second time to verify if anyone could hear him. "Your stepmother is part of them. Do not trust her. I will more than likely be killed in the next few weeks. I am truly sorry. I cannot protect you. I was hoping you would become a Blueblood Warrior, so you would have been paired with Apollo. His family could have protected you."

"What are you talking about? You work for the senate and now you are telling me not to trust my stepmother. She has never been unkind to me. Who are you?" She pulled her arms free and ran down the stairs out the backdoor of the senate building. Aquarius stood watching her run out the door. He looked around and noticed two clerks who worked for two other senators watching. He walked back to his office. He was concerned and conscious of the people watching him as he walked. He figured the Blueblood second generation warriors would arrest him and take him to the dungeon. He walked into his office and the male secretary announced, "Senator Blackmon demands to see you immediately."

Aquarius walked into the Senator's office with Senator Blackmon sitting behind his desk with a frown on his face. "Sir, I understand you want to see me."

The Senator looked at Aquarius, "What just happened? You and your daughter have embarrassed me. Do you know how hard I have worked to be selected to the Blueblood Senate? Do you realize what an honor it is for me to be in the senate?"

"Sir, I can assure you we have your back on this."

The senator looked at him with a frown, "I am not tracking what you are saying. I might need to think more about your employment."

"Your number one responsibility sir, is to serve and protect. See the insignia on your door?" He pointed to the door, to the engraved insignia. "You might be the only one that understands the threat to the City of Merlin. The citizens are counting on the senate to protect them."

"Please close the door." He readjusted his posture as Aquarius gently closed the door.

"Remember your oath. Look at your oath. The number one item listed is to serve and protect."

The senator was now caught a little off guard and agitated. "What are you talking about? Protection from who?"

"Listen Senator, we have all been told how great we Bluebloods are at fighting, and no one can come close to us in battle. We can block arrows with our swords. We have quicker reflexes. We are masters at fighting from horseback. We can take on several men at one time with a sword and win." He hesitated and then said, "It took this man from the far east eleven seconds to take down our youth city's champion. Apollo came in second to Samuel in the competition in the war tournament. My daughter has been trying to force us to listen, and no one will listen to her. I have not listened to her. We need to figure out what is going on. I would suggest we send Samuel, the man in the dungeon, and a group east to meet his tribe and find out before it is too late. You heard him say in the senate auditorium when he spared Apollo's life, we are going to need every warrior because what is coming from the east, we will not be able to stop it."

The Senator leaned over his desk and looked surprised. He looked at his desktop in thought. He was going to fire Aquarius and have the guards remove him from the building. Now, he thought yes, there might be some validity to what he was saying. He looked into Aquarius's eyes, "I will mention this to the senate tomorrow. Aquarius, you know I am your boss, and I need to be totally trusting of all my employees. I am going to consider your position and your employment working for me in the future. You may leave."

Chapter 23

Zenith decided she did not want to go home. She also did not want to walk on the sidewalks where other Bluebloods could see her. She certainly did not want to encounter Apollo's family or friends. She remembered the back alleys from when she was a toddler, and her father would take her through them as he would jog with her sitting strapped to his back in a backpack. She thought of all the time he spent with her. He would leave work early and take her to the park, and then when she got older, he would take her sailing, just the two of them. "Why did he spend so much time with me if does not love me?" She was so confused. "What did he mean when he said he might be killed in the near future? Who would kill him?" Also, he said she should not trust her stepmother. He had implied her stepmother was part of something, and he was not. She sat down on the steps under a big oak tree located in an open area in a back alley. She knew she needed time to think. She also knew the Senators would want to cover up the trial by combat, and they needed Dak out of the city. Otherwise, he would be a hero to the slaves, workers, farmers, ranchers and the common person. She felt her body go rigid as she realized another alternative. "He would be killed and made to look like another cellmate killed him or an accident ended his life. The

189

only reason Senator Dale agreed to the trial by combat was he was certain of the outcome. The Senator wanted Dak dead and that is why he was taken back to the dungeon. The Senator could not afford for him to be released and then disappear like Ivan Chezon."

She jerked with surprise when a woman sat down next to her. The woman apologized for causing her to jump and startling her. She suddenly wondered where this woman had come from, and why did she elect to sit next to her. Zenith glared at her. She was not wearing the normal maid outfit and was dirty and smelled. She was dressed as a peasant and had a hood pulled tight around her head blocking a clear view of her face. The woman looked straight ahead and whispered, "They are going to kill him tonight in the dungeon."

Zenith looked at the woman, "Who is going to kill him tonight?"

"Do not look at me. If you want to help Dak, go to this address now." She handed Zenith a note with an address listed on it near the exterior wall of the inner city. As she looked up the woman had walked quickly away and disappeared around a corner of a building behind her. Zenith jumped up and ran toward the address.

Zenith made it to the outer wall of the city and was walking toward the address listed. The numbers were getting smaller as she was getting closer to the address. The area was the warehouse district where the slaves worked making furniture and other items. She could feel her adrenaline increasing with every step. She made certain her hood was pulled tight around her head with her hair tucked down the interior of the cape. She had her right hand resting on her sword handle. As she turned the corner, a large man dressed like a custodian stepped in front of her blocking her path. She looked up into the man's eyes under his hat and noticed his long beard. He pointed across the street. He said, "Go down the alley and wait. The door will open, and you will be provided additional information." The man then turned and left walking north on the street. Zenith looked across the street and made certain no one was watching her. She noticed a wagon full of cut lumber being pulled by two mules heading her way and other workers walking on the street heading into a blacksmith shop. She could hear the hammer striking the metal on the anvil and see a blacksmith working. She ran across the street with her left hand holding her hood pulled tight against her face. She had released the strap holding her sword in place and then rested her right hand on the handle of her sword. She had heard the stories of first-generation Bluebloods being killed inside the city walls. She wondered if this was a trap. With every step she grew more concerned.

She noticed the alley had crates stacked up eight feet high and an old wheelbarrow with a broken handle. She could not see the door until she cleared the last of the crates. She walked to the back of the alley and quickly glanced in all directions and above her. She had no way to call for help, and she only had one way out-that being the alley she had just walked through. She saw the wagon full of lumber stop at the alley entrance and box her in. She pulled her sword. She anticipated a weighted net or several arrows raining down from the rooftop. She was trapped, and she could hear a portable sawmill startup next door in the building. The noise was deafening. She now accepted an attack and maybe her death. The old wooden door to the building opened an inch. The man spoke through the crack. She walked next to the door trying to hear him. He said, "The guards have been instructed to kill young Dak Donahue tonight. If you care for his safety, you will need to break him out before three A.M. prior to the two guards switching shifts. We cannot gain access inside the dungeon and help him."

She looked around again with anticipation of an attack. "Who are you? How do you know this?"

"No names. If you can get him outside the dungeon, we can get him out of the city and hide him. We will be watching and waiting."

"How do I know I can trust you?"

"He will die tonight if you do nothing to help him. That is all I have." He started to close the door and Zenith had a surge of anger and kicked the door pushing it open a few inches and rammed her sword between the door and the door jamb preventing the door from closing. She did not hesitate and rammed the door with her shoulder. The man fell backward as Zenith pushed through the doorway. It was dark in the building. She held her sword pointed at the man on the floor. She looked at the older man. He held his hand up and yelled, "No, wait."

At first, she thought he was talking to her and then she heard movement in the building. She heard someone flip a window shutter open and a sudden flash of bright light blinded her. She looked back at the man and pulled him up by his shirt. She said, "You need to start talking. Who are you?" She could sense there were men hidden in the building with arrows all aimed at her.

The man looked into her eyes as she turned toward him with his back to the window. She glanced above him and used him as a shield. She had her back to the rear of the building's exterior concrete wall. The area above her was all open ceilings and dark. She also knew she could not retreat to the alley. It was blocked. Her only way out was through the open space in this building, and she could not see the enemy. "My name is

Ivan Chezon. I am trying to help young Dak Donahue. We need to hurry. Time is running out." The man held his hand up while watching Zenith and signaled to the men behind him.

"You are the man everyone is trying to kill for treason. Why would I trust you?"

"I asked you here to help the man in the dungeon. I am the one taking the chances. You can go back to your Blueblood life of never helping anyone and living with all your servants and luxury. This was not the way the Bluebloods were meant to behave."

"What do you want from me?"

"I was hoping you could save young Dak Donohue. I owe a favor to his tribal leader. I need to meet with Dak, so he can deliver a message to his leader back east. Once you break him out, we will arrange for him to be smuggled back into the wilderness, so he can head east."

"Give me the message. I will see what I can do. I do not need your help with him."

He hesitated. "If you are identified as helping him, you will become a fugitive. The Blueblood Senate will hunt for you like they have me. They will offer a thousand gold coins for your head. The only difference is I have friends with the common people, and you don't. You need to consider this very carefully." He held up the message in a leather airtight seal. "If you are captured, you will need to make certain the guards and the Blueblood Senate do not acquire the contents of this message. Destroy the message with fire if you have too. Guard it with your life. It should be opened by the leader of Dak's tribe only." He looked Zenith in the eyes. "This message could save your father's life." He turned to his men and motioned for them to stand down. "Do not tell anyone about this message. It is life and death that the message gets through. I have been waiting for someone to be able to make the trip. Evidently, Dak's tribe knows the route by the nuclear pits and the Midlanders. This is life and death for all of us."

"What does my father have to do with this? He does not know Dak or Dak's tribe. What is so important in this message?"

"Your father, Aquarius, is a good man. You will need my help with Dak. We will have two horses saddled and ready for you." She looked him in the eyes when he mentioned her father's name. The portable sawmill started back up, and she had to lean over toward him to hear his plan. He explained the plan once she broke Dak out of the dungeon. She nodded in understanding. The saw stopped, "You must be brave and hurry. Time is not on our side."

***

Dak could not sleep. He knew it had to be past midnight. He wondered if he might ever see daylight. He tried to come up with a plan. Maybe he could act like he was sick or asleep and once someone walked into the cell and the door was left open, he would attack. Then what? He had no plan to break out of the main part of the dungeon or the city for that matter. There were always two guards at night and four during the day. The exit door from the main dungeon room was always locked from the exterior hall where one of the guards was always stationed. There was no way to break through that door. He kept trying to figure out a plausible plan. He finally accepted his fate. He had heard another prisoner being tortured when he first arrived. The man yelled for at least thirty straight minutes as loud as he could before he died. The man had kept repeating he did not know who they were asking about and begging for mercy. Dak figured a fast death was his best alternative. He would go down fighting and not beg for mercy.

His thoughts turned to Zenith and her beautiful figure and smile. He remembered her stepping out of the hot spring nude, sitting on the rock with a confident smile while placing her boots on, and then walking to the bedroll with nothing on but her boots carrying her other clothing. He knew that memory would last him a lifetime. He now realized he had a crush on her. He rolled over and thought, "She told me not to come to Merlin. The meeting would not end well."

He heard the outer door hinge softly squeak and open to the main room. He thought he heard the sound of someone being hit and the grunt by the person receiving the blow. He heard the interior door to the cell block open and then someone trying different keys to his cell. He was about to spring from his bed, when he heard Zenith's soft voice, "I am so sorry, Dak."

Zenith looked in the cell and noticed Dak was not moving. She thought he was dead. She wanted to be quiet and not wake any other prisoners. Once she opened the door, she rushed to his bed with tears coming down her cheeks. He rolled over and grabbed her and kissed her. "I am okay. They have not killed me yet."

She wiped the tears off her checks, "Come on. We must hurry. Time is not on our side. I have horses waiting for us outside the castle walls. I must get you out of this dungeon and out of Merlin as quickly as possible. They are planning to kill you."

Dak noticed the two guards were out of commission as they rushed out of his cell into the main room of the dungeon. One was knocked out and the other was tied up facing against the wall. Dak saw his belt with his swords on the shelf. He picked up his belt and fastened it around his waist. He then noticed his saddle bag back further in the shelf, his cape, and bedroll. He pulled out his saddle bag, bedroll, and placed his cape around his neck and followed Zenith up the stairs and down the hall.

She came to the rear door of the senate building. She thought if they would be caught, it would be now. She cracked the door and looked. The stairs were clear. She turned to Dak and whispered, "We will have a two-hour head start before the guards are located in the dungeon. We need to hurry. We need to go over the wall and drop down to the alley. We then will run on the back road and cross into the park. If we see guards, just act normal. No one will suspect I busted you out of the dungeon."

Dak shook his head in understanding. He watched Zenith run across the concrete stairs and jump off the wall. He followed. They landed and ran down the alley. Dak followed Zenith to the park, and she had not slowed down. She kept turning and running down one alley then crossing a street and then down another alley. She slowed and bent down on a knee in the shadows of a building once they got close to the outer wall. She knew the guards watched the exterior walls more than any other area. She was breathing hard as she looked down the street to the corner of the building. She saw two guards talking at the burning barrel stationed outside the pub. She looked the other direction and saw the silhouettes of two other guards in the moonlight at the crossroad leading to the exterior gate several hundred yards in the opposite direction. The guards were stationed in pairs around the city at different locations. Dak looked and saw the four guards. "We need to hurry. What is your plan?"

"We wait."

Dak looked at Zenith and noticed her natural beauty. He smiled at her as she was intensely watching the closest set of guards near the pub. He leaned against the stone wall smiling, "So, we are waiting on what?"

"When I say run, you need to follow me across the street and down that alley. We need to stay in the shadows. The castle is built to keep people out, not keep people in. We will climb to the roof of that building and once on the roof, we will drop down on the other side of the wall." She pointed to the building. She looked at the fur lined cape and him holding the saddle bag in one hand the bedroll in the other hand and asked, "Do you need the purse? You need to climb the wall and then we will have to drop down. It might get in your way." She started to mention the bedroll would get in the way and was too bulky to run with, but she remembered the feeling of being held by Dak in between the liner and the fur. She loved that thought.

He smiled at the thought of the saddle bag being called a purse. "I will keep the saddle bag as long as I can. Once we break free of Merlin, the contents might come in handy."

She whispered, "Here we go."

Dak saw some people come out of the bar fighting and yelling with the two guards turning toward the argument. She pulled his arm and took off bent over down the sidewalk staying in the shadows of the buildings. Once she got even with the building, she ducked her head and ran bent over across the street. Dak followed her. They climbed the ladder to the roof of the building and then jumped the three-foot distance to the top of the castle wall. Dak looked over the wall and noticed a twenty-foot drop to the ground and the large hay wagon backed up to the castle wall. Zenith said, "You go first. Hang on the ledge and try to land in the hay."

Dak did not hesitate. He dropped the saddle bag, bedroll, and his belt with his swords. He hung down and released his grip landing in the hay. He looked up and watched as she dropped her sword. Likewise, Zenith hung and dropped. He stood under her to catch her and lessen the impact.

She said, "The horses are over on the next street. There will be other guards standing at the outer castle gate." She pointed toward the direction where the two guards were standing several hundred yards away. They crawled out of the hay with the two grabbing their dropped items, and they ran around the barn and down another alley. The city was quiet this time of night, and Zenith knew two horses running down the street would awaken half the outer city. She said, "Those are our horses. Follow me. We will head south out of town in hopes we throw the hunters off our trail."

They jumped on the horses and headed south. Dak had been surprised to see General Lee, his horse, saddled and tied off for him. Dak took a second to say hi to his horse and then tie his bedroll on above his saddle bags. They then could hear dogs barking behind them as the horses were running at a full gallop. Once they were out of the city close to a half mile, they cut east at the intersection of a dirt road. They rode for another half mile and then at another road they cut north on a dirt road. "This road will lead us east of Merlin city limits and then we will intercept the Shoreline Road north of Merlin. It is the main dirt road leading north along the shoreline. That is the same road we followed when heading into Merlin. We need to make it deep into the wilderness before they start tracking us. That is the only chance we have."

"Why?"

She looked at him. "This is the right thing to do. That is why."

"You should stay here. If the guards did not recognize you, the authorities won't know it was you that helped me. This is going to be a hard trip. You can stay."

She glanced ahead of her and then turned her head looking straight into Dak's eyes, "You know I can't do that. I have no reason to stay and every reason to go."

Chapter 24

The sun had risen, and they kept pushing the horses. There were more and more people on the road as time passed. After the sun had been up for close to four hours, Zenith slowed the pace. She said, "We need to look normal and ride at a normal speed. We do not need to look like a couple of people on the run."

They came around the turn in the dirt road, and they could see the ALE House where they had stopped and eaten on their prior journey. She knew the ALE House represented the fact they had traveled one-hundred miles from Merlin. Zenith said, "Hold up. There are several horses tied up at the front. They would have known by now you have escaped with my help. They would have sent pigeons out to the outpost areas to be on the lookout for us. The fact we started south may buy us a little time, but they will send riders in every direction."

Dak adjusted his position in the saddle and rubbed his lower back. He then pointed at the ALE House, "Who are they?"

"They are the Huskie Bandits. They will be on the payroll of the Bluebloods. If the Blueblood Senate places a reward on someone's head, dead or alive, they take the bounty. No one is ever brought in alive."

"Sounds like a charming group of people. Can we backtrack and go across the farmland out of sight of the people on the road?"

"No. The farmers and ranchers all have a posse who watch their land. The Midlanders drift into the area and steal livestock and garden food. There is always a skirmish going on somewhere along the boundaries with the Midlanders. One of the posses would see us, and we don't need that trouble. The possess working for the farmers and ranchers are more like a militia. They are a very formable foe with over one-hundred fighting men with kill orders. We will have to stay on this road until we are well past the ALE restaurant. The Huskie Bandits have ridden from the north down the Shoreline Road. They are nothing but paid mercenaries." She looked at Dak. "We need to hide off the road. We need to stay out of sight for as long as we can. Our horses are tired. We won't be able to outrun them."

They led the horses over to the shoulder of the road in the bushes and overgrowth. The area was not thick once off the road past the tree line and wild bushes lining the road. There were sand dunes then the beach and ocean. Zenith said, "They are coming out. They will be headed this way."

Dak said, "They look like a war party. Hurry and bring your horse over." He grabbed the horse and pinned the head against his chest, twisting the horse's head forcing the horse to lay down. He said, "Come over here and lay across the horse's neck and hold it down."

Zenith came over and laid across the horse's neck placing her hand over the head. Dak ran and pulled his horse's head hard against his chest, twisting its head and forcing the horse down on the ground. He laid across the horse's neck. He looked over at Zenith, "Hold the horse down and if you hear me get up and head south, you wait and head north. I will meet you at the hot spring in two days." They heard the horses riding toward their direction. As the sound of over three dozen riders approached on the road, her horse tried to stand. Zenith had to struggle to hold her horse in place. There were over forty riders that ran past them on the road.

Dak announced, "The horse will get right up with you on the saddle. We can ride by the ALE House. Maybe no one is out, and the people on the inside might think we are a couple of the Huskie Bandits riding back north."

Zenith watched Dak mount his horse and stepped sideways over the saddle as the horse stood up with him. She did the same. They kept their heads bent down as they rode by the ALE House, and no one was outside. They rode hard for two additional hours.

The horses were spent. They had finally made it to the crossroad. Dak said, "They will suspect we will travel that road. I bet we have a very large price on our heads by now.

Every cutthroat on this side of the continent will be looking for us. I suggest we go further north and then go cross country. We will need to push through the overgrowth and snow heading east and find a place to hole up for a day or two. The horses are going to need to rest. It will be a hard journey forging through the wilderness."

They rode further north passing a few people pulling wagons. They tried to keep their distance and not talk with anyone. They came to a small creek at a small bridge with no one in sight. Dak said, "This is the best time to leave the road. The creek will hide the hoofprints and if they use dogs to track us, the dogs won't be able to pick up the scent in the water."

Zenith was glad they had finally stopped. She could tell her horse was tired. She and Dak had dismounted and tied their horses up near the creek and a grassy area. As they rested for two hours, they ate snacks and talked. She said, "By now, all the roads will be blocked, and the reward for just one of us would be more than these people could ever make in a lifetime. I believe they will track us until they find us. I remember listening to your friends talk about how rough the mountains are with the ice and snow." She looked at Dak and asked, "So there is no way to pass through the warm areas and stay out of the nuclear pits?"

"No one has discovered that route. I have a device in my saddle bag that will detect nuclear contamination. We could not find a route before. That is why we went north. Evidently, the nuclear bombs were targeted mostly in the middle of the continents of the old world. I have been told the Midlanders have several hundred tribes in the lower badlands, and we do not want that trouble."

Zenith looked at Dak, "I wonder why they set off all those nuclear bombs. They basically committed suicide."

"They had no trust for each other. Listening to the stories of the elders in my tribe, they do not know who fired the first missile, but it was not just the missiles, it was also the plague. The B12 virus killed more people worldwide than the nuclear war. The earthquakes were just another unforeseen problem. When the earth's crust shifted, which might have been caused by the nuclear bombs targeting underground military positions, the shift caused earthquakes and volcanoes. The bombs could have hit fault lines either accidently or intentionally. It was like God had said enough and wanted humanity to start over."

"Who is God?"

Dak looked at Zenith with a questionable look. "God is the Alpha and Omega. God is life, love, compassion and mercy." He kept eye contact with Zenith, and she smiled at him. He could tell she did not understand. "Do you love your father?"

Zenith was surprised by the question. "Yes, I love my father."

"That is God. God is the love that bonds us all together."

Zenith's head jerked around. "I heard something."

Dak whispered, "We need to get the bridles and saddles back on our horses, fast. We won't have much time."

Zenith saw the man in the brown coat as he released his arrow from next to the tree. She had already pulled her sword and blocked the arrow as it was headed toward her heart. She yelled, "Come on." and they rode northeast through the thick undergrowth and trees. The foliage started thinning once they climbed the steep mountain and rode further away from the creek. They stopped at midnight. He heard her voice in the dark, "Do you think they are still coming after us?"

"I believe they will hound us until we lose them or kill them. They will be able to follow our tracks in the morning in daylight. They know we are wanting to head east. If we had bows, we could shoot a few of them from a distance while hidden in the thick foliage and then retreat and then shoot a couple more a few miles away at another ambush spot. At some point, the posse would lose heart and go back home. I believe we will need to go to the frozen north and then we can lose them in the ice and snow. We will have to forge through the snow drifts on foot. The horses won't be able to survive in that weather. I am afraid if we keep going east, they will have more men waiting on us and have us surrounded. They know these trails and passages and could already be waiting. We cannot fight them all. They will not figure us going north. I do not see another way in which we survive."

"How far north will we need to go?"

"Past the jet stream in the atmosphere. Once we cross the jet stream, the temperatures will plummet below zero. The elders in the tribe explained in the old world the jet stream used to be so different and the weather patterns would change on a continent as the jet stream changed. Now it is constant. It is the invisible barrier where the warm climate and the very cold climate meet. We will need to take our chances on the other side of the barrier for a few days. They most likely will not follow us."

Dak looked at Zenith, "Why did you help me? You should have let me die in that prison."

"You have done nothing to be arrested. You certainly do not deserve to be murdered in a dungeon. I do not understand why the senate wants you dead. They were going to have you killed and make it look like another prisoner killed you."

"Thanks for being my friend. I do not have many, but I love the ones I have."

"How did you know how to beat Apollo? I could not beat him in our tournament matches. He was better than all of us cadets. There is only one other person who could have done that, and his name is Samuel. He is the general over the Blueblood Army. I had just assumed he would kill you. I was so scared."

"Our tribe practices all the time how to fight, how to determine the weakness of our opponent, and most of all how to win. I knew he would be overconfident. I also knew he was right-handed and would come directly for me and go for the fast kill. He wanted to impress the Blueblood Senators, the audience, and most of all you." He looked at Zenith. "I heard the guards say after you walked out of the dungeon, you were going to be his assigned mate. I did not want to kill him."

She looked at Dak, understanding what he had just said was all true. "I am glad you won. I am also glad you did not kill him. His family is a respected family in the Blueblood community. The fact you spared his life, speaks well of you. He would not have spared your life. That is why I chose to be with you." She looked at him with a sincere expression hoping he would tell her he loved her. She wanted him to confess his love to her first.

As the couple rode north, the forest got thinner with less and less trees, and the snow got deeper. On the third day, Dak saw the men. "Somehow, they have followed us and almost caught up." He knew Zenith was not used to the cold weather. He also knew she was not dressed for the below zero degrees. She could sustain the cold for a few hours but not for days. He looked at Zenith, "We have company. It looks like ten men. I will stay behind and when they get past me, I will attack them from behind the rock on the hill side. You can take my horse, and they will follow the tracks."

"No, I will stay behind."

"I will have the advantage from the high ground. I have spoken. Take my horse and ride at a gallop up the slope of the mountain."

"What do you mean, you have spoken? I do not take orders from you."

"It is not an order but please hurry." She grabbed the bridle and rode up the trail leading Dak's horse. Zenith made it across the crest of the hill just before the first man appeared. She hoped they did not see a horse with no rider. She jumped off her horse and tied both horses to a rock. She backtracked twenty yards and crawled up to the snow-covered ridge next to a large rock. She laid down and watched from behind the rock. She first saw one man and then twenty feet behind him was another man riding on a horse. The riders were spread out. They must have known to be on alert for a trap. She realized this was not going to work. Dak was perched on a large rock protruding from the slope embankment above the path which was next to the horse trail. She crawled back behind the ridge and then stood and ran to her horse. She jumped on her horse and charged back down the trail.

Dak had seen the first man pass under him and waited and then saw the second man as he approached. He jumped from the perch on the rock as the two followed the hoofprints in the snow. Dak took the second man off his horse, and they rolled over on the edge of the trail. Dak pulled his one sword and then lost his footing when he hesitated with his sword. The man grabbed Dak by his right wrist and then rolled toward the edge causing Dak's foot to slide down the embankment. He dropped his sword and reached for the man holding him tight as the two rolled over four times as they descended the snow-covered steep hill. The other man jumped to his feet, and he pulled his sword. Dak only had one chance. He pulled his knife from his boot and lunged forward stabbing the man in the chest as he tried to swing his sword. Dak slipped and fell over the dying man and then quickly turned and saw the third and fourth men coming around the corner of the trail. He panicked knowing he had lost the high ground on the trail and now he was trapped on the side of the slick snow-covered embankment looking up at the trail above. He tried to run up the hill in the snow toward their position. Both men pulled their bows and fired arrows at Dak. Dak could hardly move in the snow on the side of the steep slope embankment. He was able to jump sideways with one of the arrows cutting his coat sleeve. He crawled and picked up the now dead man's bow and arrows as he landed in the snow-covered ditch behind the rock ledge. He knew he could not hold them off with them having the high ground. The first man had retreated to his partners and had also taken up a firing position. Now the fifth and six men had arrived. Dak kept his head out of sight. He knew they would try to surround him from their firing positions on the trail. He raised up to fire and saw the men release the arrows toward him. He ducked into the snow-covered ditch behind the rock as the arrows narrowly missed him. He crawled through the snow to the other side of the large boulder and knew he would need to raise up and fire up the steep hill. He needed to take out as many men as possible to provide Zenith time to escape.

Zenith charged down the hill in silence on the horse. The five men were trying to figure out where Dak was hiding and how best to kill him behind the large boulder. They were excited and could hardly wait to kill him and collect the thousand pieces of gold. They did not see her charge until it was too late. The first man turned and fired his arrow, and she blocked the arrow with her sword. She then rode toward him leaning over on the side of the horse cutting him across the belly as she passed him. She then kept charging forward and blocked the next two arrows and cut the next two men as they stood trying to reload their bows in the cold weather with gloves which hindered their speed. The other two men had fired their arrows, and she was able to block both. She charged the two men, blocking four additional arrows and cutting both men. One she cut across the face and the other man across his belly.

Dak finally realized he had waited as long as he could and raised up to fire his bow. He saw Zenith cutting the belly of the last man. He climbed up the hill picking up his sword as he had to crawl up the steep embankment. Zenith said, "The other four men rode back down the trail." Dak looked at the five dead men Zenith had killed.

Dak asked, "What are you doing? You should have run away. I had these men trapped."

"Yes, I can see you did. At what point were you going to surrender? You gave up the high ground over one soldier. What in the world were you thinking?"

He said, "We need to move on. They will return with more men. These men are northern men. See the seal skin clothing under the large fur capes They are acclimated to the snow and know this terrain. How would the Bluebloods have contacted men this far north?"

"They would have sent pigeons in all directions. The news with the gold reward travels fast in this area of the world. Reward money is one of the few things the Blueblood Senate has not lied about to the people. They will pay the gold in exchange for our heads."

"I saw a river from the hilltop. It is a day's ride. Maybe if we can get across, we can escape the posse." Dak looked at the dead men and grabbed a better bow with several arrows. Zenith took some warmer boots, a coat, and picked up a bow. They rode double up the mountain, and Dak got on his horse.

"These men were not warriors. They hunt for their tribe. I noticed the young one I killed was dressed in seal skin garments. They most likely travel all the way to the ocean to hunt seals. I was hoping to spare their lives, so they could hunt another day."

"So why did you give up the high ground? You never give up the high ground when you are in a battle."

"When I jumped on him and knocked him to the ground, we rolled over next to the ledge, and I looked into the kid's eyes. He was scared. I hesitated and lost my footing, and we rolled down the hill." Dak did not wish to talk about the battle. He knew the kid he killed was large for his age and a bit clumsy. He had trouble pulling his sword which provided Dak the opportunity to pull his knife and kill him. Now, he would have to live with the quilt of killing a big clumsy kid. "Thanks for coming back for me. How are you able to block the arrows with only a sword blade?"

Zenith could tell by Dak's melancholy tone he was bothered with killing the one man. "Dak, I am sorry we had to kill those men. We had no choice. None of those men are innocent. They made the decision to come after us, and we are guilty of no crimes. Dak, you cannot hesitate in battle, or you will be killed." She waited to verify if Dak was going to say anything in addition. A couple of seconds passed, "We Bluebloods are taught from birth how to anticipate things before they happen. We are taught how to visualize the object coming toward us. We turn the sword, so the broad side of the blade is exposed to the oncoming arrow. Blocking arrows is one of many things we can do that a normal human cannot."

"You have better reflexes, intelligence, athleticism, senses, and appearance, which have been genetically enhanced just like your blood was enhanced to fight off viruses. Other than all that, you are normal." He smiled and looked over at her riding next to him. She did not acknowledge his statement. She kept looking ahead and appeared to be in deep thought as they rode forward.

After a few minutes, "What about you? You're smart, good looking, and you took down the Blueblood who came in second in our tournament in just eleven second in the trail by combat. You have no idea how many Blueblood warriors wish they could make it that far in the competition. Coming in second to General Samuel is an honor. How were you able to accomplish that? That should not have been possible unless you have been genetically enhanced." She looked at Dak understanding he was something special. "How do you know terms like monoculturalism? What does that mean?"

"Monoculturalism is the expectation that others will conform to your ideals and way of life. I was trying to convey to your senate not to stereotype all people. I was hoping they would realize the importance of helping us. There are some very intelligent people in my tribe. I have learned a lot listening to them talk at nights sitting around the bonfire. It is interesting listening to the stories before Armageddon. They tell the stories with a nostalgic prospective. They have learned the old days are over. The new world is harsh and violent. We have been taught how to fight since we were three years old by the best warrior on our planet. His name is Billy Ray Claiborne. He was in a couple of elite military units in the old world."

"Is he the leader of your tribe?"

"No, he is not the leader. He is the father of Hulk and Tommy Boy."

The horses had a difficult time walking through the two and three feet of snow drifts. Dak knew once they got to the river, they would need to release them. As they approached the river, Dak noted a large storm was headed their way. He could see the storm clouds and noticed the wind had picked up from the west as they kept pushing north. He wanted to keep talking, so Zenith would not allow her mind to be preoccupied with the harsh climate. He mentioned, "Wayne often talked about how the weather pattern had changed from the days prior to the new world. The storms in the north now would be more severe during the winter months but the summer months were more accommodating. The plant life and wildlife have thrived in the new world under these conditions in this part of the continent. The animals migrate to the south below the Jet Stream during the winter."

"I do not see how any living thing could live in this cold climate."

The extra clothing they took from the dead men helped, but the coldness was something that had to be embraced. Dak could sense Zenith was not acclimated to the bite of the cold. He also could tell her determination to push forward against the cold winter weather.

He looked behind them approximately four hundred yards and could see the silhouette of several dozen men pushing toward them with dogs pulling them on sleds. He announced, "We need to hurry. We must get across that river. That is the only chance we have. Our horses are done for in this ice and snow." Dak knew the men in chase had sleds pulled by dogs. They were able to travel at a faster pace. He announced, "We have men behind us. They are using sleds and dogs. We cannot outrun them. We cannot fight them from horseback in this deep snow. We will either cross the river or make a stand."

Zenith announced looking behind her, "We cannot fight all those men. They can stay out of range with the dogs. They can come at us from all sides constantly firing arrows. At some point, one will get through. I cannot protect both of us."

"We must get to the river. The dogs will not be able to cross it, and they know this. That is why they are pushing hard toward us. They want to catch us out in the open and surround us. They may have us boxed in against the river. That is the same strategy they use to hunt bears and buffalo."

By the time they made it to the cliff overlooking the river, the wind-driven snow was hampering their view. Dak had looked back and could not see the men. He knew they were not far behind. The snow provided close to fifteen feet of visibility. He jumped off his horse and hurriedly removed the saddle and bridle. He told Zenith to do the same. He hit the horses on the backside and released them. "We have to cross now." He placed the saddle bag around his neck and looked over the embankment. The drop was close to thirty feet into the pool of the fast-moving river. The visibility looking down into the water was clear, but the depth of the river under the cliff was unknown. They had no other options.

Zenith announced, "They are here." He looked, and he could see men trying to surround them with the closest man pulling his bow and loading his arrow. The man was thirty feet away trying to hold his aim still in the wind and snow.

Dak reached and grabbed Zenith's gloved hand while backing up. "We go now." They looked at each other, and the two ran and jumped outward from the top of the snow-covered rock embankment as the arrow missed by inches sailing over Zenith's head.

Chapter 25

The eight riders waved goodbye to Old Thomas and rode toward Cliff Tops. They all had been well rested and fed. The group had come to terms with Dak being on his own. They had talked about going back into the wasteland to look for him. In the end, Billy Ray and Eric of Newport had decided to return to Cliff Tops. Veronica and Hulk had led the argument of disagreement, and Tommy Boy and Trey threatened to ride out by themselves. The argument became intense. Billy Ray explained, "The winter is coming and traveling will be too difficult. We must believe he will be alright. He was placed in charge to make those types of decisions."

Veronica said, "After we met the Blueblood named Zenith, I do not trust the people of Merlin. The Blueblood Senate makes all the decisions. When we first met her, she expected for one of us to jump off our horse, so she could ride. Dak finally told her she could walk or ride double with him. We were not giving up our horses. This happened after we risked our lives to save her. There was no gratitude or thanks. It was like we were expected to die for her."

Tommy Boy looked concerned, "She expected it to happen. She acted surprised when we did not obey her. I cannot imagine how the adult Bluebloods treat the regular citizens of Merlin."

Eric of Newport looked at Billy Ray and Wayne with the three men understanding something might be amiss in the city of Merlin. Wayne had tried to stay out of the conversation because most of the talking was between the fathers and their kids. Wayne finally announced, "We need to head for Cliff Tops at first light in the morning. We must be prepared in case the Normand army returns by sea."

The group seemed to understand the situation. Dak's five friends did not agree with leaving him, but they understood the need for them, along with Eric of Newport, Wayne, and Billy Ray to return. The tribe needed Billy Ray, Eric of Newport and Wayne present to make certain the work in the city was getting completed. Some of the newer men who had fled from the New York tribe would challenge Vicky and her authority, but with the men, Little Jimmy and Billy Ray standing next to her, they would always back down.

Wayne and Billy Ray discussed as they sat around the bonfire the history of Vicky and the adult friends, and the group listened. Wayne explained, "The group of adults led by Vicky had become friends working for the United States Government directly or indirectly trying to curtail the worldwide human trafficking problem. Then they were assigned to hunt down and kill the members of a worldwide syndicate. We were the group with the sword of justice when the old world had ended. We saw the holocaust approaching and fled to one of the most northeastern parts of the North American continent and waited for the opportunity to start over. The scientists and geologists had picked the area to be one of the safest spots located above the nuclear holocaust which occurred in the old country the United States. The safe area was selected to hide from the B12 virus, and geologically secure from the volcanoes. The area was so cold, the B12 virus could not flourish in the cold environment. Now we live at the top of the cliff, and the city is called Cliff Tops. We figured there would be pockets of people and animals that survived around the globe. The earth's surface shifting into two continents with two oceans was nothing we could foresee. Seventy five percent of the earth is now land with most of the land is deserts. There is a great deal more water under the surface of the earth than on top of the surface. This is not new."

Wayne looked at Tommy Boy and Hulk, "No one knew for certain how many nuclear bombs hit the surface of the earth. The bombs created areas where nothing lived. All life was dead in the middle of the blast zones."

Billy Ray stood as he was about to go to bed, "The old-world history will be forgotten with my generation dying out. There will be no one to remember the technology industries.

Everyone who lived through the Transitional Period seems to want to move forward and live life in conjunction with planet earth and protect the environment."

Eric also stood, "The old ways will be no more. The sins of humanity killed the planet, and our gracious Lord provided small groups of people the opportunity to start over." Everyone walked to the bedrolls and cabin to sleep.

Chapter 26

Dak thought when he looked down at the cold water only of Zenith. Will her body be ready for the instant plunge into the cold river? He knew after the initial splash being cold and wet was a small part of what they faced. They must swim down river and across to the opposite side and then deal with being cold and wet for an extended period. Hypothermia would set in in fifteen minutes being submerged in the water.

He had learned as a boy, there was no training or description to prepare someone for jumping into this cold water. He and his friends would jump from different ledges along the cliff below Cliff Tops into the ocean part of their jetty in the warm part of summer. They called the jump the polar plunge. The cold ocean water stayed in the low forties year-round. After the jump they would swim to shore and then run up the trail to the top of the cliff. The run upward helped their bodies generate heat to overcome the frigid temperatures, hypothermia, and frostbite.

As soon as they hit the water, he knew he did not want Zenith to have to think about what was next. He pulled her hand down river and upward to the surface for a breath. As they both came to the top of the water, he immediately yelled, "We need to swim with the current and float down the river."

He pulled her and started swimming. He noticed she had done likewise. He was scared she would not be able to handle the shock of the coldness of the water. He figured her first instinct would be to swim back to the bottom of the cliff where they had jumped. That being the shortest distance to the bank. If she did that, they would die. They would not be able to get out of the river or hide. He knew he could not leave her, and there would be no way for them to escape the men following them. The lower part of the cliff would be the first place they would search.

As they started swimming with the current, they kept picking up speed. The current forced them into a small channel between large boulders, which lined the riverbanks on both sides of the river and produced class-five rapids. There was nothing to grasp hold of and pull oneself out of the river. He could see Zenith ahead of him. He knew he needed to catch up to her. The current changed from a swift river current to rapids dropping through a rocky area and finally to a small waterfall. Dak kept looking for Zenith. Every time she went under water she came back to the surface. She was in front, and he kept trying to catch her. The riverbanks were all steep and frozen with large boulders and snow-covered cliffs. He knew they needed to get out of the river on the opposite side and find shelter and warmth. He kept trying to glance at the riverbank ahead of them to locate an exit point from the fast-flowing river. He also knew he had to catch up with Zenith, so they could exit in the same area.

He saw Zenith trying to hold on to the top of a rock located in the middle of the rapids and her grip gave way. He pushed himself with the flow of the river in hopes of catching up with her.

After several minutes with them finally reaching calmer water, Dak thought he got a glimpse of an old shack in the woods on the far riverbank. He first thought he was hallucinating. With the snow falling, the visibility was very restricted. He turned his head and saw Zenith go under water. He frantically swam to her last position, and this time she never resurfaced. He went under water looking for her in all directions. He saw her a few feet ahead of him under water and not moving. He could see her blond long hair floating out from her head as she drifted underwater. He reached for her, pulling her to the surface.

He immediately pulled her to shore and picked her up in his arms and ran up the riverbank. He climbed the rocks and kept shaking her and telling her to open her eyes. He was pleading with her. He ran up the front stairs to the old shack and busted through the door. He laid her down and removed her heavy wet coat. He felt for a pulse. She had a faint heartbeat, and she coughed one time. He kissed her and tried to hug her. Her eyes blinked open. Dak stood her up and started telling her to jump up and down with him. He kept jumping, pulling her up and down. After about ten quick jumps with him holding her, he noticed she started jumping with him. He was pleading with her to keep jumping. She seemed to realize she was out of the water and finally started to jump on her own.

While jumping, he was looking around the old shack taking inventory of the surroundings. It appeared to be abandoned. He took a quick mental inventory of what he saw. He noticed the old wood burning stove sitting inside the bottom of the fireplace and a pack of matches on the mantel. He had started thousands of fires and knew the importance of the woodstove.

Dak took Zenith's face in his hands and pleaded with her to keep jumping. "This must be an abandoned old fishing shack from the old world. There might be some firewood stacked outside. Please do not stop jumping. If you stop jumping, you will die. I will start that wood burning stove and have it hot in this small room in a few minutes. Please keep jumping. I will be right back."

Zenith shook her head that she understood. Dak forced the front door closed and ran out the back door of the cabin. He hoped the fisherman had left extra firewood for the next trip. He pulled the old tarp off the pile of wood and picked up all he could carry. He dropped the firewood on the floor. He picked up an old cardboard box and asked her to tear it in small pieces and keep jumping. He ran back out the back door and retrieved another load of wood. He dropped the load on the floor and then pulled the abandoned bookcase from the room and busted it into small pieces. He located a small amount of paper in the kitchen area and loaded the wood burning stove. He used the matches on the hearth. His fingers were so cold he could hardly keep his hands from shacking to strike the match. The first match he broke. He noticed there were only two additional matches in the box. He held his breath and steadied his hands and eased the match across the box. The friction was enough, and the match lit and then fizzled and burned out. He picked up the last match and prayed. "Please God." This time he was able to place the burning match under the paper. He watched as the fire burned slowly. He placed pieces of the cardboard on the fire. Once the fire started, he turned his attention to Zenith. He knew she was close to dying from hypothermia. He knew they had to keep moving and to remove all of their wet clothing.

He demanded, "We must remove our frozen wet clothes. We must keep moving." He walked over to her and pulled her shirt over her head and then pulled her pants down. He bent down and pulled her boots off and then her pants. He said, "Please keep jumping. I know your mind is telling you to sit down and not move. You must trust me Zenith-keep jumping. If you die, I cannot make it without you. I love you. If you love me, please keep jumping." She looked up into his eyes and tried to smile. He stepped backward and pulled his frozen clothes off. He said, "There might be blankets in one of the other rooms."

He came back into the room with a towel and a blanket. He wrapped the blanket around Zenith and told her she was doing fine. He stressed with her to keep jumping. He placed additional firewood in the wood burning stove. He needed hot coals from the kindling to place the medium-size wood in the stove, and then a few minutes later, the heat would start radiating from the metal stove. The tarp had kept the wood dry, and the wood had started to decay. The dry wood would burn hot and fast.

He noticed Zenith had walked near the wood burning stove, and she had stopped jumping. He pulled the blanket open and pulled her underwear off her. He told her to keep jumping as he wrapped the blanket around her. He ran into the kitchen and looked for supplies. He found a plastic bottle of vegetable oil. He poured some in a pot and set it on the top of the stove. He pulled the blanket open and started jumping with Zenith up and down while holding the blanket around her.

He noticed the warm air radiating from the stove. He could hear the roar of the fire as the heat went up the metal chase inside the chimney. He laid the towel on the floor directly in front of the open stove. He placed Zenith in front of the stove while placing additional wood from the bookshelf and a rotted dry log in the stove. He held her as tight as he could with both arms under the blanket with her back to the stove. He rubbed her body and kept telling her they would be okay. He knew the wood burning stove was designed to produce more heat than the small room would need. The next few minutes would be critical for Zenith. He had to convince her to keep breathing out hot air under the blanket, and she would be okay. He had listened to the old timers talk about how the mind would give up even when the body could make it. He kept telling Zenith he loved her. He kept blowing out his warm breath under the blanket and holding her tight. He kept rubbing her back and her legs as he forced her to walk in a circle while standing in front of the stove.

Zenith looked up into his eyes and finally said, "I am so cold. I am cold all the way to my bones. I can feel the heat in the room, but I am so cold. My head is hurting." She shivered uncontrollably.

"If you love me, you will not give up. If you die, I will die. Your body temperature has dropped, and we must raise it back to normal." He reached around her holding her tight. After another fifteen minutes, he said, "Let me place some additional logs inside the stove. I love you."

He placed two semi-rotten logs into the hot burning fire. He placed his finger in the vegetable oil on top of the stove. The oil was hot. He noticed Zenith was watching him as she shivered and gritted her teeth. He knew how she felt. He had dealt with the bitter cold in the north his entire life. He also knew he loved her. He hated to see her in pain. He commanded, "You need to lay down on your stomach. This oil is hot, and I will massage it into your skin. It will help your cold bones and stop the possibility of frostbite."

He felt the heat radiating from the stove on his face as he kneeled facing the stove with Zenith lying in front of it. The room was starting to warm up. He knew the additional rotten wood would burn hot, and the room was going to be very warm. Kneeling in front of the stove he was thankful for the burning heat radiating into the room. He placed his hands in the pot and started rubbing the oil on her feet. He took his time rubbing the oil into the arches of her feet and her toes. He knew the lower extremities would be the first-place frostbite would appear. He repeated this three times and then rubbed her calves and then her thighs. He placed his hands around her waist rubbing firmly into her sides and back. "You will start to warm up soon. I am so sorry you are going through this. You should have stayed in Merlin with your parents. The Blueblood warrior would have been lucky to have you as his wife." He poured some oil on her lower back and then her upper back and rubbed the oil a second time. He rubbed up her legs, hips to her shoulders, arms and hands. He then rubbed her feet with hot oil again and then worked his way back up her body. He had moved and placed his knees between her feet and kept spreading her legs wider as he kept inching up her body. He rubbed her behind her knees, over her lower thighs, then her upper thighs, over her bottom and hips up to her shoulders with the hot oil. He kept rubbing the hot oil over her skin. The hot heat radiating from the wood burning stove against his side nearest the stove started to burn his side and face. He started over with her feet bending her lower leg upward rubbing the oil on the shins. He then slowly spread her legs again inching up the back of her legs pressing hard into both the inside and outside of her legs. Then the middle of her thighs and then her bottom and then her lower back and ribs. He kept pouring the hot oil all over her back side rubbing continuously all over her body. He noticed she had started balling up her fist and would release her fist with her arms and hands extended above her head. As he rubbed the oil into her lower back and then her upper back, he noticed she had started digging her fingernails into the wood floor and pulling her finger across the floor. Zenith finally moaned, "Please take me. I need you to consummate our love for each other. I truly love you. If you love me, I am yours for the taking."

Chapter 27

The northern leader walked up to the cliff overlooking the thirty-foot drop into the cold river. His tracker was bent down on his knees leaning over the top, peering over the cliff into the river and trying to discern if there was a body on the riverbank. The tracker turned and pointed to the horse hoofprints running down the ridge and the human footprints leading to the top of the cliff overlooking the river. "These footprints are from the two people we were chasing. They jumped. There is no sign of anyone backtracking. The horses will head for warmer weather and grasslands for food. They will run into our tribe down river. There is no way anyone can survive the jump into the cold water." The leader pulled has protected mask off his face and lifted his eye protection blinds. He could see the tracks but with the amount of the wind and snow fall, he could hardly see the river below. Three additional men walked over to the cliff and looked down at the river below. The leader cringed while considering the options. He needed their bodies to obtain the large reward and if they drowned in the river, it would make it easy provided they could locate the bodies. He knew he and his men would be wealthy beyond his imagination if they could locate the bodies. He also was aware his men had to take cover. The large dark clouds had blown in from the northwest, and he knew a large snowstorm was going to cover the already frozen ground. He motioned for them to retreat down the trail a mile and set up the tents behind the large cropping of rocks which could block the wind from the west.

The men seemed relieved at the order. They all were aware of the danger with a large storm coming in so fast. They also knew climbing down the face of a cliff in the snow and ice was difficult and time consuming in the best circumstances. One wrong step or slip could cause a man his life, falling into the river below. They further realized there would be no way to locate bodies in the ice flowing water without searching the riverbanks below, and that task was not doable with a large Northwestern storm about to drop over two feet of snow. They would need to search the area in spring when some of the snow melted. They turned and yelled at the dogs to pull the sleds back down the trail.

Chapter 28

He looked into Zenith's eyes. "I really love you. I love making love with you. You know I do not deserve to massage your feet let alone be your man." He pushed her blonde hair back out of her face and then kissed her breast and extended the moment. "But we have been here for four days, and the snow is not going to melt until spring. We might want to head southeast on this side of the river before another storm hits."

"I would rather stay here."

He pulled his lips up from her breast. "We were blessed to have found this cabin with all this fishing gear. The river is full of trout. I have never eaten so many fish, and I live on a cliff overlooking the ocean with men who love to fish. At some point when I see them, I must tell them about this fishing hole."

"What do you think happened to the owners of the cabin?"

He pulled his lips up from her breast a second time. "This was most likely a hunting and fishing cabin used by someone in the old world. The owners died with five billion other inhabitants of our planet during the holocaust. With the cabin being on this side of the river, no one could reach it. I believe the river has been rerouted from the earthquakes and the shifting of the earth's crust, and technically speaking, the river is not crossable. Someone would have to be desperate to jump into the river and then swim a mile or so down river to find this place."

"So, you want to leave?"

"No. I do not want to leave. We have been here four days and copulated thirty-four times. I want to stay, but I need to report to my tribe that the City of Merlin is not going to help with the war against the Normand army." He rolled on his back and looked at the ceiling, now contemplating the upcoming war.

"We have done more than just copulated thirty-four times. We have practiced Karate, practiced sword fighting, fished, and had plenty of exercise. Why did you not mention all that stuff? Why just mention copulating thirty-four times?"

Dak smiled, "I remember the dancing, wrestling and Karate which led to the copulating. I also knew you would track all the other stuff."

She smiled, "I love to dance with you. Dancing is not allowed in Merlin. I agree we need to go to your city called Cliff Tops. I have a message to deliver to your tribe's leader."

Dak looked perplexed, "What message?"

"It is in the airtight leather envelope. I was told not to open it but give it to your leader. The man who gave me the leather envelope said my father's life might depend on it."

Dak sat up and looked at Zenith. "Who was this man?"

"His name was Ivan Chezon. He is in hiding. He used to be in the Merlin Senate. He has been in hiding for five years. I never understood what happened. My mother told me when the Blueblood warriors took control of the senate, that it would be for the better."

"What about your friends and your father? What did they say?"

"My father never commented. He was always working. He did tell me right before I freed you from the dungeon, someone was going to kill him. He said he loved me." She looked into Dak's eyes. "I ran from him without saying goodbye. Now I have run away and have no home. I might not ever see him again." Dak could see the guilt on her face. He could see her concern for her father. He hugged her.

While being hugged she murmured, "I really have no friends. We were taught to always be in competition with our peers. Figure out their weaknesses and understand their strengths. We are taught that one of our fellow students might obtain a rank that we want, and we need to surpass them to win. Win at all costs is not a good formula to build friendships. I was very surprised with you and your friends and how all six of you worked together and joked with each other. That is not what we were taught."

He pulled away, "Where is the envelope? I want to see the message."

She pointed to her large coat. "I placed it in the inner pocket after I took the coat off the dead man at the pass. Put some more wood on the fire while you are up. It can get cold in here without clothing."

Dak jumped up, placed two logs on the fire and pulled the leather envelope from the pocket and noticed the seal. She watched him as he walked around in the nude. He hesitated before breaking the seal. He knew he could never reseal the leather envelope. He tore the seal. Zenith stood and left the covers in front of the wood burning stove. She walked over and looked at the letter. "What does it say?"

"I was hoping you could tell me. I cannot read this language. I do not recognize it. I know three dialects; Spanish, Russian and English, but I have never seen this language."

Zenith said, "I do not recognize the language either. Ivan told me to destroy the letter if I could not personally deliver it to your tribe's leader. He did not want the Blueblood Senate to have it. What could be so important?"

"Yet he trusted you, a Blueblood, with it." He looked perplexed at Zenith.

"He had no other choice. He said he had been waiting for someone who could transport the information in the letter through the nuclear pits to your tribe, and he figured you were his only hope." She looked at Dak with concern, "I do not understand what is going on. What is so important between your tribe and this man named Ivan Chezon. I have never heard of your tribe until you and your friends saved me in the valley, and Ivan Chezon has been in hiding for the past five years. The Blueblood Senate at one time posted signs inside the castle and throughout the territory with a drawing of him, offering ten gold coins, dead or alive. Then, the signs over time switched, and the amount eventually grew to a thousand gold coins. I can remember three or four years ago the Blueblood community was talking about him, and there were several bounty hunters allowed into the city to look for him. I understood they looked for him several hundred miles to the east, north and south in the territory. Then, he just appeared out of thin air and gave me this letter telling me the contents of this letter could save my father's life. My father was trying to tell me something, but he was also worried about me knowing the information. It was like he did not know if he could trust me with the secret." She looked perplexed at Dak. "I will deliver this letter to your tribe's leader. I need to help my father."

"Your father may have been trying to protect you from the information." He hesitated in thought without finishing the sentence. "The information must be very important." He looked at Zenith with a perplexed expression. "I have no idea what this is about."

Chapter 29

Senator Blackmon loved being a Blueblood Senator. The job opportunity had become open, and he felt he was literally in the right spot at the right time. He was young to be a senator and was a second-generation Blueblood. Both of his parents had died during the revolution five years prior. His brother was a colonel in the Blueblood Army. His sister was a doctor and had six kids. His three young kids were well educated, and his wife seemed to stay busy with the kids. He felt like a God. He loved the challenges and the power which came from being one of the nine who voted for the laws for the entire city. The merchants needed his vote for low taxes and the contractors needed his approval for work contracts, and in exchange for his vote he was provided young female concubines to service his desires along with financial perks. The Blueblood Senate had been a welcome alternative to being an educator in the Blueblood school system. He enjoyed living in a city with paved streets and indoor plumbing. His wealth had more than doubled since he had been elected. He had learned fast how to hold out on certain votes until someone would offer him ownership in a certain business or property. He was now part owner in three different construction companies and three large real estate ventures with farmers on the outskirts of Merlin. He also recognized who had the power in the Blueblood Senate. Senator Dale sat in the middle, was the longest tenured senator, had the most wealth, and by far was the most vicious. Three other senators were first generation Bluebloods, and the five other members were second generation Bluebloods. Senator Dale allowed the younger senators an opportunity to make money and provided them opportunities with young women if the young senators voted with him on his legislation. Senator Dale was rumored to be the majority owner in the slave industry and had diversified into several other industries. No one knew for certain how wealthy he had become. Senator Dale was one of the three Merlin Senators over the military which provided him the power to control the Security Police of Merlin. The suitable young female slaves were forced into prostitution which provided an extensive income stream for the owners and also a means to control the men of the military who frequent the brothels. The Security Police were rumored to be ruthless and the group to enforce the death penalty of the citizens.

Senator Blackmon was second from the bottom of the seniority list. He in no way could afford to make waves with the older senators. His seat on the senate bench was at the end. The closer to the middle represented the power, with Senator Dale always in the middle flanked by two other first-generation Bluebloods on both sides of him.

He knew the senators were frustrated with the debacle with the prisoner breaking out of the dungeon. One guard had been decapitated during the investigation process and the other guard's trial was pending. There was no clear explanation of what happened, or who helped Dak. There were several rumors, and Zenith had disappeared. The senate had placed a reward of a thousand gold coins for her alive, and for the man named Dak, his reward was dead or alive for two thousand gold coins.

Senator Blackmon and four others had taken their seats. He wanted to be the first to speak. He leaned forward at the committee table before the other four senators were seated and ready. "I make a motion. I believe we need to send Samuel and one other to cross the continent through the nuclear pits and past the Midlanders to this city called Cliff Tops and report back to us their findings. Just sending two men will not attract attention from the Midlanders. You have met the man from the far east here on our Senate floor. He has made the trip, and I have always heard the story that there is a map to cross the continent."

The Senator in the middle listened and was thinking when one of the other Senators third from the middle blurted out, "That is stupid. We do not need to go east. I personally do not give a cat's ass about what is happening on that side of the continent and neither do my citizens."

Senator Blackmon knew someone would want him to withdraw his request. He had planned to hold out for a business opportunity. He had no desire to see someone travel across the continent. He said, "Do not forget our oath is to serve and protect. Samuel could identify a possible threat from either that tribe or the Normand Army."

Senator Dale raised his hand to let the others know he did not want to be interrupted. He looked both ways at his fellow Senators. He knew the trip would be very dangerous and Samuel and one other first-generation Blueblood would most likely be killed. He smiled to himself as he was considering the risk. One other Blueblood had tried the journey after three different groups of castle guards were sponsored to make the trip. They were never heard of again. He picked up his gavel, "This senate has sponsored four groups to cross the Midlander territory and none have returned; however, I agree with Senator Blackmon's request. We will send General Samuel and his choice of another first-generation Blueblood to make the journey. This is urgent and the senate needs to get to the bottom of the rumors. If they locate the two fugitives, who better to deal with them than General Samuel. I agree we must know of any potential threat and also, we must know the route to cross this continent." He hit the desktop with his gavel.

No one in the room was more surprised than Senator Blackmon. He hesitated and then said, "I will have my aide draw up the order and submit it to the defense department. General Samuel will be notified shortly." He started gloating. He thought how he could spin the news that he was the Blueblood Senator who came up with the planned trip to the far east with the most well-known Blueblood warrior leading the expedition and Senator Dale endorsed his motion. He was going to contact his friend at the newspaper. He wanted his voters to know it was him.

Senator Dale leaned forward and in a harsh voice asked, "What are you going to do about Aquarius? My understanding is his daughter is still missing, and she is the number one suspect for breaking the prisoner out. How could a Blueblood have done this?"

The Senators all were quiet and contemplating the question. They also knew when he talked in this tone, he was mad and meant business. Senator Dale was visibly upset.

Senator Blackmon could feel the anger in his voice and felt it was directed at him. He stopped gloating and paused to gather his thoughts, "Aquarius is on my short leash. I will handle him when the time is right, but we do not know if his daughter was involved. My understanding is that the daughter and the father had an argument in the hall after the trial by combat. We do not know the reason for the disagreement." He hesitated and then said, "We have contacted the guard manager and the army security unit and requested they need to locate her. So far, we have not been able to capture them. The reward money has been posted as far as we have contacts. As you know the bounty on her is one thousand gold pieces alive and the man, named Dak is two thousand gold pieces dead or alive. Every bounty hunter in our region is on the job."

Senator Dale looked irate and glanced both ways at the other Senators, "We need to change her bounty to dead or alive. There is no excuse, and we must act. This session is over. We are all adjourned." The Senators had heard all the rumors about the man from the far east breaking out. There were different theories as to how it happened. The two guards either did not know how they got bested, or they had lied about the facts. The entire city of Merlin had heard about how the man from the far east had beaten Apollo in a fair fight. He had become a hero overnight with the common citizens. The Senators had hoped he would soon be forgotten and never appear again in Merlin. The fact he disappeared resolved a problem for the Senators which was what to do with him. The story had spread far past the city of Merlin into the villages miles away. Someone had carved eleven seconds into the west gate leading out of the castle yard where all the Blueblood soldiers passed during the course of a day. The Blueblood Senate and the Blueblood people knew how the normal citizens despised them.

Chapter 30

Samuel looked at his boss with a surprised look on his face. Before he could question the order, his commander announced, "This order came from the top, the very top. They know you are our best soldier, and they have asked for you and one other first-generation Blueblood to carry this task through to the end."

"Yes sir. I won't let our people down. I will take Aquarius." He turned to leave.

His commander ordered, "Stop right there. What is the meaning of this? Aquarius has not been in the field for a decade. His daughter is one of the fugitives. If you find her, your orders are to bring her back to us dead or alive. You will need to take another under your command."

"Did the order from the top, the very top not say I could select the first-generation Blueblood of my choice?" He turned and looked at his commander without looking him in the eyes. He was not permitted to look his commander in the eyes.

"Yes."

"Then you can report to the senate my selection. We will be leaving at sunrise in the morning." He turned and marched out the door.

Chapter 31

Aquarius had tried to stay out of Senator Blackmon's office. He knew no one on the senate would be there for him. He would be ostracized at the first opportunity by Senator Blackmon. Senator Blackmon did not have the courage to stand up for himself let alone someone else. Aquarius was aware of his boss's lack of character. He also knew he would try to use him to gain leverage over his family. He would try to manipulate him to perform unfair tax collections and force the business entities to become Senator Blackmon's partners in business deals. He would be forced to bully the ranchers and farmers in the outskirts to sign deals with Senator Blackmon, so the Senator could keep his hands clean. The appearance would be the business entity contacted the Senator and were not persuaded by undue influence by the Senator.

He forced a smile as he went into the Senator's inner office. The Senator did not glance up. He was reading the summons. "I asked you here."

"Are you sure you asked me, or was it an order?"

Senator Blackmon looked up. He knew Aquarius did not like being ordered to force the poor to pay more taxes than the rich. The two men had at one time been cordial acquaintances when Senator Blackmon had first been elected to the Senate.

Aquarius had been able to provide insight and predictions on how other Senators would vote and why. Aquarius had been a clerk for Senator Dale for the first five years the senate was established and thought to be in line for a senate seat. Then, for some unknown reason, Aquarius had been moved to the lower-level clerk position for the Senate and the opportunity to be a member of the Blueblood Senate had vanished. The Senator looked up. He smiled, "I cannot believe what I am reading." He chuckled.

Aquarius felt a bad omen. He knew when Senator Blackmon smiled at him, there was going to be an adverse consequence. He then realized the Senator may have heard news about his daughter. He knew of the bounty of a thousand gold coins on Zenith and the escaped prisoner's head, wanted dead or alive. He was scared for Zenith. At first the Blueblood Senate wanted her alive for questioning. Then, the news reported the two were seen riding together on the Shoreline Road before the ALE house and again after the ALE House. He knew she would die before being taken alive. Every bounty hunter and drifter were wanting to kill her for one thousand gold coins. Dead was easier than bringing someone in alive. This much bounty would make a normal man very rich. Plus, they would be a hero and a celebrity in the eyes of the people who supported the Merlin government.

The last time he saw her she was running away from him down the steps of the backdoor of the Senate building. He wished he could have held her and told her he loved her. More than anything he wished he had listened to her. His mind drifted back to her smiling when she was two or three years old playing in the park. She had been such a happy child.

The two men looked each other in the eye. "You are going east. You have been summoned by Samuel and commissioned by the Blueblood Senate to go to the tribe on the east coast called Cliff Tops and then report back to the Senate. You will be gone for an estimated four months." He chuckled. "I really did not see this happening. I did not realize you and Samuel knew one another. I suggested sending Samuel and one other Blueblood of his choice. I took your guidance and suggested to the senate that we Senators need to serve and protect. I felt we needed to know if the Normand army is a real threat and if there are other warriors better than us. Samuel picked you, and you are leaving in the morning. You need to get packed." He laughed and leaned back in his chair looking at Aquarius.

Aquarius was stunned. He knew he could not refuse a direct order from the Blueblood Senate. He could not believe Samuel had requested him. He had hardly talked to Samuel in years. He had elected to opt out of the Army. He was tired of killing the people who were branded thieves for trying to feed their families. Everyone was so poor back in those days. The people had to steal food to survive. If the B12 Virus did not kill them, they could very well starve to death. They would show up from a Midlander's camp on the run or from one of the southern cities. There were a lot of orphans. When they caught some of the thieves, they would welcome the sword to end their misery. It was basically suicide by Blueblood guards. He had thought he could help the poor working in the Senate. He felt the Bluebloods should have tried to assist with the use of their blood to at least help the people become immune from the B12 virus and other sicknesses. The only people who were assisted with an antidote were forced to give up their land, or they would have to work as slaves for the Blueblood Senate. People who had young kids were forced to decide if they wanted their sick child to live, or were they willing to give up their freedoms. The citizens were promised certain things, and the promises were all broken. Chaos ensued and the Blueblood Senate was formed with the might of the Blueblood Army. Overnight, the people lost their government and most lost their lives.

Chapter 32

Dak pointed at the river from the room in the shack. "I believe if we stay a few hundred yards from the river but follow the path of the river, we will be able to travel faster. The land is hardly passable near the shoreline of the river. If we can travel about thirty miles a day, we should be able to make it below the jet stream, to warmer weather in two days. We will need to steal a couple of horses from one of the Midlander camps. The trip is going to be difficult."

"Yes, it will be. We might be too tired after traveling all that distance to copulate." Zenith turned away and smiled to herself. She wanted to laugh. She had been surprised how wonderful the sexual encounters had been. Both had elected not to wear clothing or very little clothing during their four-day stay in the cabin.

"On the other hand, we might just travel twenty-five miles a day, so we won't be so tired," Dak said as he glanced toward Zenith and raised his eyebrow.

***

The two started before dawn and walked south along the river. They had made wooden slats to fit on the bottom of their boots. The slats helped provide traction and to keep them from sinking into the two to three feet of snow. They tried to stay within a hundred yards of the river and use it as a guide. Dak remembered crossing three rivers during his journey. He felt he could locate the marker left by Robin Hood along the riverbank, however, he did not know which river they were now following. After twelve hours of walking, the two finally set up camp in a snow-covered wooded area. Dak cooked the fish they had caught while staying at the cabin. They ate fast because once they stopped walking, they became cold. Any sweat they had built up under the layers of clothing was now contributing to the chill of their body. The two crawled into the lean-to and kissed and snuggled. They slept all night curled up in each other's arms.

Both had sore legs, and neither felt like walking that distance the next day, but both were ambitious to move further south. Dak told Zenith the hardest part of the trip would be the first couple of days dealing with the ice, snow, and cold conditions. Dak was also homesick and knew the additional difficult task they faced crossing the Midlander territory. They needed horses to head east. There was no way they could walk the distance and with winter coming, they could not be caught out in the open by a camp of Midlanders.

On the third day, Dak noticed the marker Robin Hood had cut into the Birch Tree bark along the riverbank. He had not mentioned his concern of locating the trail to Zenith, and he now remembered the area where they had avoided going south of this spot to stay clear of the Midlander's Camp. This was the middle river. The river flowed southeast and originated in the mountainous areas further north. He took a breath of fresh air. He felt the difficult part was now over.

Chapter 33

The two started out without talking. Aquarius was concerned why he was summoned to go on this trip. He had asked the Senator's secretary after leaving Senator Blackmon's office. The secretary had provided the copy of the written request from the army showing the request by Samuel. His instincts suggested at first, he would be killed, and he was alarmed after considering the possible motive. Then his concern turned to anger. He was mad at Samuel. He resented being asked to go on this journey. He remembered training with Samuel when both men were young. Samuel always beat him in the tournament rings. Samuel always intentionally hit the opponents hard in the training, and his bruising lasted for weeks. He did not like Samuel, and he did not want to be on a long journey across the continent with him. Samuel was a proven killer, and the men under him had to prove they could kill without hesitation, or he would beat them. He was a hard man who did not like conversation.

They rode fast for the first ten hours, and Samuel finally dismounted. Aquarius stopped and dismounted. He was tired of eating Samuel's dust from the dirt road and having to push his horse to keep up with the fast pace set by Samuel. Samuel did not seem concerned with Aquarius's ability to ride for long distances. Samuel said, "We will allow the horses to drink and rest for an hour and then we will head further north." Both men also drank water and filled their canteens. Samuel could tell Aquarius was mad about being picked for the trip.

Aquarius asked, "Why go further north? When are we going to start heading east? What is the plan?"

Samuel did not like being questioned. The men who rode with him were never allowed to question him. "I will let you know when I am ready to head east. Your time in the senate has made you soft. A true Blueblood warrior should be able to ride for twenty-four hours straight."

"You should have selected someone else." The two men stared at each other.

"Senator Dale was on to you. He was going to have you killed."

Aquarius was shocked by the nonchalant statement. "What do you know about Senator Dale?"

"I know he believes you are the one who helped Ivan Chezon escape during the coup five years ago. He thinks you know where Ivan is hiding. Your wife reports to Senator Dale."

Aquarius was stunned by what Samuel said. He was the general of the army, and everyone feared him. No one would challenge him. The citizens outside the castle walls always stayed clear of him. He had hunted down and killed hundreds of men who had avoided paying taxes and crimes as set forth by the Blueblood Senate. He would bring the heads of the guilty to the senate floor leaving the bodies of the men and women on the ground where they laid. He had never shown mercy. He was known as the man who never smiled, and the human slayer.

Aquarius thought, "I have been summoned out in the wilderness to be killed by Samuel." He paused, "I guess we need to start riding again. The horses should be able to hold up until dark."

Samuel looked at Aquarius knowing he had just changed the subject. He also understood Aquarius did not trust him. He now assumed the rumors were correct that Aquarius had been the leak inside the senate from years past.

Chapter 34

The seven men and one woman rode into Cliff Tops. Two of the older men came out and greeted them and secured their horses. The kids ran alongside the horses and yelled hello to the riders. The parents were expecting their teenagers, and everyone was hugged. Vicky walked out and watched the riders. Billy Ray hugged Delores and Delores broke off and went and hugged her two sons. Little Jimmy had been working in the lumber yard. He walked from the sawmill area and hugged Veronica and Trey. He told them he loved them. He then walked over and asked Billy Ray, "What is the news of Merlin helping us?"

Billy Ray looked at his friend and shook his head no. "How is the work going on the platform? We need to harvest the steel from those boats before the Normand army returns. We need to have the blockade set. We cannot allow them to make landfall, and they might return before winter. We are in for one hell of a war. This is going to get bad."

Little Jimmy turned and yelled his commands to the loggers to bring in fresh cut logs. He knew they needed to have the boats lifted by the next day and then use the platform to hold the ships in place while the metal was cut and harvested for the underwater blockade. He also knew with Billy Ray returning from his trip, he would be ready to start molding and forming the needed rigid metal structure to place in the ocean in front of the opening to the jetty. The design of the metal structures was to form welded large metal I-beams with three legs and two sharp points. The points were going to be hidden below the surface of the ocean during high tide to stop any large boat from entering the jetty. The metal structures would make a hidden underwater barrier and tear out the bottom of a steel or wooden ship. If they could prohibit the foot soldiers from reaching the beach, they could win the battle and maybe the war. The ocean was too unpredictable with twenty-foot-high swells up to fifty-foot-high swells for a ship to anchor for an extended period. The beach area provided the tribe the needed access to the ocean to fish from their small two men rowboats to harvest the fish to survive.

Billy Ray walked toward Vicky's home. The home was a fourplex. She lived on the top level with Dak until he moved out to live with his friends. Wayne lived in the back on the main level by himself. Eric of Newport and Casey lived in the section to the right with their one child. Robin Hood had moved out with Dak. Delores and Billy Ray were now empty nesters and lived in the section to the left. Hulk and Tommy Boy had also moved out with Dak. Dak and his friends had built a hang out on top of the cliff overlooking the ocean and then as they got older, they wanted their freedom and lived with each other for the past two years. Veronica, being the only female of the group, had started visiting with Vicky and talking with her at night for hours. They had become friends, and she often would sleep in Dak's empty bed.

Vicky walked down the stairs and looked at Billy Ray. "Based on what the kids have reported, we will not be receiving any help from Merlin. The Blueblood girl was trying to complete her training to be a Blueblood warrior. They saved her life from a large group of Midlanders. She told the group they would be hauled away to the dungeon and beaten if they went to Merlin. They would be treated the same as Midlanders or drifters, and they would be provided no mercy." He kicked the dirt with his boot and glanced at Vicky. "Dak cut them free and ordered them back home to protect them." Vicky turned and almost cried hearing the news. "We will try to set the platform tomorrow and pull the first boat up. We need to start cutting the metal by the end of the week. We need the barrier set by next week."

"It will not be enough." She looked at Billy Ray. "I believe the Normand army will try to hit us from the west and north with their main force coming from the east through the sea. We cannot count on the harsh climate and terrain to protect us from the north. They might have some men die, but it would only take a few to break through our defenses and hit us from the back. That is what I would do."

Eric walked over and heard the last of what Vicky said. "I do not trust the New York Tribe. If the Normand army made them an offer, us or them, they would sell us out. We keep taking on refugees from them which might be part of the plan." He looked at both Vicky and Billy Ray. "We might already have some elements of the Normand army in our tribe. Those last four guys that came across the bridge just do not seem to fit. They are always watching and seem to have a separate agenda. They did not bring with them a family. Just four men. They say they are from the New York tribe, but they are intentionally vague. I am willing to bet they come from the deep south. They have aged suntanned hands and necks. Their accent is an accent from the southern region."

Vicky asked, "Billy Ray, what do you think?"

"I will work two of them cutting the metal. The other two will be sent back into the woods to cut timber. We have tried to keep them all separated doing different jobs. They have not tried to be social with anyone else in our tribe. I do not trust them, but we need everyone we can get."

"Do you think they are spies?"

He hesitated and then said, "We might want to interrogate one of them in an isolated location by ourselves." He looked at Vicky like this should be urgent.

"Go ahead. Let Wayne in on the plan. I will set up a conference with Zorro. The next time we meet the New York Tribe at the bridge to exchange fish for metal, I will ask for a conference with him. We need to see where they stand. We have been neighbors with little conflict with them for years."

Billy Ray blew out his breath. "It has all been one-sided. We have tried to help them. They have done nothing for us. The amount of steel they provide us is a fraction of the fish we provide them. I agree with Eric. They will sell us out in a heartbeat."

Vicky knew the truth. She also remembered the first time they had met Zorro, and he kept bossing them around. They were at the large gorge which separated the two territories and the bridge which had been built with the work of both sides. Finally, Billy Ray and Little Jimmy had walked across the bridge and beat and killed his ten men, and then Billy Ray held his knife to the throat of Zorro. Vicky had stepped in and then asked him if he would like to live and be neighborly or did he want his head cut off? They had been neighborly ever since.

She walked over and hugged Veronica and then the boys. She forced a smile as she welcomed each of them. She was worried about Dak, and if Zorro was working with the Normand army, she would kill him.

She had known Zorro for sixteen years. He had killed everyone who challenged his authority in his tribe. He possessed very little passion for someone who did not do as he said. His tribe had grown over the years because the refugees had to escape the Midlanders and the southern warring tribes. People had walked on the newly discovered road leading from the mid continental area north to the New York Tribe, and the path is named such. The Continental Trail had been discovered a few years ago. It travels around the nuclear waste areas and, in places, the path proceeds underground through dug out tunnels to avoid the radiation from the ground level above. The most northern part of the Continental Trail is the old railroad tunnel from the old world and the tunnel exit that is located on the western edge of the New York tribe boundary. The tunnel had to be dug out to form a cave which is several hundred feet long and big enough for wagons, cattle, and horses to travel.

No one had been able to connect directly with the people located on the west coast and the city of Merlin. The city called the Southern City had been able to sail ships north along the coast to Merlin. The rumors were that King Solman had taken the Southern City along with several other smaller communities. His empire was growing daily. No one knew where he originated. He seemed to appear from thin air with a few men and then his group grew into armies and these armies were ruthless.

More and more people were using the Continental Trail to move livestock and other goods, and some were fleeing King Solman's wrath. For the most part, no one came as far north as Cliff Tops by boat. There was one captain, Captain J.J., who would brave the harsh sea and sail into the jetty about once every four months. He would bring fruit from the south and trade for fish, coal, and seal furs. He would take the traded items south. Cliff Tops was the only provider of coal and Captain J.J. helped keep the origin of the coal concealed from the larger tribes in the south. Cliff Tops was located just south of the jet stream. North of the jet stream was an extremely cold, harsh territory with wind gusts of sixty miles per hour and heavy snowfall on the glaciers. The only way to reach Cliff Tops from the south by land was through the New York Tribe Territory, and Zorro ruled with an iron fist. No one entered his territory unless he approved, and they paid his tariff. The New York tribe had grown to double the size of Cliff Top's Tribe with the influx of people migrating north.

Chapter 35

Dak looked around as he was trying to peer through the small trees and bushes. "We are close to the small camp. They will have guards. We can crawl into position and then wait for nightfall."

"How can you tell we are close? I cannot see anything."

Dak responded "I can smell them. They are different from us. If they walk up to a nest of baby birds, even the women would reach into the nest and eat the baby birds alive."

Zenith could not tell if Dak was joking or not. "Maybe we need to hide the bird nests instead of trying to steal two horses."

Dak kept his eyes focused trying to make certain the area was safe. "Once we get closer, we should be able to crawl up to the fence and take two horses with saddles. They leave the saddles on the wooden fence. They are not very smart."

"Watchout." Zenith could sense movement from her peripheral vision. She immediately pulled her sword and blocked the arrow headed for Dak's back. "Run. Follow me."

They ran up the hill and through the pine thicket. Both were breathing hard and out of breath. "We cannot outrun them on horses. They will cut us off." Zenith looked at Dak as he was bent over holding his side.

Dak said, "I counted ten of them. We need to attack them before the entire tribe is alerted and comes for us. Follow me."

Zenith could not believe her ears. She ran after Dak. He charged into the open field and was staring at ten men on horses four hundred feet away. "What are you doing? This is your plan? We are in the open."

"Stay behind me."

"What are you talking about? You need to stay behind me."

"Here they come. I will take the five in the center. The other five will run off once they see the five comrades fall. You capture two of their horses."

Zenith looked at Dak on one knee in total disbelief. Dak jumped up and charged the ten men. He dropped to one knee and reached for the arrows as the riders were fifty feet away, charging on horseback. Dak pulled the bow and stuck three arrows in the ground. He stayed on one knee. The front rider in the center took the first arrow in the chest. At forty-five feet, the second rider to the right took the second arrow in the chest. Dak pulled the third arrow from the ground and loaded his bow. He released the arrow with it striking the now front rider in the forehead. He pulled his sword with his right hand and charged toward the riders.

"Dammit. What are you doing?"

As the horse and riders were heading directly toward him,

Dak squatted close to the ground to the left of the front horse. At the last second, he jumped to the right, taking out the front leg of the horse with his sword as it passed him. The rider had leaned toward his right and anticipated swinging down at Dak. When the horse fell, the rider flew headfirst turning a summersault in the air and landed in the weeds on his back. The other riders were not prepared to fight Dak. They had assumed their front rider would take him out.

Zenith knew she had to capture the first horse. If she could corral a horse, she could take these men out. One of the skills in training to become a Blueblood warrior, the cadets had to master riding a horse and fighting from horseback. She ran into the path of the first horse and slowed it down to a trot, so that she could jump on it while it was still moving. Once on the horse, she turned the animal and charged the men. She saw the last man to pass Dak slumped forward in the saddle after taking an arrow in the back.

Dak had immediately pulled his bow and loaded an arrow and fired at the fifth Midlander striking him in the back as he rode past Dak. The man slumped over and held onto the horse's neck as the horse trotted off into the woods.

The five remaining men noticed the one charging was a Blueblood. They did not know if they should break off the attack or try to capture a Blueblood. They hesitated as Zenith charged at the front two riders. As she rode between the riders, she swung her sword catching the rider on the right in the chest and the one on the left ducked and rotated to the side of his horse. Zenith remembered her training. She did not swing for the torso. She swung low for the exposed thigh. The rider had no way to protect his leg. Her sword sliced deep into the femur. The Midlander rode his horse into the woods while he hung over the side. She knew he would bleed out if he did not have someone stop the bleeding in the next few minutes.

The rider who landed in the weeds had risen to his knees. He was disoriented after the hard fall. He reached for his head to check for blood loss. Dak did not hesitate, and his arrow went through the man's back, heart, and stuck out his chest. He fell forward dead in the weeds.

The other three Midlanders saw the five dead riders and two who had ridden away injured. They kicked their horses and ran off into the woods headed for the main camp. Zenith rode up near Dak, "Get on. We need to find you a horse. They ran off toward the wooded area."

Dak knew they needed to go back to the trail and head east. The main Midlander camp would now be on alert. "We need to head for the trail. We need to ride off on one horse. We do not have time to look for a stray horse. We will be surrounded by a thousand mad men in a few minutes. These people are not our enemy. I do not wish to kill any more of them."

Chapter 36

Little Jimmy looked at the man, "Listen Hershel, you are going to tell us the truth, or we are going to hurt you and make you bleed. We know you are not from the New York Tribe. Tell us the truth."

The man looked at Billy Ray, then Wayne. "Please. I just want to live in your tribe. I work hard. I do what I am told."

Billy Ray and Wayne did not move. Little Jimmy lifted his steel rod. He poked the spear end in the dirt while staring at Hershel. "Where did you get the suntanned neck and hands?"

The man stuttered, "I have always been dark. What does that have to do with anything?" He looked scared.

Wayne said, "Take your shirt off. I want to see your tan." The man looked worried.

Billy Ray walked toward the man and grabbed him by his neck and squeezed. "He said he wanted to see your tan." He pulled Hershel's coat off and then his two wool shirts and then his wool undershirt. He pushed Hershel down on the cold ground.

"That is a brand from the Normand army. You are a spy. You have three seconds to tell us all, or I am going to smash your head with my hammer."

271

***

Vicky looked at Zorro. Ever since Billy Ray had held a knife to his throat, and Zorro watched as Little Jimmy threw three of his men into the gorge headfirst, he had been very nice to her. Zorro yelled from his side of the gorge, "What can I do for you on such a beautiful day?"

Vicky watched his men for any action. She knew Zorro had to be strong in front of his guards. In the New York Tribe, only the strong survived. Zorro had surrounded himself with trusting guards, and the men were ruthless to the emigrants fleeing from the south. The people were stripped of all assets and searched by the guards. If a man fought back, he would be forced to leave and go back to the south. Vicky had heard stories from the few who had escaped to her village over the years. There was no fairness with the decision of the leadership of the New York Tribe. The new world was a harsh place to live.

"Please come over to our side. I need to conference with you."

Zorro looked and raised his hands palms up. "I can hear you just find. What can I do for you?" He looked at Little Jimmy standing with his steel spear. He then glanced at Billy Ray with his sword and bow strapped to his back.

272

"Come over here now. I will not ask you again."

Zorro looked concerned. He knew he had forty of his best guards, and he was facing just two big men and five teenagers. He said, "Certainly I will be happy to talk with you." Vicky watched as Zorro walked across the wooden bridge. When he got to the middle of the bridge, he turned the revolving gate and walked over to Vicky. "What can I do for my friends?" He looked at Billy Ray and Little Jimmy. He remembered the men, and how they had killed ten of his best guards and wounded four others. He also recalled Billy Ray's knife piercing his neck until Vicky asked him, did he want to be friends or have his head cut off?

"Zorro, what do you know about the Normand army?" Little Jimmy walked behind him, cutting his path off from escaping across the bridge.

He glanced behind him at Little Jimmy blocking his path, "I know what I hear. They are forcing their way north from the southern continent. We have a few refugees that bring us news, but we do not know if the news is reliable."

"What are you going to do if the Normand army comes north? Are you going to stand and fight?"

"We will close the Continental Trail at the tunnel. We have made certain the security at the gate is well maintained. We have your smoke bomb sitting next to the metal bars in the box covered for protection against the rain and snow. They won't be able to get through. We will fight." He turned and looked at Wayne and Billy Ray for reassurance. He could sense something was askew.

"Bring the men." The four men were led from the hidden embankment tied with ropes. Zorro watched and did not seem to recognize the men. They walked into the middle of the area and were forced to sit on the ground.

"These men have each provided their statements. They were captured approximately one-hundred miles north of Southern City by the Normand army. They say they were farmers, and their kids and wives have been taken as slaves. They have been branded as soldiers by the Normand army." Vicky motioned for Billy Ray to pull up the shirt of one of the men. Vicky watched for the body language of the men across the bridge. She wanted to see if any of the guards recognized these men. She noticed the guard third from the middle glance around. She turned to Billy Ray, "Third from the middle, right side."

"How did these men make it to your tribe?" He looked concerned.

Billy Ray walked by the first man. "Hershel. Is he the third man from the right center?" Hershel glanced up at Billy Ray and shook his head yes. Billy Ray quickly pulled his bow and fired the arrow the one-hundred-forty-feet crossing the one hundred seventy-five-foot-deep gorge, striking the third man from the center in the chest. Everyone watched as the man fell backward on the ground with Zorro turning to look at Vicky. Zorro turned to his guards and held his hand to hold their position.

Vicky said, "These four men are spies. They have told us you have several spies in your tribe. The Normand army will attack you at some point. They are trying to figure out your weaknesses and strengths."

Zorro looked at Vicky and then the four men. He yelled at the men and pulled his knife. He walked over to the man next to Hershel and scalped him. He said, "You will tell me who has betrayed me," as he held up the man's scalp. "We will deal with these men. I will assure you; I will get to the bottom of the treason."

Chapter 37

Samuel looked at Aquarius as he rolled out of his bedroll. "Why did you not re-enlist in our army? You could have been a general by now."

Aquarius hesitated as he considered the question. He knew he would die trying to protect his daughter, and he knew Samuel would kill her. He had always killed people that had a warrant wanted dead or alive. "There were too many unnecessary killings. We should have been trying to help the poor." He looked at Samuel. "On patrol one day my squad walked up on a merchant who was holding an eight to ten-year-old boy. He was yelling that the kid had stolen an apple. He wanted justice. He mentioned we Bluebloods had agreed to provide justice, and he was right, our senate had agreed in exchange for taxes, we were to uphold the law. The merchant was a worthless piece of shit, but he held the boy. The penalty as you know was for us to cut the kid's hand off. I tried to reason with the merchant and while I was talking to him, the boy's father arrived. He was a poor man and had several smaller kids. He tried to intervene. In the raucous, the man was killed by one of the young guards. The man laid on the ground dead in front of his crying wife and three very young daughters. The sergeant in my squad walked over to the boy

276

and cut his left hand off. All for an apple. I filed my paperwork the next day to resign from the army. I wanted to work in the senate. I thought I could make a difference. I just do not hate everyone like you do."

***

Samuel did not fall asleep until he watched Aquarius fall asleep. He placed his sword on his chest holding the handle with his right hand. He pulled the cape over his chest and fell asleep. In the morning, the men rose from their bedrolls and hardly talked. Neither man had slept very well. The cold temperatures prevented either man an opportunity to become comfortable. Samuel looked at Aquarius, "I do not hate the people. We must have laws and enforce the laws. That is the reason the old world ended. The entire world was corrupt. The news media shows were all propaganda and after so many years of the unjust influence of the propaganda on the citizens, the propaganda became reality. I am not corrupt, and I will not be influence by propaganda. My actions deter crime. Now we must ride."

Aquarius saddled his horse. "You are delusional if you believe your actions are in any way preventing crime. The old world fell because of the sins of the men and women who ran the governments. Our senate is a bureaucracy led by criminals.

The same as the governments in the old world and that much is true about the news channels in the old world having unjust influence. The people did not realize they were listening to propaganda which became the reality of the world." Samual did not speak. He seemed to consider Aquarius's comments as he mounted his horse and started riding east.

They rode hard for another twelve hours. They started east with neither man speaking. The cold climate and the terrain took a turn for the worst. Neither one was acclimated to the sub-zero weather, and the windchill factor made the temperatures feel ten-to-twenty degrees lower. They passed a small hunting group of Northern people. The group had crossed the north territory from the shoreline where they had been hunting seals. Samuel asked for further directions, and Aquarius traded his pearl handled knife for an old fur coat and better socks.

Aquarius figured he was meant to die on this trip at the hand of Samuel. He could not understand why Samuel summoned him to come along. There were several hundred Blueblood warriors a lot more experienced and deadly than he. He finally figured if Samuel wanted him dead, there was nothing he could do about it. Samuel was too good of a warrior for him to kill, and Samuel knew this.

The next morning the two men got up from their bed rolls and Aquarius warmed him some coffee. He rekindled the fire. He heated the last of the bread he had packed. He noticed Samuel had eaten something from his saddlebag and saddled his horse. He looked at Aquarius and ordered, "We ride now."

Aquarius was tired of taking orders with no explanation. He was also sore from the prior days of riding and looked forward to his cup of coffee. "You go ahead. I will catch up after my coffee."

As soon as he said it, he knew he was going to regret it. Samuel turned, took four large steps, and kicked the hot ashes in Aquarius' face, forcing Aquarius to spill his coffee and burn himself. "We ride now, and you better not tell me what you are or are not going to do one more time."

Aquarius brushed the ashes out of his face. He looked at Samuel with contempt. He thought about his options then went and got on his horse. The two men rode for two hours when Samuel motioned for Aquarius to stop. He watched as Samuel checked the air for nuclear waste and knew something else was bothering him. He turned and said, "We go north."

Aquarius punched his horse and followed. They came to a river after another two hours. The ride was brutal with the cold temperature and rough mountains. Both men dismounted and drank some cold water from the river. Samuel looked up stream and then downstream. "We will need to go further north to locate a place to cross."

"Why?"

Samuel looked at Aquarius. He started to say something and then he drank some more water.

"What is your question?"

"There are over three thousand Blueblood warriors. Several hundred would have been honored to ride with you east. Why me?"

"You are my brother. I was not going to sit back and watch a second-generation Blueblood kill you."

"You did this to protect me? Are you certain I was going to be killed?"

"You know what I say is the truth."

"If we make it across the continent and somehow do not walk into a nuclear waste pit or be killed by the Midlanders, what are your plans? I mean, you might need someone better with a sword than me."

"We were sent on this mission to die. The last few missions I have been summoned to go on, I have gone with not nearly enough support. The main body of the Blueblood Army is second and third generation Bluebloods with another four thousand regular soldiers all controlled by three senators." Samuel looked down and then glanced up. "I figure the best chance we have is to keep moving fast. We should be able to detect the waste pits, but the chance of us making it is not measurable. If we do make it, I will do my duty as I have always done."

Aquarius watched and reflected back sixteen years ago, when the two men attended training for the army. Samual was bigger, faster, and stronger than he. Samual was brutal in the tournament ring either fighting with his hands or wooden practice swords. He would intentionally hurt his opponent. No one wanted to spar with Samual. His personality was one of never giving up and never admitting defeat. If you bested him, you would have to kill him, or he would not stop. Several Bluebloods received broken bones after sparring with Samuel. The bruising from the wooden swords where Samual would relentlessly strike his opponent would last for weeks. "Your duty? Based on who?" Aquarius was now getting agitated. "I have one question that really matters to me." The two men looked at each other. "If we meet up with my daughter and the man named Dak, what are your intentions?"

Chapter 38

They rode back to the river and the marked trail. Dak jumped off the rear of the horse and quickly retrieved his saddle bag, bedroll, and cape. He could tell Zenith wanted to be in the front by the way she shifted her body up next to the saddle horn. He placed the saddle bag on the horse, tied off the bedroll, and jumped on the horse sitting on the back of the saddle. She kicked the horse, and they galloped up the side of the mountain. Once they made it to the top of the hill, "You know it would be better if I was in the front. The constant moving of your body against my body is distracting to me."

Zenith felt his hands drop to her inner thighs. "Better for who? I am still mad at you for charging those ten Midlanders. What in the hell were you thinking? I am so mad at you. No, you need to be taught a lesson. You need to ride in the rear for a while."

"You are mad at me?" He pressed his fingers tighter on her upper thighs. He slowly rubbed up and down her inner thighs. "I thought you loved me?"

She smiled, "I do love you. That is why from now on you need to listen to me. You do not charge ten men on horseback while you are on foot. You do not charge one man on horseback. You know something. I am getting madder by the

282

second thinking about how reckless you are. Do you know I never used to cuss? Hell. I didn't even know what a cuss word was until I met you and your friends, and now you make me so mad I cuss every other word."

"There was a place in the old world in the Smoky Mountains which overlooked other mountains and a huge forest. It was said that the view was perfect, and the view could not be improved. That is what love is. When you would not change anything about the other person, then you know you love them."

Zenith smiled as she kept feeling his hands and fingers rubbing on her inner thighs. "I do love you, but you are going to have to start listening to me."

"I think you are perfect just the way you are. At least one of us loves the other one." She laughed.

The journey started getting easier with flatter and warmer conditions, and they could ride faster on the marked path. The two talked the entire ride, then snuggled and copulated every night inside the large fur bedroll. As they rode along a mountain ridge looking down at the valleys below, Dak asked, "Have you ever made love outdoors in the daytime on a beautiful day overlooking the mountains?"

Zenith smiled as she felt Dak's fingers pressing in on her upper thighs as they rode along the trail. He would release his fingers and rub downward and then push inward and rub back upward and stop at her most inner area. "No. Since I have never been with another man before, I believe you know the answer."

"Well, I believe this open area in front of us would be a good place for the horse to rest. I believe the horse is tired. We need to think about what is good for the horse."

She felt his fingers pushing in and him breathing hot air into her ear. "Yes, I do believe the horse is very tired. We need to lay the bedroll out on the ground and turn the horse facing the other way. I do not want her watching us copulate."

"Maybe we should copulate horse style, and the horse would be okay watching."

Zenith laughed, "You are so bad." She stopped the horse, and they dismounted. The warm sun on a cold day felt good to their nude bodies as they laid on the bedroll holding each other.

A few times they would stop in a pretty spot in the mountains and copulate out in the open in the warm sun.

***

Dak announced, "I can see the roof of Old Thomas's house. We are about home." Old Thomas saw them coming. He was surprised when he saw Zenith jump off the back of the horse. He had never seen a Blueblood up close. He welcomed the two and told Dak his five friends would be happy to see him. "They were very worried about you. They argued with the tribe's men about going back into the waste land looking for you."

He looked at them closely. He could tell they were tired and hungry. Old Thomas announced, "After dinner I will release a pigeon, and let everyone know you made it." Old Thomas told them he would loan them a horse for the journey to Cliff Tops. When he came back to the house, he noticed Dak, and Zenith were fast asleep in the bed he had set up for company. They had eaten some of the pheasant he had cooked for them and fell fast asleep.

Chapter 39

Vicky was never so happy to see someone in her life. The two had ridden into Cliff Tops after lunch on a perfect cold sunny day. The kids had come out and followed the two horses yelling hello and laughing. The town's people all walked to the side of the trail and watched them pass while they all greeted Dak. When they arrived at the main house, Vicky and Delores rushed out and hugged Dak. Delores said, "The men are not here to greet you. They are trying to set the metal underwater structure to prevent ships from entering the jetty. They are rushing to get that task behind them. Billy Ray has indicated they are days behind. We are so happy to see you."

The two women turned and looked at Zenith. Dak smiled, "This is my girlfriend, Zenith. She broke me out of prison, and I owe her my life." The two women looked at Zenith and then greeted her with a hug. They welcomed her to Cliff Tops. Zenith was surprised with the hugs from the two strangers as she stood still and smiled.

Some of the town's kids had run behind them while they rode into town. They ran up to Dak, and he had taken turns picking them up and throwing them in the air and asking them to grab a cloud as he would then catch them under their arms.

After a few times each, the kids laughed and started to return to their homes.

The town prepared for a large bonfire with food. Zenith was surprised with the party, and how happy everyone appeared. All Dak's friends had hugged him when they arrived from the beach. After the dancing and fun, Wayne finally announced, "It is late, and we have a hard day ahead of us tomorrow." With that the town's people started heading for their homes.

Vicky said, "Zenith you are welcome to stay with me. Dak normally sleeps in The Dive with his friends. You can sleep in his old bed."

Zenith did not hesitate. "I will sleep in The Dive with Dak. He and I have bonded."

Vicky's eyebrow involuntarily raised as she was caught off guard. She hesitated and tried to think of what to say.

Dak could feel the other adults and his friends staring at him in the awkward moment. He reached and took Zenith's hand and pulled her toward The Dive. He said, "We will see you in the morning." The group watched as Dak and Zenith walked toward The Dive.

***

Wayne and Vicky met in the kitchen and made breakfast for themselves. The elderly cook walked out to the hen house.

Vicky had two cups of coffee, and Wayne was not talkative. Delores and Billy Ray walked into the kitchen and then Eric of Newport and Casey. They poured some coffee for themselves. Casey finally said, "Our kids are all grown up. I am proud of that group of kids. I hope the younger group are as good."

The elderly lady who cooked the breakfast walked in and immediately placed additional wood in the wood burning stove. She began fixing eggs and making biscuits. The group watched, and all were deep in thought.

Delores finally said, "The kids have matured a lot faster than we did. They were not given an opportunity to be teens. They were forced from childhood into adulthood. War is coming, and we better think of something."

Wayne said, "That is what has me baffled. I am not certain what to do. In our past, we always had a plan. We were always working together to remedy the situation. Now, this is so different."

Eric asked, "How is this so different? We have always been behind the eight ball, and we always won."

Billy Ray said, "We need more allies. The bottom line is we do not have enough people who can fight. Half our tribe is either elderly or young kids."

He poured himself another cup of coffee. The elderly cook said, "Your eggs and biscuits are ready." She looked worried and hurried out the door." The group watched as she left. They knew she lived to gossip, and the entire tribe would know their concerns within an hour.

Wayne announced, "Telephone, telegraph or tell the cook are the three ways of communication."

Delores added, "Yeah, and we don't have the first two. So, the third one will let the entire tribe know our concerns. Maybe they will work harder." She drank some of the coffee and glanced at the others.

Vicky realized the situation, "You are correct, Eric of Newport. In the past, we were always the aggressor attacking and killing people on their soil. We did not sit still like ducks on a pond to be shot. We have become passive."

The exterior door opened and in walked Dak, followed by Zenith. Zenith appeared to glow with her beautiful wide smile and dark skin and long blond hair wearing a dark thick shirt with white fur around the neck. Dak looked at his mother, "We need to talk about the city of Merlin. It was not what I thought, or how you all described it. There is no help coming from them. Matter of fact, we need to prepare to defend our western front."

Zenith pulled the note out of her shirt pocket, "I was told to deliver this note to the King of Cliff Tops. She was looking at Wayne. It was given to me by a man named Ivan Chezon. He is an ally of yours. He was concerned about Dak being killed while in the dungeon. Without his help arranging for us to scale the castle wall and providing us horses, we would not have been able to escape. He told me this message meant life and death. He said the note had to get to you." She handed the note to Wayne. Wayne took the note and handed it to Vicky. Zenith glanced at Vicky and then at Dak. She was surprised. Dak had not mentioned his mother was the one in charge.

Vicky noticed it was addressed in German to Christine Crus. Only five people knew her alias she used when working undercover in the CIA years ago. She also noticed the seal had been broken and the letter had been opened. She acted like she did not notice the broken seal and read the note.

Delores walked behind Vicky and looked at the note over Vicky's shoulder. "Is that written in German?"

Vicky read the note a second time. She did not say anything for a few seconds and turned and looked out the window in thought. "This news is worse than I ever thought possible." She turned and walked out of the kitchen door and up the stairs to her room.

Dak looked at Wayne and the others. They all seemed to be surprised. The group all sensed something horrendous. No one said a word.

Dak led Zenith up the stairs to his old apartment. He knocked on the door and then opened the door. His mother was looking at a book. Dak remembered the book of science. He was forced to read books at a young age. He was not interested in books and could not remember the contents of this book. He was more interested in learning how to fight, hunt, fish, work and have fun with his friends. He never had an aptitude for school.

The tribe had taught the kids how to read and basic math, but given the time limits with them all trying to survive, they had spent very little time learning from books. His mother had kept this book from the old world.

Dak walked into the room holding Zenith's hand. Dak said, "I opened the note back at the beginning of our trip home. Back when we were not certain we would make it. Neither one of us could read the language. I guess I should have shown more interest in your teaching when I was younger."

"Dak you were a loving kid." She smiled. "A parent could not hope for a better child, and now you have grown into a nice loving young man. You make me proud."

"Zenith was told the information in this letter could save her father's life. She is afraid he will be killed. She has a right to know what is in the letter. She risked her life for me and also to bring you this message. Now, she has no home. She would be executed if she returned to Merlin. The Blueblood Senate has no tolerance for anyone doing what she had to do to save my life. There is a reward for both our heads, dead or alive, in exchange for a wagon load of gold."

Vicky studied the two as they held hands standing in front of her. She could tell they were in love. They seemed to be in-tune with each other's emotions and thoughts. They seemed to consider the others' point of view before they spoke. She remembered when she and her late husband had first dated and the sexual excitement they enjoyed. She quickly changed her thoughts back to the present. Vicky looked at Zenith. She stared into her beautiful eyes trying to decide if she should tell anyone what was in the letter. War was coming, and there would be no way to survive.

She smiled at Zenith. She went over and hugged her. "You do have a home with us." She then stepped back and looked at the two. "Do you two love each other?"

Dak looked at Zenith and then his mother. "I think she is perfect, and I do love her with all my heart and soul."

"Yes, I love Dak. I would die for him in battle if needed, but he has some issues with charging on foot an enemy on horseback while being outnumbered. We have some work to do."

The two smiled and Vicky laughed, "Yes. He does have some issues you need to help him with. I watched him jump over the jetty rock wall and attack ten men in a rowboat. For heaven sakes, he takes chances."

Dak started feeling outnumbered. "There is a male way of doing things and then there is a female way of doing things, and you two need to respect the difference."

Zenith looked at Vicky. "Has he always been this stubborn? I promise I never cussed until I fell in love with him."

Vicky smiled and then got serious. "Dak, you two and your friends maybe should leave and seek a way to fit in with the common people of Merlin. You would be safe there."

"What? I love it here. Zenith mentioned last night how happy everyone seemed here in Cliff Tops. There is no comparison with Merlin where no one is happy except for a few people at the top who have all the wealth. I cannot live like that."

"War is coming, and we are not strong enough to defend our city. We cannot trust the New York tribe. We found spies from the Normand army in our city. Zorro indicated he would fight, but we cannot trust him. If they do fight and are overrun by the Normand army from the south, the men and women of the New York tribe will come north to the huge gorge and seek refuge from us. We do not have the resources to support that many people. The Normand navy will cut us off from the ocean and the supply of fish. We do not see how we can survive. I want you two to be safe. You two and your friends, Dak, deserve to have happiness in your lives and live without the threat of constant war. I want you two to go to Merlin and live in hiding in one of the out-skirt territory."

"No, we will not go back to Merlin. I would rather die here than live in Merlin."

Zenith looked at Vicky. "Can you tell me the contents of the message? I was told by a man named Ivan Chezon that my father's life might depend on me being able to deliver this message to you. The king of Cliff Tops."

Vicky knew she could not conceal the secret. "King Solman is a Blueblood. He is working with Senator Dale to conquer our world. We cannot fight both of their armies and survive. Ivan is asking for my help to overthrow the Blueblood Senate. I do not have the resources to accommodate his request."

Dak looked at the book of science turned over with the pages marked for reading. He walked over to the table and turned the book over. He read the words, "Gunpowder." He read the formula and how to refine it. He turned and looked at his mother. "This has been outlawed by our world."

Vicky said, "Being able to produce gunpowder may be the only hope we have. We have the right to bear arms. I always believed in the second amendment in our old country's constitution. I wish we had not lost all our weapons at sea when several of the boats sank during the Transitional Period."

Chapter 40

The two men started traveling at night. They were following horse tracks they thought might have been riders from the east. Samuel noticed older tracks heading west with six riders and then five riders with fresher tracks heading east. He could see the tracks with the help of the moonlight, and they wanted to stay clear of the Midlanders. Traveling by night was the only alternative. After the first night and part of the next morning, Samuel knew these tracks were the tracks he had been hunting. He did not mention anything to Aquarius about the significance of locating the tracks. During his tenure as a commander, he had never shared his plans with any of his subordinates. He always made certain they followed his orders to the letter. He was accustomed to the ill feelings of his soldiers with his authoritarian style. Now, he could feel the ill will coming from Aquarius. On the eleventh day, he noticed footprints leading down the riverbank and then one set of hoof prints heading up the river north and then turning east over the mountain following the same tracks. Aquarius sat on the ground and watched as Samuel studied the ground and considered the options. He was tired and wanted to rest. It was going to rain and maybe snow. He was always cold. He wanted to build a fire and cook something. Samuel would not allow a fire in fear of attracting attention. They kept pushing east.

On the twentieth day, Samuel held up his hand for Aquarius to stop. Aquarius looked east and could make out the roof of a log house, and a trail that led to the rear yard. Samuel glanced back at Aquarius. "Be ready. Keep your eyes open and pull your sword." The two rode slowly east. As they got closer, they heard dogs barking and someone yelled for the dogs to be quiet. Both men looked in all directions as they approached the home.

As they came up the hill and rode around to the front of the home, they saw an old man sitting on the front porch chewing tobacco.

"Welcome. You can put your horses up in the corral, and I will feed them." He hesitated. "Or at least what is left of them. Those horses have been ridden too hard. Shame on you for treating an animal like that. I can see their ribs from here."

Samuel looked around. "Old Man. Our horses are not your concern. How many people live here?"

"Just me. Where are you headed?"

"Cliff Tops."

"Why?"

Samuel dismounted. "We are looking for a couple of riders. Have you seen a Blueblood girl and a young man?"

Old Thomas got up from his chair. "No. Let me take your horses, and there is food inside the home. I just killed a turkey for dinner. I heard you coming from the west yesterday and have been smelling you two for a couple of days now. You can wash up inside. We can talk after dinner. Now give me your horses. They need food and rest. I have never seen two horses so tired."

Old Thomas took the two horses and looked back as the men both walked into his home. He placed the horses in the corral and provided three times the normal amount of food for them. He brushed them as they ate and felt bad for the two animals. He understood Blueblood warriors had no concern for their animals. He cursed them for the abuse. He walked behind his barn and wrote a note and released the pigeon. He walked back to his home.

Chapter 41

Vicky read the note. She reached up and rubbed her cross. Wayne said, "I can take some men and go meet them on the trail. I can tell them they are not welcome. This cannot be good."

Vicky turned, "They might be bounty hunters. We need to meet them. We need to discuss our position from one of strength and not weakness. We need to negotiate with them on our terms. I will send a pigeon to Old Thomas advising him what to do."

***

Vicky looked at her seventy riders on horseback, "Let's go." Little Jimmy rode up next to Vicky after the five-hour ride. "I am wondering why you insisted on the stable boy to saddle you with that horse? She is nothing like your horse. She is not nearly as fast."

Vicky smiled at Little Jimmy. He had always shown concern for her. He had always done as she asked. In the old world, he had been her trusting bodyguard when they went on assignments for the CIA. He had never backed down from anyone. He was a true friend and now their kids were best friends.

"She will get the job done today. When we get to the end of the gorge, make certain everyone stays hidden. We do not want to engage a couple of Blueblood warriors in combat with them on horses. They are too good at fighting from horseback. We have to get them off the horses to have a chance."

"So, you believe Captain J. J. has accurately described the Blueblood warriors? I guess I have some reservations about what he said."

Vicky said, "It is not just Captain J.J. I saw them before the Transition Period. I talked to the doctors that worked with the genetic engineering. I suggest we handle them with care."

Little Jimmy looked around at the men riding behind him. He asked, "What do you think she will do?"

"I believe Zenith will do the right thing. She is a fugitive from Merlin. We might as well determine what it is they want, while we have them out numbered and trapped inside the canyon." She looked over at Little Jimmy and kicked her horse in the side with her heels. The rest of the group followed.

***

Old Thomas said, "I normally do not come this way. It is shorter but a little more treacherous." He glanced behind him at the two Bluebloods, then turned and kept riding at a slow pace. He knew he needed to buy time. Once he got down and acted like he had to use the bathroom behind some bushes.

Now, as they entered the mouth of the gorge, he checked his watch and the time. He hoped the plan would work. The two men did not appear to anticipate a trap. They turned a curve in the gorge, and he turned around to let the two Blueblood riders pass him. He pointed, "Right up there at the next curve we will climb out of the gorge and ride on flat land. This route saved us a half of a day." He sat still and watched.

Suddenly, the two riders stopped and looked up at the top of the gorge on both sides. They were surrounded by men armed with arrows aimed at them. Most of the men were on horses with their bows and crossbows aimed in their direction.

There was a pause, and Vicky rode to the side of the gorge and looked down. "You are welcome to visit our village. We are peaceful people."

Samuel looked at her, "You could have fooled me. All of you need to drop your bows, crossbows, and your swords in the name of the Blueblood Senate. We will not tolerate this action. This is an act of war."

No one moved. Vicky commanded, "You will get off your horses, and you may walk to our village. We are gracious hosts."

"We will not get off our horses, and if you do not tell your men to drop their weapons, we will be forced to defend ourselves."

Aquarius looked at the back of Samuel. He whispered, "Are you kidding me? They have us boxed in here like two mice in a shoe box. We walked right into this trap. Remember Apollo, you fool."

Samuel turned and glanced at Aquarius, and in a harsh tone, "Keep your mouth shut."

The men heard another female voice from the other side of the gorge. "Father, please do as they ask."

The two men looked up to the left side of the gorge, and there stood Zenith with her sword in its sleeve. She was standing next to several young warriors.

Samuel looked at her, "You two are under arrest."

Vicky felt a surge in her temperament as she looked across the gorge at Zenith and Dak. She turned her horse into a dead run and ran it down the upper right side of the top of the gorge approximately one hundred yards and then down the steep embankment. Everyone watched as she leaned back in the saddle as she descended the steep embankment and then turned the horse and raced past Old Thomas and up to the two Blueblood warriors. She demanded. "You are our guests. You will dismount your horses and walk to our village. No one is going to be arrested. You try to arrest anyone in my village, and you will die. We do not trust you and your Blueblood Senate. Do I make myself clear?"

Samuel was surprised a woman was giving him orders and threatening him. He glanced up at Little Jimmy and then over at Billy Ray and the other men. He started to turn to look at Vicky and Zenith yelled, "Father, please."

Samuel turned his horse, and the horse seemed a little jumpy. He had trouble holding it still. He was trying to discern what had spooked his horse. He glanced at the ground looking for a snake. Vicky turned her horse around in a circle with it standing in front of Samuel and his horse. The white stallion was a large horse that stood eighteen hands high and only a strong rider could control it. Samuel, while sensing something was spooking the horse, leaned forward. The horse bucked with the hind legs raising forward and upward. Then the horse raised up on its hind legs causing a collision between Samuel's forehead and back of the horse's head. The sudden impact knocked Samuel backward off the horse. He flew in the air landing hard on the ground. Vicky immediately looked at Aquarius, "You, sir, can ride to our village if you leave now. He will walk. Now follow me."

Aquarius did not hesitate. He wanted to see his daughter. He kicked his horse and followed Vicky and Samuel's horse down the canyon trail.

Samuel was a little rattled by the hit on the head. When he landed, he hit on his sword and the handle rammed into his ribs. His muscles were already sore from the long journey and the cold weather added to the aches and body pains. He rubbed his hurting ribs and checked his head for blood as he looked up and noticed he was alone. He sat still feeling his aching muscles and listening for riders. The tribe disappeared just as fast and quietly as they appeared. He got up and started walking.

Chapter 42

When they rode into Cliff Tops, Aquarius was surprised. The people in the village lined the dirt road and greeted them. The kids were running alongside the horses laughing and cheering at the riders. He watched as Zenith rode several yards in front of him with several riders between them. She rode next to the young warrior who had fought Apollo in the senate auditorium. He turned in his saddle and noticed no one was watching him as he rode into the city. The tribe did not seem to be worried about what he might do or not do. He still had his weapons, and the tribe did not appear to consider him a threat. He tried to judge their ability to wage war, but he was having a hard time getting a read on them. When he arrived at the main building, he dismounted his horse and gave the reins to an older man. Some of the horse riders had separated as they approached the city of Cliff Tops. Some went north and others had ridden south with a few riding into the city. He stood and watched the people of Cliff Tops. An elderly lady walked by and announced, "We are going to eat in just a little while. You can walk over to the tables and have a seat."

Aquarius walked to the table and sat on the bench. Four children came over to him and started asking him questions and talking with him. The children all seemed inquisitive and happy. He smiled and answered the kid's questions. One of the little girls brought him some water. He learned the ages and names of each kid as they each took a seat around the table looking at him as they talked.

He asked about the attack from the sea. "I understand your city was attacked by an army from down south."

All the kids were excited to tell the story of the battle and tried to talk at the same time. Finally, the little girl spoke up and said, "There were not a million Normand soldiers, Jordan, there were three hundred that died. They never made it to our shore."

"Where were you guys when this was going on?"

Jordan announced, "We were all in the church. We were not allowed to fight."

***

The tribe within the Cliff Tops inner community prepared a feast, and the residents joined in eating the meal. There were a lot of happy faces at the festive dinner. The tables had been lined up in rows with three tables placed end to end facing the other tables. The evening weather was cold but sunny. Zenith sat at the head of the table next to Dak. Aquarius looked at her from time to time as he sat at the end on the back row, and he noticed she seemed to be smiling and having fun. She had avoided talking with him. He had tried to approach her once they arrived, and she turned and walked away. He observed her as he ate while watching the other people. Finally, when he was done with his meal, he noticed Samuel walking toward the feast from the dirt trail leading from the west. He watched as the kids ran up to him and welcomed him. The people in the village acted as if it was normal for a Blueblood to walk into the village area. He noticed Vicky and the people at her table however were all observing Samuel as he approached on foot.

Samuel looked down as one of the smallest of the ten kids stood in front of him and smiled and offered him a drink of water. "Mister, would you like a drink? You look thirsty." He smiled back and took the drink. He observed the child was very cute and friendly. He glanced at the other kids and noticed they were all friendly and curious. He drank the water and pondered. He then saw Aquarius sitting at a table eating, and his irritation flared. He was the Blueblood General, and no one under his command had ever ridden off and left him. He thanked the girl and the other kids. He walked toward the table. He demanded in a loud authoritarian voice, "You left me. You do not leave me. I am going to teach you a lesson."

The entire group of people got quiet. Vicky from her sitting position declared, "He is our guest, the same as you. Do not overstate your welcome and do not think for a second, we will tolerate rudeness."

Vicky got up and walked toward Samuel. Some of the men appeared with swords and bows. She turned to them, "Those will not be necessary." They all backed down and walked away. Samuel stood looking as Vicky approached and glanced at the men of her tribe. He had heard the story of the man from the far east beating Apollo in eleven seconds. He knew someone must have taught him how to fight. He noticed the huge black man and the other large warrior sitting with a group of teenagers all watching. They all seemed relaxed. He then turned back to Aquarius, "I will teach you a lesson." He then looked at Vicky, "This is not your concern."

Aquarius answered, "I do not work for you. Remember, I am a member of the Blueblood Senate staff. I am not one of your soldiers you can order around. I decided in the gorge when you were lying on your ass, I would rather ride with these villagers instead of walk with you." He glared at Samuel. Vicky could tell the two men did not like each other.

Samuel's nose flared, and Vicky could tell he was ready to fight. She stepped in front of him with her palms of her hands up. Her body language was telling him to halt, and she demanded, "There are small kids watching you. You will not fight in our city. I will not tolerate it. Matter of fact, you need to hand over your weapons or leave. Do I make myself clear?"

Samuel looked at the group of people, the food, and then glared down into Vicky's eyes. He considered his options. He was starving for good food as he looked at the fried chicken. The food he had eaten at Old Thomas's was over cooked, burnt, and not tasty. The journey had been harsh with very little to eat. He had been reluctant to start fires because of possibly alerting the Midlanders to their positions. He stared into her eyes and reached and unbuckled his sword and pulled his bow over his head and handed them to Vicky. She took them, "You need to give me your two knives." He reached behind him and pulled the knife from the sleeve he had strapped to his back. He then pulled the other knife from the top of his boot.

"Samuel, you may help yourself to the food and drink." She turned and took the weapons to the front and gave them to the older man who carried them to the fourplex.

Samuel stood and watched as an elderly lady approached him and handed him a plate with utensils. "We heard you would be here soon. We left the food out for you. Please help yourself."

Samuel took the items and considered what she had said about leaving the food out for him. He loaded his plate. He walked over and sat across from Aquarius. Samuel proceeded to eat as fast as he could. Aquarius mentioned, "The food is very good." Samuel glanced up at him. Samuel looked around and noticed no one was watching him. Aquarius had his arms crossed sitting and watching Samuel. He added, "You know when you walk around in Merlin and the surrounding territories, how everyone acts like they are scared of you?" Samuel looked up with a mouth full of chicken and stared at Aquarius.

"Samuel. These people are not scared of us. I still have my weapons. They do not consider us a threat. A word of advice. Before you start demanding your will and trying to arrest someone, you might want to consider the situation." Aquarius looked around and then poked his index finger hard into the surface of the table trying to capture Samuel's attention. "The Normand army attacked these people, and not only did they win the battle, but they had no casualties. They killed over three hundred Normand soldiers in less than thirty minutes. Some of these men look like they could be very skilled at combat. They have that look of both warrior and killer."

"How did you find out that information?"

Aquarius hesitated to tell Samuel three four-year-old children and two five-year-old children were his source. He whispered, "Jordan and Emily Sue told me." He knew Samuel would not know who they were.

***

309

After the sun started setting, the bonfire was lit, and the music started playing. Some of the people started dancing. Vicky saw Dak talking to the singer and was surprised when Dak walked up to her while a slow song was playing and asked her to dance with him. She was taken back by the request. He was a young man and being seen with his mother was not cool. She smiled at him as they danced, and the singer was singing, "Strawberry Wine". The song she had loved to sing when rocking Dak as a baby. She realized while dancing the transition for her son from being a teenager to an adult had been complete. He now was a mature man. She also realized she had just handed Dak off to Zenith. The transition from mother to girlfriend had been finalized. She knew Dak loved Zenith, and she loved him. She knew given time; she would grow to love Zenith. She and Veronica over the years had become friends when Veronica would come to her room and talk all afternoon about their day. She figured the three would become friends.

After the dance, Dak leaned over, "I love you, Mom." The group watching had stopped dancing and all watched the two dance. When the song ended the crowd cheered with Delores, Casey, and others crying happy tears. Vicky was intrigued by what had just transpired. She knew Zenith and Dak would be looking to build a small home for themselves. Wayne had offered to give them his apartment, and he would move into the small room at the church for a temporary period. Vicky stood back and watched the teenagers start dancing and having fun. She watched as Zenith and Dak laughed as they danced. She noticed Veronica talking to Aquarius and both were smiling. She looked and saw Samuel standing in the shadows of the barn with a stern look on his face staring directly at her. She thought, "That man never smiles."

She could feel the cold air, the cold wind as her body ached from the horse ride and the long day. She turned and walked into the common area in her building and up the stairs. She started the fire in the wood burning stove and turned on the bath water. She waited until the tub was full and the fire was burning hot. She undressed removing the layers of warm clothing and stepped into the hot bath water. She poured the liquid soap and liquid cream into the water and sat down. She slowly leaned back while allowing her body to adjust to the hot water. She thought about how happy her son appeared. She had never seen someone that happy. She glanced out the window noticing a full moon on a cold clear night and knew the party was over for the young kids and the older adults. She thought about raising Dak by herself. She knew she had a lot of help from her friends, but that part of her life was now over. She leaned back in the hot water and relaxed for the first time in several weeks. She slowly took the oil-based lotion and rubbed it on her legs and then she took her razor and shaved her legs while she considered her sexual needs. She had not dated anyone since her husband had been killed over twenty years ago. She wanted a man to hold her, keep her warm at night, but mostly she wanted men to quench her sexual needs. Her thoughts drifted back to her college days when she was eighteen and started dating. Her then boyfriend liked to set her up with other guys and watch her perform. He would coach her, and then he would make love to her after the other male had left. The sexual encounters had been exciting, and the anticipation leading up to the encounters were always difficult for her to control her sexual desires. Then, her boyfriend became her husband and a preacher. That way of life had become very addictive, and she fought her desires over the years. Now, she kept thinking about the swimming pool and all the men watching her in the yellow thong two piece. She smiled to herself as she remembered the males at the pool staring with pure hunger in their eyes as they watched her. She slowly placed her feet on the top of the tub spreading her legs, laying her head back and closing her eyes. She started inching her fingers down past her belly eager as she anticipated the climax, knowing she needed to release herself at least once.

The stern knock at her door startled her. She almost jumped out of the tub with surprise. She slipped her feet and legs back under the water and thought at first it would be Zenith and Dak. Then she thought they would stay out late and head back to The Dive with their friends. She stood and reached for the sheer thin cotton gown and pulled it over her head as she walked toward the door. She then thought it would be Veronica coming to sleep in Dak's old bed. She hurriedly walked to open the door.

She pulled the door open and looked up at the man standing in her hall. She tried not to be scared. She asked, "Are you here to assassinate me? What did you do, kill all my guards?" She knew she had no guards. Samuel turned his upper body and looked back down the hallway toward the empty stairs. He turned and faced Vicky and smiled, "I have not killed anyone yet. I did not see any guards. May I please have a word with you?"

Vicky could feel the cold air coming up the stairs and hallway as she stood in the doorway. A chill swept over her body. She was somewhat surprised at his request to talk with her, and he had not ordered her to listen. She stepped to the side and motioned for him to walk in. "Have a seat. I was about to pour myself a drink of blackberry wine. Can I get you a glass?"

"No thank you. I do not drink." He walked into the room and noticed the candle lights and one lantern. He scanned the room for danger. He noticed the two other doors closed and the window. He elected to sit facing the two closed doors.

"Well heck, Samuel from what I understand, you never have fun." She looked at him, "You know I insist you have this drink. It may help you." She poured both of them a drink and sat down on the small couch facing the wood burning stove next to him. She crossed her legs and hung her bare foot partially in front of him.

He looked at the glass and considered the drink. She took a drink of hers, "I insist." She watched him drink a small amount.

"Now was that so bad? Did the world end? It is okay for you to relax with a little self-indulgence."

He drank another drink and announced, "This is very good."

She smiled. "We have some very crafty people in our tribe. Some of them really like to have a good time. I love the blackberry wine the best. It is the sweetest. Here, I will get you another glass."

Vicky got up and walked over and placed the two glasses on the ledge. She bent over and opened the door to the wood burning stove and placed another log in the fire. Samuel watched and when she stood in front of the fire, he could not help but notice her nudeness under her pull over from the light of the fire. The material was see-through with the light of the fire glowing from behind her. He liked the view but tried not to stare. She poured another glass of wine for both. She sat down and this time he watched her cross her legs and noticed her bare foot with the red nail polish as his eyes shifted upward looking at her leg to her midthigh where the fabric parted. He noticed the smooth wet skin and the top buttons on the sheer cotton pull over were unbuttoned with the top portion of her breast visible. He noticed the drops of water pooled on her chest where the lotion had been rubbed into her skin. Her legs were glowing with a shine. They both took a drink. "So, you had something you wanted to talk to me about?"

He looked over and started to loosen his coat. "You may take it off if you like. I enjoy a warm room after being cold all day every day. We are now in the extreme north. Even on warm days, it is still cold. Some of my youth was spent in a very warm climate. I miss the warm weather. So, I guess with your winter clothing this seventy-eight-degree room is a little warm." He pulled his coat off and then his top shirt. She glanced at him as he laid them on the floor.

"So, you, a woman is the leader of this tribe?"

She raised her left eyebrow and took a sip of wine. "Yes. I am."

"That young man you were dancing with, I understand he is your son. Did you know there is a very large reward for him dead or alive?"

"Yes. I heard all about your city and your corrupt Senators. I believe he was forced into a trial by combat, and it took him eleven seconds to complete the combat part of the trial and took your Senators less than a minute to show they are corrupt. He spared the Blueblood warrior his life and should have been granted a pardon by your senate in reward for winning. Instead, he was arrested. They went back on their word." She took another sip of wine. "They were going to have him killed in the dungeon if Zenith had not broken him out." She took another sip of wine.

Samuel shifted the conversation quickly. "My horse is a stud. I was wanting to know if you knew your horse was in heat earlier today?"

She accidentally spit her wine out and laughed. She leaned forward touching his arm gently. She thought to herself about the expression on his face as he went flying backward in the air and hitting hard on the ground. His forehead had bumped into the back of his horse's head after it bucked him forward in his saddle and raised its head backward. She tried to stop laughing, "Lord have mercy, Samuel. Where are my manners." She kept trying to resist laughing as he watched her. "Yes. I received a message from the outpost, two Bluebloods were heading our way, and the one in charge was riding a white stud. I thought you could use a little humble pie. That was not what I thought you were going to ask me." She tried to stop laughing.

He glanced at her with a slight smile. "Why did you let me in your apartment? Are you not scared of me?"

"I know you are the general of the Blueblood Army and the greatest warrior on the planet. You have been credited with killing thousands in battles. You do not seem like the type of man who sneaks around and kills defenseless women while they are bathing. Should I now fear you?" She sipped her wine looking at him over the rim of her glass of wine. He smiled and did not answer.

He hesitated and then asked, "The boy Dak, he took down a competition champion Blueblood in our senate auditorium in front of a large contingent of on-lookers in a trial by combat." He looked Vicky in the eyes. "He has been genetically enhanced and well trained with a sword and martial arts."

"I taught him how to attack his opponent's knees." She thought back to her training in Karate years ago in Butler, Tennessee and her retired Army instructor. "All of us are trained to fight. We now know war is coming. We have isolated our tribe trying to protect ourselves from the B12 virus. Now, we realize we need allies to help us battle the approaching armies. You know, I was present in Germany and then in Russia and saw your colony. I was the one who suggested your group needed to be moved north away from the pending collapse of the world governments. When we realized the world as we knew it was not going to survive, we came here. We were lucky. We were somewhat prepared. We lost a lot of people and technology. We lost boats full of supplies in the ocean which we certainly could have used. We were all surprised to have lived through the Transition Period. The B12 Virus we discovered does not transfer from person to person as efficiently in the cold climates."

He looked at her, "and your son?"

"Genetic scoping of the chromosomes was being improved at different locations around the world. I carried Dak for nine months. His father was selected from a panel, and I was impregnated by a doctor in a lab. Some of the other kids here also were treated similarly. A man could supply the sperm, and the scientist could cleanse the male sperm and female egg and impregnate the mother. It was old technology which had been upgraded. In addition, the scientific breakthrough was a game changer. The human genes could be enhanced either by chemicals or by a process taking out the master genes and then shaving the master genes and then installing them back inside the body."

He listened and observed her as she talked. He was enchanted by her sex appeal and her looks. She was also very educated and intelligent. He could not help but be attracted to her. "So, you were there. How old are you?"

She smiled at him, "Well, I am not telling my age. I know you were developed to help, to have empathy, to follow orders, and to be loyal. I remember talking with the scientist. So, what happened? You Bluebloods took over." She looked at him. He had perspiration on his forehead. "I love the heat. After being cold all day, I enjoy coming into my room and warming up."

He glanced at her foot and nail polish and then her bare leg. "We also struggled during the Transition Period. Several of our people starved when the stored food started running short. When the earth's crust shifted, the land rose from the ocean depth and became deserts. There were barren mountains that just appeared, rising through the ice-covered tundra in the north and south poles. Some of the land masses around the world fell below the ocean levels and just disappeared. The ocean floors in other areas had been pushed upward in the middle of the new world creating deserts and barren land. I have traveled and seen some of the changes in our world." He hesitated and appeared to be considering his next statement with concern. "It is true. The first generation of Blueblood people were created with hopes of creating a superhuman race without the negative characteristics as defined by the creators. The science was not perfect. Some of us have more intellect, are stronger, quicker, have more empathy, are more loyal, and driven more to be successful than others produced in the same lab." He looked her in the eyes, "There were ten separate labs, and we are all different. Consequently, we all have our vices in addition to the preferred character traits as set forth by the creators. Some of us suffer from being prideful, envy of others, greed, gluttony, sloth, easy to anger, and have trouble with sexual lust." He looked away, "They made us stronger by providing our cells with additional amounts of testosterone produced in our adrenal cortex. We are constantly at war with ourselves and our lust for power and other desires." He turned and looked at Vicky.

Vicky reached down and pulled the cotton material down further covering her upper exposed thigh. She had heard the stories. No one had predicted the earth reforming during the Transition Period. Some of the survivors had blamed the earth's crust moving due to the nuclear Armageddon with the nuclear bombs exploding on the geographic fault lines. The good news had been with all the movement of the continents, the dust and dirt pushed into the atmosphere had been no worse than the sandstorms reported in America in the 1940's when the farmers in the Midwest had stripped the ground of all vegetation preparing to plant the ground the next year. The reports had indicated in the 1940's, the wind had picked up the soil and carried it eastward as far as the east coast, which created very little visibility, causing people to have to wear masks to breathe. She thought there was no reason to relive the days of Armageddon. Her tribe had survived and adapted the best they could while groups such as the Midlanders had reverted to only the strong could survive, and reports of cannibalism and horrible tales were not uncommon.

She smiled and very much desired to change the conversation. She was now concerned about being able to understand the Blueblood community. She had never considered the vices and the problems the negative characteristics could cause in dealing with these people. "I hate to say this, but you really stink. I guess you have not had a bath in three weeks?"

He smiled and finished his drink.

"I have a full tub of hot water. That was what I was doing when you knocked. You are welcome to use it."

To her surprise, he stood and walked over. "Yes, I do stink. I can smell myself. You know you stink really badly when you can smell yourself." He pulled his two other shirts off. Vicky noticed his broad shoulders and his muscled arms. He pulled his boots off with dirt falling from the inside of his boots to the floor and tugged his pant legs pulling off his top layer of pants and then removed his bottom layer of pants. He stood naked and removed his hair tie that held his long hair in place. He reached and noticed the water was still warm. He looked at Vicky. "How is this water hot?"

"We are over a hot spring. There are several in the area." She stood, which provided her an excuse not to stare and walked to the wine bottle.

He turned and watched her. "May I have another glass?"

Vicky had heard the first-generation Bluebloods would all bathe together. She had been told prior to the Transition Period they were genetically engineered not to have any sexual deviations or impurities. Delores and Mia had told her what their kids had mentioned about Zenith walking around inside The Dive in the nude before Dak explained to her that was not normal. Delores and Mia were laughing so hard they could not control their laughter. Trey had turned over in a chair when he saw Zenith walking naked in the hall. Tommy Boy had told his father he had never seen someone so pretty without any clothes on, and Billy Ray had asked him how many naked girls he had seen prior to seeing Zenith. The two women could not stop laughing.

Vicky knew it was not unusual for Bluebloods to be naked in front of their family members. She tried not to notice and acted like his nudity was normal. She also knew this was the general of the Blueblood Army, and her tribe needed their help. She noticed as he stepped into the tub, he was very buff. His six-foot-five-inch frame did not fit in the tub like her five-foot-four-inch body. He was forced to sit erect in the small tub. She walked over and handed him his glass of wine.

She pointed, "The soap and hair wash are sitting on the floor on the other side of the tub. He reached over the side of the tub with her watching his nudity. She walked to the far side of the tub and pulled a towel from the shelf. She had not realized when she walked in front of the window in the moonlight, he could see through her sheer pull over. She noticed he watched her as she stood in front of the window and the moonlight folding the towel. "We have geothermal heating in pipes underground which heats the water and our rooms. The hot springs in the area are a blessing. I also like the wood burning stove to make it warm when I take a bath and sleep." She noticed he finished his drink. "Let me get you another glass. I will wash your clothes and hang them up in front of the fire. I am not certain which smells worse, you or your clothes."

"Only if you have one also. I do not want to drink by myself."

He could not take his eyes off her. He felt his body growing stiff as he watched her walk in front of the fire with the doors open to the wood burning stove. She was beautiful with the perfect lips and smile, but he could not help but be attracted to her confidence and intelligence. She was in charge of all these men and her tribe. He again could see through her sheer pull over. He tried to fight his sexual urges but could not control his desires.

She filled his glass to the top and gave herself a small serving. She wanted to keep her wits in dealing with the general. She walked over to him and bent forward, handing him his glass of wine. He noticed her chest cleavage as he reached for the glass looking at her breasts with just the top of her pull over covering her body. He immediately drank some wine and watched her pick up his clothing and start submerging them in the large bucket and then hanging them up one at a time near the wood stove. He washed himself and then stood and reached his now empty glass and set it on the table. She noticed his demeanor had changed. He seemed friendlier. He was hard with no body fat and had several scars from arrows and swords. She had completed washing his clothes and sat on the couch. She then opened another bottle of wine and poured him a drink. She watched him dry off. He then came and sat on the couch with a towel around his waist next to her and drank his wine. She could tell he was aroused, and he was trying to hide himself under the towel.

"Your clothes will be dry soon hanging by the hot fire." She sensed he was in a hurry as he walked over and placed his underwear and his other clothes on. He picked his shirt and coat up and said, "Thanks for the drinks, washing my clothing, and the use of your tub. I will see you tomorrow. I must go at once."

"What are you doing?"

"I am getting dressed and thanking you for your hospitality."

She stood up and looked into his eyes. "I mean, what is your mission? I must know. My people, my family, my friends are counting on me to make the right decisions. You must tell me why two Bluebloods came all the way to Cliff Tops. When we sent an envoy to meet your Blueblood Senate, he was imprisoned and almost killed. How should we treat you? Should we throw you in a prison cell for four days?" She clenched her jaws. "That was my son."

He paused and looked at her in her thin pull over and long hair hanging down over her shoulders. He was internally fighting his sexual desires, which were hard to control. He had never felt this surge inside his body. He wanted to grab and kiss her. He knew he needed to leave as soon as possible. He looked at the door as he talked. "We were not meant to survive the trip. I discovered the monitor to detect radiation had been tampered with. I had hidden a second one in my saddle bag and used it, but we had no way to recharge the battery. Once I was able to locate the trail your riders took, we followed it. I pushed Aquarius hard to reach you. Time was not on our side. I must now go and rest."

"What about Aquarius? You two do not seem to be friends."

"We are not friends." He looked at Vicky like he wanted to say more. "Aquarius is a good man. I believe in him. He needs to stay here with your tribe and his daughter. This is where he belongs. When I am ready in a few days, I will return to Merlin. I will report both have been eliminated. Now I must go."

"Why should he stay, and you return? What are you not telling me?"

He walked toward the door. He turned, "Thanks again for your hospitality. I have my duty, and my duty is to return to my command."

"Your horse won't be ready to leave for a couple of days. We are using him." She looked into his eyes. "We have several mares in heat."

He smiled and walked out, closing the door behind him. He walked swiftly down the stairs and out the front door and into the cold air in the middle of the empty compound. He removed his coat and allowed the coldness to cool his body as he noticed the stars, the moon, and the smell of the fragrance of honeysuckle on his damp clothing. He turned and looked at her window and realized he had just had an enchanting moment with a beautiful lady. He reflected on the woman he had just talked with and knew she was the most beautiful woman he had ever met. She was truly special.

Chapter 43

Wayne poured himself another cup of coffee. "They are going to try and set the barriers today. They've cut the end of the large I-beams sharp and have the foundation reinforced. We can only hope it works. There is no way to test it. In World War II, the German army built smaller types of structures to keep the Allies from landing with larger ships on some of the beaches before D-Day. The engineers know the depth of the bedrock is eleven feet under the sand and the I-beam will not break with the impact of a ship."

Vicky looked over at Billy Ray. "How many steel tipped arrows do we have?"

"We've made over ten thousand tips. The workers are placing them on the shafts. They have also made extra spears. Everyone has a sword. We have been training nonstop for ten days. We just need more men. We need more workers and warriors. I do believe our people will fight. We are just so outnumbered."

Little Jimmy looked at the rest of his friends sitting at the table. "What about the two Blueblood warriors?"

"I have not told them about King Solman being a Blueblood and that he is working with Senator Dale." She looked at her council, "I just do not know what they would do. Anyone who knows this information could be killed. There is no way Senator Dale could afford for anyone to know King Solman and himself are conspiring. He will order the entire Blueblood Army including the regular standing army to attack us if he finds out we know or even if he suspects we know. That is why Ivan kept this information a secret, but now they will know the hidden path to reach us. Our world is getting smaller with the hidden passage from our city to the City of Merlin."

Delores looked up, "What about Samuel? Do you not need to tell him? He is the general of the army. We will at some time have to face him and his army on the battlefield."

Vicky said, "If he knows, he is part of the cover up, and if he finds out, he will be killed. The information is toxic. He came to my chambers last night and told me he suspects someone in Merlin is trying to kill him. He told me his radiation detector was sabotaged before he left Merlin. He had a second one hidden and before the batteries died, he and Aquarius located the trail made by our riders. His detector is not like ours where we can recharge in the rivers. He will head back in a couple of days to Merlin by himself. He will report Aquarius, Dak, and Zenith all have been eliminated."

Wayne looked surprised, "He came to your chambers?"

"Yes. I asked him about his mission. He did not seem to know about King Solman. He is a soldier, and it appears to me he follows the orders provided by the Blueblood Senate."

Wayne wanted to change the subject and address another topic before the meeting was over. He seemed irate but interjected, "There are a few that believe we should sign a treaty with King Solman before the next battle."

Billy Ray snarled in anger and hit the wall with his hand.

Vicky said, "The definition of being an idiot is to know someone is lying to you and then believe them anyway. Take Hershel to our villages and force him to tell the people what happened to his tribe." She looked at the group. "If they want to leave, let them leave on the next boat or allow them south to the New York tribe, but if they stay, they will fight. We will all fight."

***

Vicky saddled her horse for the mid-morning ride and started to lead it out of the stables. She heard the voice behind her. "Where are you riding? Do you mind if I ride along with you?"

Vicky was somewhat surprised she had not heard Samuel approach. "Certainly. I am just going for a ride along the mountain overlooking the ocean and then cut back into the wilderness before I reach the deep snow line. It is a beautiful fall day, and winter is coming. The opportunities to ride will be few unless one waits until spring."

They rode for a couple of miles north on the ridge through the large hemlock forest. The area was beautiful with a small amount of snow on the ground, with the green forest and the view overlooking the ocean. Vicky had been a little preoccupied and frustrated with her tribe's situation and their options. She figured a ride would help her relax. She wanted to be hospitable, and she was not certain what they had in common. She finally asked, "So, what do you think of our defenses?"

"You need professional soldiers who are better disciplined. The fighting men need to be pushed harder and taught there will be punishment for failure in practice. The attack will come next spring when the weather is more suitable in the ocean. If they wait until the spring, it will reduce their casualties. Your army is not getting stronger. There is no need for them to attack this winter."

"We have a trade ship from the south which brings us news about every three months. We anticipate over ten thousand Normand soldiers who have been trained to kill and hardened by all of the slaughtering of innocent people, will arrive by ship. We do not trust our neighbors to our south to close the tunnel on the Continental Trail to keep the Normand Army from approaching from the south. I believe they will also hit us from the north. The north is a frozen tundra, but they will figure out how to sneak a small band of soldiers to simultaneously attack from our north. That is what I would do."

Samuel looked at Vicky. "I have watched your soldiers in training. I watched as the barrier was being placed in the sea blocking the passage inside your jetty. That is a great idea. It will stop one or two larger boats. Then, they will realize how to defeat the barrier. They will drop rowboat after rowboat with soldiers or just run their large ships during high tide into the outward wall of the jetty and unload large numbers of soldiers. You will have to fight them from the jetty, and once they break through your defense line on the jetty, your soldiers will be cut off from a possible retreat. They will be killed or forced to surrender and then decapitated while you, from the top of the cliffs, are forced to watch. They will attack you from the frozen north tundra and scale the cliff walls. Some of your soldiers are very good, but you don't have enough. You need to sink their ships at sea. You need bigger catapults to hit them further out as they approach the jetty. The cold ocean will do the rest. They will also attack the New York tribe. There is no need to conquer one without the other."

She felt her anger spike, then, she felt frustrated. He was very direct and precise with the details of the pending attack. She glanced over at him as he looked ahead. She already understood these facts. She also understood they could not hold out under an extended siege. They had very little chance to survive. She loved her tribe and her friends. They had struggled to live through the Armageddon from the old world, and now they were going to be killed defending their homes. The tribe had planned to live out their lives in isolation. They had never been involved with the world governments or concerned with building rapport with possible allies. Cliff Tops was a remote location positioned at the top of a cliff with the sea to the east, frozen tundra to the north, nuclear waste pits to the west and one neighbor to the south with a large gorge separating the two. The location provided a certain amount of natural security from attacking armies.

Samuel added, "The attraction to the location is the natural resources, and the jetty provides a natural dock and protects the larger boats in the calm waters near the beach at the bottom of the cliff. The mountains provided timber resources and coal is the hidden resource. I saw the pile of coal next to the black smith building. The natural resources are plentiful, and the desiring armies of the south are after the resources."

Her feelings had changed again and now she was upset and aggravated with his observations, "You better hurry and leave before you get trapped here. I cannot protect you. I would not want you to get injured while we all die in battle." She kicked her horse which ran ahead.

He was surprised with her actions and punched his horse racing after her. They rode across a meadow and into a forest, into the hills and down the hills through another forest. Every time he got close, Vicky would punch her horse and head in a different direction. Samuel finally caught up with her and reached over and grabbed the horse bridle pulling her horse to a stop. "What was that all about? You could have been thrown from your horse. That was reckless."

Vicky reached and pulled her bridle free and goosed her horse in the sides. She headed west at a full run. Samuel kicked his horse and took off after her. They rode close to two miles through all types of terrain. He finally caught up with her. "Will you please stop?"

"No. I won't stop." He reached over and grabbed her by her arm as she started to ride off again. He pulled her off her horse with her landing on her feet. The horses were tired, and when Samuel jumped off his horse and faced Vicky, the two horses galloped off into the field. She clenched her jaws. "How dare you touch me."

"Listen. You asked me my opinion, and I told you. What you are doing now is suicide. Your tribe is going to need you, and you falling from a running horse is not going to help."

"I want to be left alone, and I do not want you to touch me."

He looked at her angry expression. He thought of her beautiful body, and he was attracted to her. "Look, I will go retrieve the horses. Please do not run off."

She waited and watched. He led the two horses back to her spot. He tied the horses up and asked, "What was that all about?"

She had settled her rage. "Samuel, you cannot understand. This is not your fight. I sent my son to Merlin to recruit an army. I found out the Blueblood army is my enemy and now I am standing in the middle of a cold wilderness with you, the general over that Army. I now know I will have to face you on the battlefield at some point." She stared into his eyes.

"What are you talking about? I have no order to face you on the battlefield. I am going back to Merlin and tell the Senate, Aquarius, Dak, and Zenith are dead, so they can remain, and no bounty hunters will be sent after them. There is no threat against your tribe from my City of Merlin. The Blueblood Army is not going to be ordered to march east."

Vicky had a tear in her eye, and it rolled down her cheek. She knew she could not defend herself in the middle of the northern wilderness against a male Blueblood. He had to know what was happening with the Blueblood Senate. He had been assigned to locate and exterminate Ivan Chezon and his associates. Lucky for Ivan, he was able to stay hidden. She glanced at his sword and then his knife on his other side. She could see the handle of the second knife strapped to his upper back where he could reach it over his shoulder. She knew he was a complete warrior and a killer. "Why would you leave Zenith and Dak? Why do that for those two? When you first saw Zenith, you wanted to arrest her, and you're not friends with Aquarius."

"Sometimes a soldier must look the other way. Command does not need to know. They are not a threat against my people. You are not a threat against the City of Merlin. We have no reason to cross the waste lands and fight your tribe."

She looked him in the eyes and blurted out, "I do not believe you." She hesitated. "King Solman is a Blueblood warrior. He is one of you. He is working with your Blueblood Senate to take over the world. We have captured some of his slaves which were forced to fight in King Solman's army. King Solman sends the men off to battle and holds the wives and children hostages, forcing the men to die in battle. If they die with honor, the children and wives are provided for, but if they die without honor, the females and children are used as prostitutes for the armies. There is no mercy, only death and misery. You are a general in the Blueblood Army. How could you not know?"

Samuel did not seem surprised with the news about King Solman being a Blueblood. Vicky had observed him closely trying to judge his body language and expression. He stared at her without blinking.

He reached over and removed the teardrop from her cheek.

She was surprised by his gentle gesture, "My tribe, my people, my family, and friends are all going to be slaughtered. They are counting on me." She kept staring into his eyes without backing down. "It will be just a matter of time before your Senate gives you the order to kill me. You might as well go ahead and be proactive. Pull your knife and cut my head off. Take my head and present it to them as a trophy, but I beg you leave my son and Zenith alone."

He thought about the little girl when he first walked into the camp and how sweet she was offering him water. He looked into Vicky's eyes, and his heart sang seeing her tears. "They will not be slaughtered if I have anything to say about it. I can help. I have never met anyone as beautiful and as appealing as you. I will fight for you."

"Why would you help us? You do not look surprised about King Solman being a Blueblood. Did you know your Senator

Dale is also a Blueblood, but not one like you? They both are renegade Bluebloods."

"He looked to the side, breaking eye contact and answered, "I suspected Senator Dale was from an outside lab."

"What about your wife and family in Merlin? How can you protect them and help us at the same time?"

He somberly said, "My wife was killed eight years ago. I never had a child. We never emotionally bonded. It was an arranged marriage. I have not remarried."

Vicky looked up trying to hold back her tears. "I am sorry to hear about your wife."

"I talked with Wayne. He explained you were present when your husband was assassinated. I was sorry to hear about your loss." He pulled her into his chest and hugged her while she cried. He gently lifted her chin and looked into her tearing eyes. He slowly leaned over and kissed her. The kiss extended with him bending over her, holding her tight for several minutes.

Chapter 44

The large guard yawned and watched the traders walk through the gate. The old trader did not attempt eye contact when he handed the guard a gold nugget to ensure he could pass and not be ordered back through the tunnel. The guard saw no threat from the older man and waved his hand for him to pass as he pulled his small cart. He yawned again. The next traders were a group of four younger looking men pulling a covered cart. The one trader walked to the bars of the fence and likewise handed the guard a gold nugget. The guard yawned again. He looked at each man with a questionable expression. He knew he had been trained not to allow anyone through the gate unless they had a product the New York Tribe needed. The tribe craved certain items, but they desperately needed food, steel, and leather more than other items. He motioned for them to pull down their masks. Everyone from the south wore a mask to prevent contracting the deadly B12 virus. No outbreaks had been observed in the New York Tribe or with the traders moving north in over a year. The guards had kept a watchful eye for the signs of the traders having the B12 virus. The easiest symptom to spot the deadly virus was coughing. In the early stages before the infected person was contagious, the person would be forced to cough. He hesitated and looked at his gold nugget. The guard did not recognize the four men. The guard hesitated. The leader smiled and handed the guard a second nugget. He thought about getting up from his chair and inspecting the cart, which he had been trained to do. After seeing hundreds of carts just like this one, he did not see the need. Besides, the time to look through the cart would hold up the traders waiting in line. He noticed while glancing into the tunnel the next people in line were three young ladies. He was impatient to look at them closer. He was ambitious to see what they were trading. The sooner the better. He could see the cow hides on top of the cart, which would be used to make leather clothing. His gate had been set up for only traders with carts and animals. They would return heading south after a few days of trading through the other gate. He recognized most traders as they crossed through the tunnel weekly, and he had not bothered to search their carts. If refugees came to his gate, he would either turn them away or order the other guards to handle them. Some would be allowed to stay and work, and others were sent back to the southern tribes. He liked working the gate. He made a good living taking gold under the table. He motioned for the four men to walk through. While sitting in his chair, he hit the latch with his foot and opened the first gate. The gate would automatically swing close from the pressure of the hinge once the person and the cart cleared the entrance and then he would motion for the other guard to open the second gate about ten yards further ahead for them to enter the New York territory.

The large guard yawned again, and he smiled this time as three women approached. He had seen them standing and waiting their turn when they were seventh in line. The one in front smiled. She handed him a small gold earring through the iron fence window and winked at him. She spread her large fur robe open revealing she was carrying only a small sword on her left hip. She also was displaying to the guard what he wanted to see, that being her firm young-looking body in her tight-fitting leather jumpsuit. He allowed his eyes to drift down her body checking her out as she held her robe open for display. He then glanced at the other two young women. He smiled again as they opened their robes. He noticed they were also carrying swords which was not uncommon. It was about lunch time, and he thought he might make more today than any other day of working the gate. He knew where the three women were headed, and he thought he would meet them when he got off work. The first lady said, "Maybe I can earn my gold earring back after you get off work." He smiled at the other two women and knew the females did not have a product to sale, but he knew the service they would provide. He also knew he would bend the rules for the victimless crime which they offered. He motioned the three females through the first gate and then motioned the second guard to open the second gate.

The iron gates were located at the north end of the tunnel with a one-inch iron bar fence welded together and anchored with drilled spikes and brackets into the rock cave floor, walls, and ceiling. The people would lead their animals and walk close to five-hundred-yards underground to cross under the nuclear waste area located above the cave. The large mountain above, shielded the radiation from above. The Continental Trail had been a great discovery to link the New York Tribe to the south region and the southern tribes. The commercial trading and selling of goods had helped all the people. Gold was established worldwide as the measurement of trade.

She walked out of the tunnel and through the gate. Once she and her two partners cleared the gates, she noticed the older man had walked near the other guard post. The four young men were walking slowly as they progressed toward the north road and the guard house. She turned, smiled, and walked back toward the big guard as her two friends smiled at the second guard and approached him.

The large guard stayed in his chair and smiled at her approach. He could not help but be excited, and he anticipated an opportunity for a date. Sexual favors were always welcomed. He knew he would spend his gold tonight with these women. As she straddled his lap placing her left hand around his head, the short blade knife caught him in the throat as she kept eye contact and pulled the knife from the liner of her left sleeve with her right hand and sliced his aorta and windpipe. He saw her sword on her left hip when she lifted her robe. He never saw the small, concealed knife, and he instantly reached for his neck and started making a rasping noise. She then stood and pushed him backward, turning him over in his chair as she hit the lever for the gates to open. She wedged the chair down onto the lever to make certain the gate was forced open and the spring in the hinge would not close the gate.

The second guard did not have time to prepare for the blade hitting him in the upper arm as the female close to him had pulled her sword and swung it with great force. As he was falling, he looked at the first guard bleeding from his neck lying on the ground and grunted, "You fool. You just killed both of us."

The old man turned and threw a knife and hit the guard in front of the guard post center chest. The knife sank all the way to the hilt with the guard's eyes rolling back into his skull as he fell dead.

The four men pulled their swords from under the cart and ran toward the guard standing in front of the second guard house. The New York guard yelled with urgency in his voice,

"Sound the alarm and close the gate." as the sword cut him across his chest.

Chapter 45

The men walked over to the lunch table. Billy Ray announced, "We set three huge barriers today. We did more than I thought possible."

Tommy Boy smiled, "Holding that rope and then lowering the heavy steel beams has tuckered me out. I am starving to death."

Trey smiled, "You make it sound like you did it all by yourself. I have news for you, I was on the end of the rope doing most of the heavy lifting. Me and my horse."

Wayne thought about the group of young men and Veronica. They had always worked hard without any reservation about working a task until completion. He smiled, "Yeah, we could not have done it without your muscles. I was tired just watching. We will be able to allow Captain J.J. to enter the landing without damaging his boat. Everything works perfectly."

Eric of Newport said as the food was being carried to the table. "I was doing my best to be the manager of this job. I am not tired at all." The group laughed and started eating.

Little Jimmy had not been talking much. He knew Vicky had gone on a horse ride with Samuel. He worried about Vicky. He had no trust for the Blueblood government, and Samuel was the general of the army. He glanced up, "Look at the pigeon flying into the loft. He turned to Mia and yelled. "Mia, can you or Delores bring us the message on the carrier pigeon?"

The men kept eating as the talking and joking died down while everyone ate. Mia ran out the door of the barn and approached the table holding the note. "King Solman has attacked the New York Tribe. They have broken through the tunnel on the Continental Trail. They are pleading for our help."

Wayne jumped up and yelled, "Sound the alarm. Everyone to battle stations."

Little Jimmy yelled, "We need to go to the gorge gate. Get your swords." They all ran toward their rooms to get their equipment and protective clothing.

Billy Ray yelled at the stable guy. "Saddle the horses. Everyone, prepare for battle."

Chapter 46

Zorro ridden into the fray with his thirty best warriors. Over a hundred of his soldiers had already met the Normand Army and were fighting in the open area outside the gate entrance. He yelled, "We have to close that damn gate." He headed for the gate and his men were confronted by arrows and swordsmen. The horses and riders were shot with multiple arrows, and he and his men ended up in the middle of the compound fighting with swords on foot. At that point, they could not run, and they could not push forward to the gate. They could only fight to the death.

Men from the south kept pushing through the tunnel entering through the narrow entry and the two open gates. Additional men from the New York tribe kept entering the battle with arrows firing into the middle of the compound hitting both the enemy and their comrades. The bodies were lying all over the ground as the battle proceeded with wounded men and women fighting to the death.

***

Billy Ray looked at the bridge. He then looked at his two sons and their friends. He looked at Zenith and Aquarius. He said, "We need to stop the advancement on that side of the gorge. We cannot allow the New York tribe to lose this battle."

"I agree. Follow me." Dak yelled at the people fleeing from the New York tribe to clear the bridge. "We are coming over."

The group rode hard for close to half an hour. They passed several families heading north away from the battle.

Aquarius had been the last to cross over the gorge and pass through the narrow gate located in the middle of the bridge. He wanted to catch up with his daughter. He could remember his earlier years fighting the bandits and gangs in and around Merlin. He knew the younger Blueblood soldiers were fearless and some would be overconfident in their abilities and end up getting killed taking on too many warriors. He wanted to tell Zenith this was not their fight. He wanted her protected. He tried to catch her to tell her to stand down. His horse could not catch her. She was at the front several hundred yards ahead.

Dak was first to reach the compound. "Follow me. I am going to close that outer gate." Dak headed for the north side of the fighting and then once he circled behind the fighting he commanded, "We need to take out those archers." He jumped off his horse and pulled his bow. His five friends rode in behind the Normand archers and each jumped off their horses. They stood in a line and fired four arrows each killing the Normand archers. They then proceeded to the gate. They ran into the mayhem with their swords cutting the enemy in their path. They had not hesitated, and the Normand soldiers had not met an opponent who fought as a team and was so fierce. The group was lethal as they would team up on a soldier, kill him and then move forward to the next and then the next.

Aquarius knew he wanted to protect his daughter. He yelled at Zenith to attack from the fringes. He knew once in the middle of the fighting her horse would stall, and she would be a sitting target. He followed her with her leaning over her saddle hitting King Solman's men one after the other. Aquarius leaned over his saddle and did the same. They cut a trail around to the rear with Eric of Newport, and Wayne shooting arrow after arrow into the soldiers. Billy Ray and Little Jimmy headed for the gate entrance trying to catch up with Dak, Veronica, Hulk, Trey, Tommy Boy and Robin Hood.

At first, there was a stalemate with the large number of Normand soldiers, but Dak was able to slice through one soldier after another. Hulk and Trey followed up on both sides. Little Jimmy and Billy Ray fought the Normand soldiers in a frontal assault and ended in the middle of the compound and then realized they had been cut off from the gate. They could not forge through the carnage and fighting warriors. The ground was stacked up with bodies falling constantly in battle.

Dak jumped over the last soldier at the gate after cutting him nearly in half and pushed his dead body back across the threshold of the gate entrance. The man landed in the tunnel. Dak pulled his bow and fired his arrow into the face of a charging soldier from the tunnel. He dropped his bow and blocked several arrows with his shield all coming from inside the tunnel. He closed the gate, locking it. He yelled for Hulk to help him with the gas ball. "We must ignite this smoke bomb. Trey and Tommy Boy, you need to protect our backs from the Normand soldiers already inside the New York Territory." He pointed for Veronica and Robin Hood to fire arrows through the iron fence into the dark tunnel to stop the forward movement of the Normand soldiers. "I need a few seconds to ignite the gas bomb and roll it into the tunnel." Dak had helped Wayne deliver the oil bomb two years ago and knew the oil bomb was sitting at the edge of the gate and was engineered to burn while inside the tunnel producing smoke and stopping any advancement of soldiers from the other end.

Wayne had explained the need for the oil bomb to Zorro and had engineered it. The bomb was made of alcohol and seal oil-soaked leather strips rolled tight around a cowhide ball held together with four-inch leather bands with small chunks of coal placed under the strips of cowhide. The fuse would ignite the alcohol and slowly burn the coal producing an abundance of smoke. The cowhide would burn, and the leather bands would smolder which would hold the ball compressed together and the coal produce a toxic smoke inside the tunnel.

Chapter 47

The couple walked holding hands for close to an hour while leading their horses. Samuel was interested in hearing about Vicky's life story. She looked at him as they stopped walking. "I am not what I seem. I never confessed to my prior husband until right before he died. Samuel, you do not want to fall in love with me. I am not worthy of your love. In my prior life, I worked for the Central Intelligence Agency (CIA) as an assassin. My team would hunt and kill individuals in the worldwide human slave industry. I was a sword of justice for the ones who could not protect themselves. One Catholic priest compared me to one of our Lord's Avenging Angels. I have killed, and I never felt ashamed. Matter of fact, I would thank the Lord for giving me the fortitude to carry out his work providing lethal justice."

"I love you. You will be my Queen." He looked at her in her boots and tight-fitting pants with her tight-fitting blazer trimmed in fur around her neck. Her hair was pulled back in a ponytail. He noticed her curved body and beautiful smile. "I am in love with you. Will you have me?"

She blinked her eyes from his surprised response. She was trying to make him understand she blamed herself for her husband's death. She lived with guilt. "You were correct with your assessment of the tribe's ability to wage war. These people are my family and friends. We have some very educated middle-aged and older people in the tribe. They were not accustomed to working with their hands. I had to finally tell them they were either going to have to learn to hunt, fish or discover a trade where they could assist the tribe, otherwise the tribe did not need them." She smiled, "That is why we have all the picnic tables and wood burning stoves. They were made and forged by one man with his doctorate in sociology and one with his Ph D in psychiatry. Once they started working with their hands, they discovered they liked the manual labor. We had to accommodate them by making certain types of bolts for the tables and other concessions for the wood stoves, but it all worked out. As far as pushing these types of people into being soldiers, that is not going to work. I thought once we survived the Armageddon event and the earth seemed to be cleansed, we could live in peace. I never dreamed we would need to fight other people to survive. The history of humanity has always been one of extreme violence. Cain killed Abel. My deceased husband was a preacher, and he would say the Bible was the most violent book he had ever read. The Bible does a great job of not only teaching about our Lord, but also the Bible depicts our history four thousand years ago."

"It is you who should not accept me. I have done unthinkable things." He told Vicky how his wife had died trying to help an orphan when she was cut down by a Midlander east of Merlin. He had arrived too late to help. He thought about his wife, looking back in time remembering how he held her as she died. "The Midlanders were trying to drink her blood with her injured lying on the ground. With her last breath, she had asked me to live with grace and those were her last words. I instead rode after the dozen Midlanders to seek my revenge, killing every single one of them, even the kids." He looked at Vicky, "I bare my sins to you. I killed the Midlanders in a state of hatred and revenge and that hatred has fueled me and now has made me, over time, feel worse. My dying wife asked me to live with grace and courage, to use my wisdom to change the things I could and accept the rest. My late wife would not have wanted me to have done what I have. The orphan had been abandoned from his tribe and the Midlanders had attacked. She tried to protect the innocent and was killed when she did not run. She decided to fight against overwhelming numbers. Now, I am willing to be your servant, if you will accept me."

She looked down as they walked. She could tell this man meant everything he was saying, but she knew for her, romantic love took time. "I am sorry about your loss. Your wife sounds like the type of person I inspire to be." They walked in silence for a couple hundred feet with Samuel reaching over and holding Vicky's gloved hand as they walked. He turned to her and looked at her. He pulled her against his body and stared into her eyes. "I am truly sorry for all I have done. I have followed my orders and now I stand here with you. I have fallen in love with you." He kissed her.

Vicky liked this man. He appeared humble and loving and not the killer he had been portrayed as being. She loved his kiss. However, she broke off the kiss and smiled looking into his eyes. "We just met. I do not want to be one of your many concubines."

"I have no concubines. I have never met anyone as beautiful and as confident as you. You are brave and intelligent. My wanting to kiss you is real. I know how I feel. I really care for you. I could not sleep after we talked in your apartment. I could only think of you."

She jerked her head around. "Listen. I thought I heard the high pitch sound of the alarm." The high-pitch whistle sound meant only one thing. She stopped staring into his eyes and pulled her hand from his, placing it on her cross and started rubbing the cross hanging around her neck. She asked Samuel, "Did you hear the whistle?" She suddenly looked over at him and quickly mounted her horse. "We are under attack."

Samuel jumped on his horse and followed. They rode swiftly, and Vicky ran her horse into the main area of Cliff Tops. She jumped off her horse, and the small boy reached and held her horse in place as she ran into her apartment building. Samuel dismounted and noticed the entire village streets were empty. He noticed men at the top of the cliffs looking over the ocean watching for ships and older men pulling wagons and other equipment into the street blocking off the passage. Vicky ran out wearing her protective padded vest. She had a bow over her head hanging down to her side. She had placed a strap with a knife around her lower leg on the opposite side of her sword. Vicky looked at Samuel, "The Normand army has breached the tunnel entrance on the Continental Trail located in the New York territory. We should have set our defenses at the gorge. This is not your fight." She took off on her horse headed for the gorge. Samuel followed.

When Vicky reached the gorge, she noticed her men arguing with people on the other side of the gorge wanting to cross the bridge. She demanded, "Where is Billy Ray and Little Jimmy?"

She looked around and noticed most of her soldiers were stationed behind the barriers on her side of the gorge and prepared to fight anyone trying to cross the bridge. They were also spread out in both directions at observation stations watching the gorge as it extended through the bottom of the valley. There were already some families that had crossed the bridge and were waiting to head toward Cliff Tops. The gorge was located between two large cliffs with a narrow path on the New York side leading to the bridge which provided access from the New York tribe territory to the Cliff Tops territory. Once one crossed the bridge from the New York Tribe territory, the area opened into a clear area and a path ascended a few yards over an embankment. The distance from the bridge was close to fours mile to the Cliff Tops community.

Her soldier in charge yelled. "They told us to hold the bridge and then they went to assist Zorro. At the first sign of the Normand army, we were instructed to burn the bridge. They have been gone for two hours. What are your orders?"

Vicky noticed the families on the other side of the gorge fleeing the battle. They were backed up on the narrow path. She knew Billy Ray and her other men could not get through the large number of people and wagons if they returned. The fleeing families would be in their way blocking the passage. She commanded, "Open the gate and allow them through. We need them out of the way for our soldiers to be able to cross the bridge if they retreat."

"Yes." He yelled, "Open the gate. Search everyone coming across."

Vicky thought about Dak and his friends. She had told Little Jimmy and Billy Ray no matter what, they had to hold this gate here at the gorge. She looked at her gate commander as his troopers were watching the people come across. "Have you heard any word about the advancement of the Normand army?"

She heard Samuel yell, "Watch out," and heard his horse head her way. She turned to look at him as the arrow hit her in the back. She slumped over as the second arrow hit her in the thigh. She kicked her horse to turn away from the archers. She felt the impact and the sharp pain. The arrows struck with such force, she felt she had been hit by a hammer. She never saw either shooter. The instant pain caused her to be nauseated, and she leaned over on the horse's neck and held to the mane.

Samuel ran his horse toward the first shooter blocking two arrows with his sword. The shooter realized his arrows had failed, and he turned to run up the embankment. As Samuel approached, he reached over and cut the shooter's head off. He immediately turned his horse to face the second archer and yelled to get her to safety as he headed for the other shooter. The other shooter had likewise shot two arrows, and Samuel blocked both arrows as he approached. Samuel ran his horse over the shooter as he tried to run, knocking him to the ground. Samuel jumped off his horse and hit the shooter in the head with the grip of his sword, knocking him out. He quickly looked around for additional threats. He then pulled back the face mask and grimaced at the foreign assassin. He looked at the men fast approaching and yelled for them to close the gate and search everyone. "Be on the lookout for additional assassins. Make everyone remove their mask. These men are Persian assassins from the Pacific Continent."

He then looked at the commander and yelled for two of the soldiers to take the assassin as a prisoner for interrogation. "Tie him up and take him back to Cliff Tops. Do not allow him out of your sight. He will need to be interrogated." He ran over to Vicky who was slumped over in her saddle. He saw the arrow sticking into her shoulder and leg. She grimaced, "I need a doctor." She turned and headed to Cliff Tops. Samuel ran and jumped on his horse and turned the horse spurred the sides and took off at a run to catch up with her.

As they ran into the main street by the blockade, he yelled, "We need the doctor." He pulled her off the horse and carried her into the fourplex and laid her on the kitchen table. Casey and Mia ran over with clean rags and water. Samuel cut away the vest, two other garments and the silk undershirt and noticed the silk had not ripped or been torn. The arrowhead had pushed the silk into her body. The silk had kept pressure on the wound area and helped control the bleeding. He cut off the arrow sticking out of her back and then grabbed the remaining end and pulled the arrow out and then gently pulled the silk material out of the wound. He studied the arrowhead and stem and then threw it on the floor.

Delores watched and noted the puncture wound. She felt relieved the arrows did not appear to be life threatening. She announced the silk shirt worked. Samuel looked at her understanding now why she had on silk. Delores reached for the clean wet cloth from Casey and with pressure pushed the rag onto the wound in her upper back. "The great Genghis Khan and his soldiers took over the world in 1100 A.D. with his soldiers wearing silk to protect wounds from arrows. The arrows would not tear through the fabric, and this helped in removing the arrows and protected the soldiers. The silk garment would be held in place by the arrow and the pressure helped control the bleeding."

Samuel looked at Delores, "She has been hit by poison arrows. They are very deadly." He set Vicky up and held her in place. He pulled her vest off and then her long sleeve jacket and then her seal-lined shirt off her other arm. He placed the clean rags over the puncture and told Delores to hold the rag in place tight with pressure. He yelled for Mia to bring him the alcohol. He commanded, "Pour it on the wound. The arrows are tipped with a poison harvested from sea snakes. The alcohol will slow the poison from spreading and cleanse the wound."

He then bent down and looked at her leg. The arrow had not come out the other side. "We need to remove this arrow." He cut her pants back exposing the impact area. He looked at the arrow trying to figure out how deep the arrow had penetrated when the door burst open and in ran Doc Johnson. Delores announced, "Doctor we got one arrow out and the other is stuck in her thigh. Samuel explained they were shot from assassins with the tip of the arrows coated in poison obtained from sea snakes. We poured alcohol on this one and have stopped the bleeding. She will need sutures."

Vicky was nauseated with the pain. When the alcohol was poured into the wound on her back and leg, the pain spiked. She leaned over on the table. Samuel said, "We will need to cut it out from the top. The tip is stuck against her femur."

Doc Johnson pulled his knife and cut the flesh around the arrow as she yelled.

He said, "You two hold her down. The barb on the arrowhead will need to be exposed, so we can pull the arrow out." He handed Vicky a leather strip, "You will need to bite down on this."

Mia and Delores laid her on her back and held her down. "I will cut and open the area with my knife, and you pull straight up on both the arrow and the silk material when I give the word. The arrow is stuck into the femur." The doctor cut around and deep into the hole. He looked at Samuel. Samuel pulled the arrow out. Vicky screamed and then passed out from the acute pain.

Samuel looked at the arrowhead, "The poison is deadly. If it gets in her blood stream she will die within a couple of days. There is no known cure."

Doctor Johnson looked at the arrow and then at Vicky and her bleeding leg wound. "She is strong and healthy. The wounds are not life threatening unless the poison has transferred from the tip into her blood system. We have no way to know when the tip was rubbed with the poison. The poison would have an incubation period and could have evaporated from the arrowhead prior to being shot."

He looked at Delores, Mia, and Casey, "I am sorry. The Blueblood is correct. There is nothing else I can do once I place sutures over the wounds." He looked somber again at Delores, Mia, and Casey, understanding his patient had been poisoned. "You need to get young Dak and bring him at once. She might wake up before she dies. We will try to make her comfortable and turn the healing over to the Lord."

Delores looked at Samuel, "How do you know so much about these arrows, and how they are coated with poison?"

"The one dead assassin and the one captured are both from the Persian territory from the Pacific continent. They are paid mercenaries and very deadly and very expensive. I have killed several of them on the west coast. We need to find out who hired them. They always work in a group of three. One master and two apprentices."

Samuel stood abruptly, "We can give her some of my blood. Hurry, my blood will help her."

Doc Johnson did not hesitate. He pulled the syringe and tube from his bag.

While his blood was being fed intravenously into Vicky's arm, Samuel did not speak. He contemplated his next move. After the pint of blood was provided, he walked out the door with the others watching him. They quickly turned their attention to Vicky, trying to make her comfortable. The doctor and the three women carried her to her upstairs apartment.

Samuel knew he needed to know who sent the assassin, and where the additional one might be hidden in the Cliff Tops community. He knew he needed to find out how they entered the community. He had listened to Mia and Delores talking as he was giving blood. He just was not certain he agreed with the two ladies about the assassins entering from south along the Continental Trail and crossing the bridge which connected them to the New York tribe. These two assassins came from the other continent, and they had to travel by ship to reach Cliff Tops. He knew they were ordained in the Persian religion. They were taught how to specialize in assassinating non-believers and promised to receive glory of their God after they successfully killed their assigned target. The more targets they killed, the more glory from their God they were blessed.

Chapter 48

Zorro was about to give up from exhaustion. He was bleeding from his forehead and an arrow had entered him in his upper shoulder. He had been swinging his sword for over two straight hours and was now fatigued. His throat was dry from lack of drinking and his body was covered in sweat. Some of his men had died, but not before they had killed several Normand soldiers. He looked at the ground around him, and there were dead and injured soldiers all around. Some were missing arms, and some had deep puncture wounds. Others were cut deep into their flesh, and all were bleeding. He knew for them to win, the gate would have to be closed to stop the intrusion of the Normand soldiers coming from the south. He looked at the gate and saw Dak fighting two soldiers at the entrance. He then noticed two Blueblood soldiers on horseback riding down the backside of the Normand army cutting men down one right after another. They had outflanked the Normand army and had made it to the gate. He yelled with renewed enthusiasm for his men to fight. "The Cliff Tops Soldiers are here to fight with us. We are winning. The gate has been closed." He saw the Normand soldier approach. Zorro stumbled as he backed up trying to create room for himself to swing his sword, and his feet tripped over a dead man and then his left foot tripped over another dead man, causing himself to fall backward close to five feet. As he fell on his back, he became panicked with anticipation knowing he could not defend himself while lying down. He felt the surge of fear. He blocked the first swing of the sword, but the force of the swing pushed his right arm out wide. The Normand soldier was to quick and powerful. His sword blade hit him in the lower right side. Zorro clenched his jaws and held the sword in place by grabbing the sword blade with his gloved covered hand and then pulled the man down on top of him with his other hand. The Normand soldier tried to break his sword free and lift himself upward. Zorro released the man with his right hand and pulled his knife from his boot. He rammed the knife under the armor into the man's ribs. He grunted and pulled the knife out and rammed the knife a second time as he gritted his teeth looking at the now dying soldier through his face shield into his dying eyes. Zorro pushed the man off him. Zorro pulled the sword from his side and waited for death.

The second wave of the Normand soldiers that had cleared the gate were well protected by additional armor. An arrow had to be fired from a compound bow to pierce the metal chest plate or helmets. A hard swung sword would knock a man over but could not cut through the metal protected armor. The Normand soldiers had waited in the darkness of the cave until the first squads of Normand soldiers had opened the gate and cleared the path. The plan had been for the Normand army to move a battalion of soldiers into place in the Midnight Hole region without the people who were supporters of the north to alert the New York tribe.

Billy Ray had hit a large soldier from the rear in the back of the head and the man had adjusted his helmet and turned to fight him. Billy Ray had ducked under the large man's swing and lunged forward. He was quicker than the large man and rolled toward the man and then reached around his body and sliced the hamstring muscle in the back of the femur with his knife. The large man lost the support of his leg and fell on his back cringing in pain. Billy Ray had not hesitated and rammed the pointed end of his sword through the man's eye hole. He yelled for the others to attack them on the backside of the legs. "There is no protective armor on the back of the legs."

Robin Hood and Veronica ran to the gate to provide additional support for Dak and were firing one arrow after another through the welded iron fence into the tunnel and the darkness at the Normand soldiers who tried to advance to the locked gate. While Trey, Hulk, and Tommy Boy fought back Normand soldiers who were trying to keep the gate open, Dak rolled the gas bomb into place, struck the match igniting the wick, and pushed the ball through the small gate opening in the bottom of the fence next to the larger gate. He quickly glanced around to verify if there were any Normand soldiers about to kill him. He then turned and watched as the bomb rolled down the path inside the cave. The bomb rolled and first collided with a dead Normand soldier lying on the ground inside the tunnel at the fifteen-yard mark. The bomb then ricocheted off the leg of the dead soldiers and then stopped when it wedged against the body of another Normand soldier. Dak watched as he observed the flame on the outside of the ball appeared to burn out. He did not see a flame of light in the dark cave. Hulk was fighting two Normand soldiers who were trying to push forward to the gate. He yelled, "You need to hurry."

Veronica was aiming her arrow down the tunnel looking for a target. "Did the flame go out?"

Dak glanced around to determine if he should unlock the gate and enter the cave and light the bomb. Then, he noticed a burst of light, and the flame suddenly ignited. Within a second, the entire ball was engulphed with a flame and abundance of black smoke started rising. The bomb worked perfectly as designed, and the smoke billowed out and filled the tunnel. The Normand soldiers positioned further inside the cave started retreating from the smoke and coughing while they ran back to the other entrance.

The Normand soldiers emerged from the tunnel into the fresh air, they were out of breath, coughing, and covered in soot. There was no mercy for retreating. They were killed by the waiting army. The penalty of not winning was death, and the captain knew when General Cuez heard of the terrible blunder, he would be decapitated in front of the command team. He was in charge, and his men should have never attacked until all units were in position. His main army had been in hiding and could not advance quick enough to the tunnel entrance. As he stood and watched the men retreat out of the tunnel covered in soot and coughing, he realized there was nothing else he could do to win the battle.

Dak looked at Hulk, Trey, and Tommy Boy, "Let's end this." Dak threw his pouch of arrows to Robin Hood, and Hulk gave Veronica his arrows. The group ran into the battle of the Normand soldiers, fighting them, using their quickness to kill several Normand men. The Normand soldiers wearing the heavy armor could not match the speed of their assault. When the opportunity presented, they would slice into the back of the legs of the Normand soldiers and then ram their swords through their face shields. Robin Hood and Veronica fired arrow after arrow into the legs of the Normand soldiers. Once on the ground, the other soldiers would finish them.

Aquarius blocked arrows and kept taking out soldiers. He tried to stay close to Zenith and watch over her. She could sense incoming arrows and block them with her sword. Zenith would turn her horse at the last second as she was charging toward a target and use the horse to run over the Normand soldier and then swing the sword while hanging over the side of the horse holding onto the saddle horn as she rode, hitting the soldiers. Her horse had been hit in the hips and neck with arrows, but she kept riding blocking arrows aimed for her.

Veronica ran behind Aquarius as a soldier was about to throw a spear and shot the spearman in the temple. Aquarius nodded his thanks and watched as Veronica and her friends killed Normand soldier after Normand soldier. He admired their ability to wage war.

Aquarius turned his horse and watched with concern. He watched as Dak was about to be killed. Dak instead caught the swing of the longsword in between the short blade and long blade of his sword and in one quick motion twisted the blade of the Normand soldier causing the soldier to grimace with acute pain in his wrist as he lost his grip and dropped his sword. Dak rammed his second sword into the top of the man's foot, cutting his foot in half. The man fell backward off balance screaming in pain.

Dak rotated and ducked as the sword missed his head. He stuck the soldier under his breast plate, and he fell dead. Aquarius thought to himself, "So that is how he beat Apollo in the Trial by Combat. He is very gifted with his swords."

Dak ran through the middle of the battle zone killing men as he reached Zorro who was lying on his side. Dak bent down and inspected the wound. "Put your arm around my shoulder." Dak helped him to walk to the rear line of the battle and placed pressure on the injury. Zorro's face was red, and both his hands were bloody. He looked like he understood he might die. "I believe you will be okay once we can get you to the doctor in Cliff Tops. I will have one of the Bluebloods provide you a pint of blood."

Zorro tried to smile, "I like your positive outlook."

Little Jimmy and Billy Ray decided it would be safer in the middle of the fighting than standing on the edge of the battle where the Normand archers could pick them off. The archers would rather not shoot into the middle of the fighting and chance hitting their own soldiers. The two men had been taking out Normand soldier after Normand soldier. Little Jimmy had seen the archer run into the mayhem and fired the arrow. Little Jimmy pulled the shield from the dead Normand soldier and blocked the arrow. He took off running toward the archer. The archer fired another arrow and then realized Little Jimmy was able to block that arrow. The man stumbled and fell into the back of one of the Normand soldiers fighting a New York soldier.

Little Jimmy changed his mind at the last second and hit the soldier in the ribs with the hammer end of his spear. The force of the blow broke several ribs, and the man fell as the New York soldier finished him. The archer fired his arrow at point blank range while lying on his back, and Little Jimmy pulled the shield up just in time in front of the arrow. Little Jimmy stepped on the man's stomach, dropped his shield, and then used both hands to sliced downward with his spear into the archer's face killing him instantly. Little Jimmy turned and tracked the next man, who was the captain of the Normand army as he killed two New York men. Little Jimmy ran toward the large soldier.

The commander saw Little Jimmy running toward him and had timed his swing. Little Jimmy placed both hands on his spear and blocked the sword and then kept his momentum forward and kicked the commander in the chest knocking him backward to the ground. Little Jimmy did not hesitate as he slammed the sharp end of the spear into the man's eye hole, killing him instantly. Little Jimmy pivoted and blocked the sword from the second Normand soldier, and then he hit the soldier in the head killing him with his twenty-four-pound eight-foot solid steel rod. The blow dislodged several teeth which fell inside the helmet as the second in command fell dead with his helmet bashed inward.

The Normand soldiers who were still standing realized they were surrounded, and the New York Tribe had stepped back and watched as Little Jimmy rammed his spear through the helmet of the commander of the Normand army and then he hit the next soldier in the head killing him. Little Jimmy had made the custom spear with a sharp bladed edge on one end and hammer on the other. He could swing the metal spear with great force, he could block sword swings with the steel spear, and either end of the spear were deadly. He could stab with one end or punish a soldier with the heavy hammer on the other end. He worked out with the spear one hour every day and had learned how to defend himself against single attacker or multiple attackers. He stood and looked at the Normand soldiers dropping their weapons in retreat.

As the rest of the Normand army laid down their weapons, the New York Tribe roared a cheer. The fighting was over.

Dak yelled for Veronica to bring a bandage. He cut back Zorro's coat and shirts. He placed his fingers on the wound holding the pressure on the artery. Veronica reached the two and immediately and clamped off the bleeding artery. She worked quickly and placed the bandage over the clamp protecting the wound.

Dak stood and yelled for Aquarius. "He needs your help."

Dak turned to the second in command of the New York Tribe. "We will take Zorro with us. We have better doctors, and once he has sufficiently healed, we will bring him back.

You are now in charge of the New York Tribe until such time as he returns."

Dak knew if he left Zorro in this condition he would not survive. The law of the land was that the strong lived and the weak either obeyed or died. Dak knew his tribe needed Zorro healthy and in charge, and they needed him to be the leader of the New York Tribe in future battles. There was too much at stake, and the next leader might not fight the Normand army as he had just done. "You will need to take the prisoners and secure them. We will need to interrogate them. We desperately need intel on the Normand Army, General Cuez, and Southern City. Do you understand?" Dak knew the prisoners would be executed. The New York Tribe would not provide mercy for anyone let alone Normand soldiers who had just attacked them and killed their friends.

Aquarius looked at Dak, "He has lost too much blood. He will need blood immediately. We have stopped most of the bleeding, but the kidney is damaged, and he needs a nephrectomy. I would suggest immediate surgery."

"Can you give him a pint of your blood to stabilize him? We have a line and a syringe in Veronica's saddle bag." Aquarius nodded yes.

Billy Ray and Little Jimmy walked over and looked at Zorro. Wayne commanded for the men of the New York tribe to bring a wagon and a horse. He then yelled for medics to help the injured. Dak looked over at the New York Tribe's second in command, "He said he needs a wagon and a horse. I told you to provide the injured medical help and secure the prisoners."

The second in command was a large man in his forties. Dak observed he had on clean clothing with no sign of being involved in the fighting. He had stood back and watched the battle and tried to organize the incoming New York soldiers as they arrived at the battle. They had been alerted for the call to arms from the forest, towns, and farms all over the area. He had witnessed Dak and the other young soldiers approach the Normand archers from the rear, and they had taken out over twenty of them in a few seconds with their bows and then pushed a path to the tunnel entrance and closed the tunnel while protecting their own backs. He had also watched as the two Blueblood warriors attacked on horses and rode down the flanks of the Normand army cutting them down while blocking arrows. He had never met a Blueblood warrior, but now he had witnessed them in action, he understood they were as good in combat as he had been told. He had further observed as Billy Ray cut down over a dozen Normand soldiers and everyone had watched the end of the battle with Little Jimmy killing the leader of the Normand army and taking out his second in command with the hammer hit to the helmet. He looked at young Dak and wondered if he should take orders from him.

The two Bluebloods were not giving orders, and he knew of Little Jimmy and Billy Ray. Every soldier in the New York tribe knew of those two. He glanced over as the female Blueblood who rode up next to Dak and walked her horse in behind him while Little Jimmy and Billy Ray also walked up next to Dak. All were staring at him. He hesitated while considering his options. Should he take orders from this young man who he had just met? He glanced at the people and the situation. He noticed Zorro was now being placed in a wagon and the male Blueblood was providing him blood intravenously through the clear tube. He knew Zorro would never elect him to be the leader of the New York Tribe, but this young man from Cliff Tops had just endorsed him as the temporary leader. The tribe was aware that Zorro had three sons and one of them would be the leader of the New York Tribe.

He turned to his men and gave multiple orders to tend to the injured and secure the prisoners. He looked back at Dak, and Dak raised his voice for all to hear, "You men and women of the New York Tribe fought valiantly today. You were brave and protected your tribe. These men you have beaten here today were professional soldiers, which illustrates how good we all are at fighting together. We thank you. If you lose, we all lose. We will take care of Zorro and return him once he has healed."

The New York tribe personnel seemed to take pride in what they accomplished. Dak walked over closer to the second in command, "We won the battle. The war still looms. Keep the gate closed. We will be back to interrogate the Normand soldiers. We need information. Do not kill them. The Continental Trail is the only road for the Normand army to advance north. You will need to double your guards here at the gate." Dak turned and walked over to Zenith and her horse and jumped on the back of the horse. The two headed toward Cliff Tops.

Chapter 49

Samuel walked out into the cold air. He felt the dread feeling of death and was convinced Vicky was going to die. The poison was lethal, and there was nothing he could do to save her. As he walked toward the garrison, he became overwhelmed with rage knowing the woman he had just fallen in love with was dying. He knew the assassin would not talk. They had tortured the zealots in the past for information. They would chant a prayer to their God while being tortured and never break. He had not understood their religion but had discovered the zealots were more fearful of swine and being placed in a pig pin then being tortured. He pulled his knife and considered his options. He had decided he was going to cut the man and force him to talk or kill him before the people of Cliff Tops wanted to spare him the pain. He knew there was only one chance for him to talk, and he was about to administer the extreme pain. He walked at a fast pace with clinched jaws toward the garrison close to one-hundred-yards away and saw a shadow of someone running into the woods near the garrison which housed the two-prison cells and the front office. He walked to the door and noticed it was locked. He peered in through the glass door window and noticed the guard was lying on the floor. He pulled his sword and forced the door. He entered the garrison front room and saw the guard lying dead on the floor. He looked around expecting an attack, and there was no one else in the room. He knelt next to the guard as he watched the interior doorway to the two cells. He cautiously turned the guard over. His mouth was stuffed with a rag, and his eyes had been cut out and his three fingers cut off, which were lying on the floor next to him. Samuel pointed his sword toward the interior doorway and pulled his knife. He eased over to the doorway and walked through the door entrance with his sword held in front of him. The prisoner was in the room chained to the large post, and he was also dead, with his throat cut. Samuel felt the immediate feeling of being tricked. He turned and ran back out of the garrison and toward the four plex and Vicky's apartment. He burst through the exterior foyer door and climbed the steps two at a time. He opened the door with his sword pulled. Casey screamed with fright as Delores pulled her sword. Both women were standing next to Vicky's bed waiting for her to wake.

Urgency was in his voice, "Your guard has been tortured to death, and the prisoner has been executed. There is a Persian assassin in the area."

To Be Continued

ACKNOWLEDGMENTS

✳✳✳

To my editor Carolyn Pegram for all the hard work.

To Chesnie Nichols for the book cover and formatting the book.

To big sister, Sherrie Rutherford, for all the loving help in writing book five.